THE THIRTEENTH PETAL

THE THIRTEENTH PETAL

CEDAR CREEK LEGENDS BOOK ONE

CEDAR CREEK LEGENDS
BOOK 1

JORDAN JACE

Print ISBN: 978-1-967657-56-8

EPub ISBN: 978-1-967657-55-1

CONTENTS

FOREWORD

Some towns keep secrets in locked archives. Cedar Creek hides them in plain sight—painted in stained glass, whispered in bread blessings, and carried by families who would rather forget than remember.

When **Miriam Adler,** a recently widowed woman searching for renewal, arrives in the quiet town of Cedar Creek to claim her great-aunt's metaphysical shop, she expects only dust, crystals, and a few wary neighbors. Instead, she steps into a legacy. The townsfolk whisper of "the Adler gift," a strange intuition passed through generations. Miriam dismisses it—until she unlocks the shop's attic and finds her aunt's trembling letter: *Seek the thirteenth petal.*

At first, Cedar Creek seems welcoming enough: lantern-lit festivals, fresh bread from the bakery, a café alive with gossip. But unease runs under the cobblestones. Old family rivalries stir at the edges, and the chapel's rose window—a masterpiece glowing with twelve perfect petals—suddenly cracks. Miriam alone sees the shimmer of a hidden thirteenth.

Haunted by dreams of a long-ago bride, guided by cryptic notes, Miriam turns to **Julian Roth**, the local historian and museum curator. Divorced, cautious, and tethered to rationality, Julian distrusts mysticism. Yet he cannot ignore Miriam's courage—or the uncanny ways the past responds to her presence. As they sift through brittle journals, missing records, and a rose-shaped pendant etched with thirteen petals, Julian and Miriam uncover an ancestral pact of silence binding Cedar Creek's founding families.

But some want the past buried. **Pastor Elijah** warns that truth may unravel the town. Skeptics mock Miriam in cafés. Allies urge caution. And yet, with every clue—the fragment of a bride's journal lamenting her vow, whispers at the chapel at midnight, sabotage during the town festival—the threads pull tighter around Miriam. To abandon the mystery is to betray the gift she was chosen to inherit. To pursue it risks unraveling Cedar Creek's fragile peace.

What begins as curiosity becomes destiny. The thirteenth petal is not just a symbol hidden in glass—it is the missing piece of wholeness, the broken promise of unity silenced generations ago. Only by speaking truth aloud can the town heal.

At once a cozy mystery, a slow-burn romance, and a lyrical exploration of belonging, *The Thirteenth Petal* brings Cedar Creek vividly to life: its market square full of quirky characters, its bakery fragrant with challah blessings, its chapel trembling under centuries of silence. Readers will be swept into a story where history and legend intertwine, where love grows from shared vulnerability, and where courage means choosing truth over comfort.

The novel crescendos in a luminous climax inside the chapel: Miriam reading from the bride's hidden journal, Julian standing at her side, the rose window glowing as the thirteenth petal finally reveals itself. The families are forced to confront the pact they kept, the silence they maintained, and the possibility of redemption through truth.

And just as Cedar Creek begins to breathe easier—its window restored, its community bonds renewed—the story leaves readers shivering with anticipation. On the night of the festival, Miriam discovers the ceremonial basin at the river mysteriously empty, a strange spiral carved into the dry stone. The rose has spoken; now the water waits.

Perfect for fans of **cozy mysteries with mystical twists, heartfelt community drama, and tender second-chance romance,** *The Thirteenth Petal* is both satisfying in its closure and irresistible in its invitation forward. Book One of the **Cedar Creek Legends** opens the circle, reminding us that wholeness is not symmetry—it is courage, truth, and the willingness to keep each other.

The legend has only begun.

PROLOGUE: THE PACT BENEATH THE ROSE

The storm had gathered without warning, tumbling down the slopes of the Cascades and sweeping across the wide, braided rivers that met at Cedar Creek. By dusk, the winds had found their way into every shutter, rattling against the clapboard homes of the settlement and bending the trees that ringed the old chapel. It was 1846, and though the town was scarcely more than a cluster of cabins and a fort still smelling of fresh-hewn timber, its people felt the weight of permanence in every stone they laid, every vow they made. The land was raw, the rivers wide and temperamental, but the settlers had learned quickly that survival here demanded more than muscle. It required unity—and unity was fragile.

Inside the chapel, candles sputtered in the draft, their flames bowing toward the tall rose window above the altar. The window was their pride, shipped in pieces from Europe and assembled pane by pane by patient hands. Even in the dim flicker of candlelight, the glass shimmered with muted hues: blues like the river at dusk, reds like wild berries crushed in a child's palm, golds that caught fire when the sun was right. But tonight no sun warmed it, only lightning splitting the sky, illuminating for brief seconds the twelve-petaled rose that bloomed in the center.

Twelve petals, perfectly symmetrical, glowing with holy resonance. And yet, those gathered in the chapel knew another secret, one that did not belong to the records or the sermons or even the town's memory. For beneath the painted lines, faint enough to be missed by casual eyes, was a thirteenth petal. A fragment of design, older than the rest, its existence whispered only among the founding families.

Three families now stood before the altar, the storm's growl pressing against the walls. The Wagners, their patriarch with a beard gone white before his years, hands clasped like roots pulling tight into the earth. The Dubois, French traders who had taken wives from the Chinook people and bore children who straddled both worlds with an ease their parents sometimes envied. And the Adlers—soft-spoken, sharp-eyed, their matriarch with a prayer shawl wrapped close as if to shield herself from more than the chill.

They had come not for worship, but for covenant. Between them lay a small table, upon it a sealed box of cedarwood and iron, smelling faintly of resin and smoke. Inside, as they all knew, was a diary. The inked confessions of a young bride, words written with trembling hand. Words that, if ever revealed, could divide Cedar Creek before it was even fully born.

"We must decide," Matthias Wagner said, his voice nearly drowned by thunder. "The window cannot be spoken of. Not the petal, not the meaning it holds. And not this diary. If word spreads, we invite suspicion, rivalry, and ruin."

"You fear ruin more than truth?" asked Elise Adler, her dark eyes lifted to the rose window as though she saw more than glass. "If there is a thirteenth petal, it was placed there for a reason."

Matthias's hand slammed against the cedar box. "Reason or not, it will tear us apart. Do you not see? Twelve is order. Twelve tribes, twelve apostles, twelve months. A thirteenth unbalances the world. Best to seal it and speak no more."

Silence pooled between them, broken only by the groan of the rafters. It was then that the bride stirred—a girl no more than sixteen, her gown still smelling of lye soap, her face pale as the lightning through the window. She had not been meant to be here; the pact was for elders. Yet her diary had brought them, and so she stood, trembling, her hands knotted in front of her.

"It is not the petal you fear," she said, voice barely audible. "It is what it reveals of us. That we are not whole. That there are parts of our story we have hidden, parts we are ashamed to name."

Her father hissed her quiet, but the words had already unsettled the chamber. Elise Adler regarded the girl with quiet sympathy, while Henri Dubois shifted uncomfortably, his fingers tracing the edge of a carved cross around his neck. Outside, rain slashed against the window, and for one breathless instant, lightning revealed the faint shimmer of the hidden petal. It gleamed as though alive, as though reminding them it could not be erased.

"Then let it be sealed," Matthias said again, his tone final. "We three families will swear tonight. By this window, by this storm, by God Himself. We will protect Cedar Creek from the chaos this knowledge would sow. The thirteenth petal will be buried in silence, as will this diary."

The bride began to weep softly, tears slipping down her cheeks and darkening the lace of her gown. No one reached to comfort her; the pact was already weaving itself around them like invisible chains. Elise closed her eyes as if in prayer, her lips moving with words no one could hear. Perhaps they were words of resistance, perhaps resignation. None would ever know.

The cedar box was carried to the wall, where a stone near the altar had been loosened. With effort, the men pried it open, slid the box inside, and sealed it again with mortar still wet from their hands. As the stone settled, thunder cracked so violently that dust rained from the rafters. The bride flinched, clutching at her skirts. Somewhere in the storm, the rivers answered, their waters rising with a voice older than any family gathered here.

"Let it be sworn," Matthias intoned. "We guard this silence. For our children. For their children. Until the day silence itself breaks."

Candles guttered, nearly extinguished, and for a moment the rose window appeared to shimmer—not with twelve petals, nor with thirteen, but with something more. A wholeness that none of them dared name.

The pact was sealed. The silence began.

THE OTHERS DRIFTED from the altar like figures withdrawing from a painting—their voices a hush behind closed mouths, their lanterns listing in the drafts. Only the bride lingered, swaying in the seam between light and dark, one hand gathered at her collar as if the bone there might break. Her name was Leah Adler, and when she lifted her eyes to the rose window, she did not see twelve. She saw the ghost of the thirteenth, the line no one would name, a whisper-petal nested just beyond symmetry, like a breath held too long.

Leah knew what it was to be a hidden thing.

The storm was burrowing into the chapel's joints. Wax slid down the candles' sides in patient rivers and pooled on the altar cloth with the stubbornness of choice. She had not been meant to stand in that room, to watch the men place her words in a cedar box and wall it into the stone like a sin. The diary—her diary—felt heavier in its absence, as if the world had tilted slightly to keep her from falling toward it. Somewhere beyond the glass, the two rivers pawed at the banks, fat with rain, muttering to each other like people too long married to be kind.

Leah wore the Adler heirloom at her throat—a small silver pendant pressed into the shape of a rose. When she was a child, her aunt had rubbed it between finger and thumb and told her there were ways of seeing that had nothing to do with eyes. That truth could hide itself and still be true. That some petals only opened in moonlight.

"It is not the petal," Leah had told the elders. "It is what it reveals of us." The sentence still trembled in her bones. Her father's warning hiss—hush—still lived at the edge of her tongue. She could obey a hush. She knew obedience, how it soothed older hearts the way a hand smooths creases from linen. But this hush would not smooth; it would harden. It would turn the town to a stone with a secret sealed inside, and she could not bear to think of people building their lives on such a weight.

She crossed the nave to the basin near the door—rainwater and river water, blessed that morning, now shivering under the bell-rope's sway. Candlelight scattered across its surface. She cupped a hand and dipped. The water was cold enough to make her gasp, and in that shock she had a flash of meaning that was not hers alone: I will bring you out. It arrived as if the river itself had put it there. She did not know from where, only that the words were true in a way that made her throat ache. The water slipped through the lines of her palm and down her wrist, a wet thread drawing a path she could not yet follow.

Leah turned. The bell's rope dangled, frayed near the knot where children had tugged at festivals. There was a hum in it, a quiet restlessness as if the bell were listening. She imagined it refusing one day to speak—refusing to lift its voice for promises that did not honor truth. Not out of spite but fidelity, the way a heart refuses to say yes when yes would make it small. She shivered and pressed her pendant against her skin.

At the altar, the last candle faltered, then recovered. Leah stepped closer to the window. In the lightning's slash, the thirteenth petal revealed itself for a heartbeat: a filament-thin arc tucked between red and blue, subtle as mercy. She thought of the hiddenness that lived in this land—the salmon smooth as light sliding under black water, the mycelial rumors passing from root to root deep in the forest soil, the stories traded in whispers between traders and keepers and mothers with flour on their hands.

"Leah," her aunt Elise said gently. Leah started; she hadn't heard her return. Elise's shawl was drawn up tight, gray hair threaded into a coil like a thought too long considered. "We must go."

"They sealed it," Leah said. She was surprised to hear her voice steady. "They sealed what I wrote. They sealed the petal too, in their way."

Elise did not contradict her. She glanced at the wall where the stone was already darkening as the plaster drank the wet. "Some truths have weather like this," Elise said. "They are not persuaded by doors."

Leah's defiance, which had burned hot while the men argued, softened at her aunt's voice. Elise had taught her to read symbols as one reads faces: with patience, with humility. She had shown her that covenant was not an iron lock but a bridge—suspension and tension, a humble engineering that let people cross wild water together. Leah had believed this. She still did. But bridges could also be closed.

The door groaned. Matthias Wagner, hat pulled low, paused under the lintel as if he might say something fatherly. He did not. He looked at Leah the way a man looks at a hearth he cannot approach without burning. Then he was gone, swallowed by the rain. Henri Dubois lingered a moment, crossing himself, the gesture awkward on a body made for barter and story. "Pardon," he whispered reflexively to the air. To Leah he said, "Forgive them. And if you cannot, forgive them later." Then he followed Matthias into the storm, his son's shadow vanishing after him like a young promise trailed by duty.

Leah pressed her palm to the cool stone above the sealed box. She saw in her mind the neat pages of her hand, now buried—her small defiance of ink, her attempt to assemble what had been scattered. The diary had begun as any girl's—scraps of the market, names for the shadow-puppy that chased her across the square, sketches of the fort's bell because she loved its voice. But this last week, as whispers of the window reached her and the elders' faces closed like shutters, the diary had changed. It had become the only place where Leah could set down what she knew and did not know: that silence could be a virtue and a cowardice, that truth could heal and also split, that love required a voice and so did a town.

"Some truths have weather like this," she repeated, and the words steadied something inside her. She looked again at the window and thought—perhaps madness, perhaps faith—of petals beyond counting, of circles nested inside circles the way a life nested inside a family nested inside a town. She imagined a time when a woman not yet born would stand under this same window and feel the same thin arc of light. She did not see her face, only the posture of her —spine like a vow, eyes taking in what others had learned to ignore.

Elise touched Leah's sleeve. "Come. The mud will swallow us."

They stepped into the night. The rain had a feeling of argument—insistent and repetitive. At the chapel's threshold, Leah lifted one of the wall lanterns. Its flame stuttered, then caught, and for a moment the glass chimed with a tone she felt in her ribs. She lifted it higher—an instinctive, primal gesture, as if a signal were called for. The river answered with a low rush. Leah imagined a line from the lantern to the bell to the window to the water, a stringing of lit beads that a child might call a game and a scholar a map.

"I will deliver you," she breathed without meaning to, not certain who the you was—herself, the town, the truth sealed in the wall. The rain blurred everything except the lantern's small sphere. In its circle, Elise's face was both mother and commander. "We cannot keep you dry," Elise said. "But we can keep you unbroken."

They cut across the square toward the Adler house, skirts slick with mud, hair stuck to cheeks. The fort's blockhouse brooded on the bluff, a geometry of protection that comforted exactly no one in a storm like this. Leah saw a spill of light where the Dubois lodge faced the river— someone singing very soft in a language she did not know all the words to. She thought of the basin in the chapel, the way the water had seemed to lower under her hand as if obeying some command not given by men. I will bring you out. I will deliver you. The lines kept threading themselves through her without asking permission, as if the weather had learned letters.

Inside the Adler rooms, the lamplight steadied. The smell of cedar lives in such rooms the way grief does—subtle, stubborn, not unkind. Leah's father had banked the stove and set out a goblet from the chest, a thin-stemmed thing more special than practical. It caught the light without consent. Elise saw Leah looking and smiled. "A cup is a promise," she said. "Even when empty."

"Will he forgive me?" Leah asked. She was not sure which he she meant—her father, God, her betrothed, the bell. A face flashed—kind, earnest, too prepared to stand on his father's side. Elias Wagner had not spoken in the chapel. He had taken off his hat and watched the walling as if it were a useful fence. Leah could love a man like that. It would be simple. She might have to become simpler to do it.

"Forgiveness is not the work tonight," Elise said. "Tonight we hide what must be found."

Leah stood very still. Elise drew from her shawl a little bundle of oilskin—the thing the elders had not seen or perhaps had chosen to see and choose again. Elise set it in Leah's hands. "Not all of your words are in that wall," she said. "I told you we would keep a page."

Leah unwrapped it and saw the single sheet, dry and white as if it had not been born from the same paper as the rest. Her handwriting, small and orderly, had not yet learned to be brave; but the words themselves had tried. She traced them with a fingertip and felt an almost physical relief—as if a bird she had watched caged had flown, very quietly, while no one was looking.

"Behind the shelf," Elise said. "Second plank from the back. Your uncle left a gap when we built it—a foolishness we were grateful for later. Nail it in. Say nothing. Not to husband or father or priest. Not even to me once it is done."

Leah lifted the lamp. In the corner, the shelves waited, obedient and dumb. She set the lamp on the floor, knelt, and ran her fingers along the plank's lip. Her nail found the soft seam. She worked the nails out with the stubborn competence of someone who has watched men build and never been invited to try. The board loosened with a sigh, revealing a pocket dark as a closing eye.

She slid the page inside. Before she replaced the board, she hesitated, then unsnapped her pendant's clasp. The silver rose lay small and living in her palm. Elise inhaled in surprise but did not stop her. Leah pressed the pendant flat against the page—a weight, a sign, a soft knock on a future door. "If someone is meant to find this," Leah said, "let her find it by touch."

She hammered the board back with the butt of the lamp. The sound was not loud, but it was honest; it belonged to work and not to argument. The second nail bent and resisted; Leah leaned into it and it yielded, a small capitulation like a person beginning to say yes.

When she finished, she sat on her heels and closed her eyes. The storm's voice kept its own counsel. She thought of the concealed box in the chapel stone, of the basin, of the bell. She thought of the lantern she had lifted in the rain, of the cup waiting empty on the table as if for a guest who arrived only in stories. She thought of the thirteenth petal lying quiet in its web of twelve like a secret muscle the town did not yet know it had.

"I will redeem you," she whispered, and this time the words did not feel like theology. They felt like a promise the land itself had made through the mouths of rivers and bells and girls who hid pages where men could not find them. She opened her eyes and saw Elise watching, unafraid.

"Sleep," Elise said. "Tomorrow we will go on pretending. It is a skill that can be practiced without becoming a habit."

Leah lay down in the small bed by the window, though there was no sleep yet for her. The pendant's absence was a bright ache at her throat. She touched the skin there and felt the remembered cool of silver and then the remembered chill of water. Her hand smelled faintly of resin from the cedar box she had touched earlier. She pressed her palm to the sill. Outside, rain braided itself into the night; the rivers argued and agreed and argued again.

The lamp guttered low. Lightning lit the room soundlessly for a single breath, and in that unnoised light Leah saw again what she had seen in the chapel: the thirteenth petal like a faint arc between colors, a hinge on which the window might someday swing. She imagined it blooming fully not for the elders but for someone who would need it like a door. She did not know her name. She saw a corner of a shop she had not yet seen, shelves that would one day hold stones and books and small, implausible comforts. She saw hands, different from hers and yet kin, prying up a board, breath catching the way a person's breath catches when the story they have been given acquires an echo.

Leah closed her eyes and let the words come once more, quiet as the last wax thread giving itself to the wick. I will take you to me. I will bring you in. The sentences unspooled in her mind like river lines, five in all, though she could not have told you why that number mattered. She fell asleep inside them, the storm gentling its palms against the house, the thirteenth petal lifting in her dream to meet the others as if to say, We are not unbalanced; we were simply unfinished.

In the morning, Cedar Creek would rise wrung-out and blinking. Men would nod at one another across the square, having survived both weather and ceremony. Women would begin the day's bread. Children would chase each other with the wild kindness of those who have not yet been taught what not to see. The bell would ring, obedient, because there are seasons of obedience before there are seasons of refusal. The basin would be refilled by steady hands. The cup would return to its chest. The lantern would dry its smoke-smudged glass. The stone in the chapel would cool and harden and take on the memory of new mortar until only fingers with a certain way of touching would suspect the seam.

But in the wall of the Adler shop, behind the second plank from the back, a page would begin its long patience. A pendant would lie face-down on Leah's neat letters. Truth would live as a seed lives—husked, not dead. And when, many years later, a woman with a spine like a vow and eyes that had learned to see would place her hand in that pocket of wood, the town would feel the first quiet loosenings of its sealed hush.

Leah slept. The storm receded to the edges like a conscience appeased for a time. In the chapel, the window gathered up the early gray and made something merciful of it. For a blink, when no one watched, the hidden line of the thirteenth petal brightened—then settled again into its work of waiting.

THE STORM WITHDREW toward the mountains as the night's last hours thinned, leaving Cedar Creek hushed, its streets strewn with broken branches and mud slicks that gleamed faintly under the paling sky. The chapel stood at the town's center like a sentinel that had endured both weather and vow, its rose window clouded by mist yet strangely unbroken. Inside, the smell of wax and cedar lingered, mingling with mortar dust from the wall where the box lay hidden. The pact was sealed, but silence, like rainwater, has a way of seeping through every crack.

Leah stirred before dawn, her sleep shallow, her dreams tethered to half-heard voices. She rose quietly, careful not to wake Elise, and pulled her shawl tight. Something compelled her back to the chapel—as though the stone itself was calling her to witness what the elders had done. Her slippers grew heavy with mud, but she pressed on, following the rivulets that threaded downhill to the river, following too the rhythm of words she did not invent yet could not silence: *I will bring you out. I will deliver you. I will redeem you. I will take you to me. I will bring you in.*

The bell rope swayed gently when she entered. Its fibers were damp, and she thought of how easily a voice can fray when stretched between two duties. She placed her hand upon it and closed her eyes. For an instant, she saw not the chapel of her present but something future—light pouring through the rose window, colors sharper than glass should allow, and a figure standing beneath it. Not herself. A woman older, dressed not in linen but in something stranger, her hands steady, her presence calm. She bore the same eyes Leah saw in her reflection when courage flickered against obedience. The vision passed, leaving Leah breathless.

Her gaze lifted to the window. Dawn's first light threaded itself through the glass, a subdued radiance. Twelve petals took on color. The thirteenth, though faint, seemed to catch a separate gleam, like a secret flame refusing extinction. Leah whispered the words she had not been permitted to speak aloud in the company of elders: "We are not broken. We are unfinished."

Behind her, the door creaked. A shadow stretched across the nave. Matthias Wagner, hatless, his hair plastered by rain, stood uncertainly in the doorway. He had followed her, perhaps out of duty, perhaps out of something more tender he could not name.

"You should not be here," he said softly. "The pact was sworn."

Leah turned to him, her shawl slipping from one shoulder. "And do you believe silence makes truth vanish?"

He hesitated, his mouth opening then closing. He was young still, not yet hardened into his father's sternness, but loyalty bound him tight. "It makes peace," he said at last. "Peace enough to build a town."

Leah stepped closer, searching his eyes. "Peace built on silence is not peace. It is waiting for the silence to break."

Lightning no longer split the sky, but the words lit the air between them as though charged. Matthias's gaze faltered. For one unguarded moment, she saw the boy in him, the boy who might have wished for courage but had learned obedience instead. He reached as if to take her hand, then withdrew, fingers curling into his palm. "Please," he murmured, "say nothing more. For your sake. For mine."

He turned and left, his boots striking the threshold like punctuation. Leah remained, her pulse trembling. She pressed her hand once more to the cold stone concealing the cedar box, then stepped back. It was not courage to stay, she realized, nor was it cowardice to leave. It was simply unfinished, like the thirteenth petal.

· · ·

By mid-morning the storm's wreckage was being cleared: wagons righted, fences mended, laughter forced into the day to mask the night's unease. Cedar Creek's people were practiced at labor, and labor often disguised wounds. Yet the chapel carried its secret, and Leah carried hers—the single page and pendant hidden behind the shelf, her private covenant with the unknown. The elders believed silence had triumphed; she knew silence had only been delayed.

At the riverbank, she watched driftwood spin in eddies, watched gulls circle where salmon might surface. Water had a memory, she thought. It carried not just silt but whispers, fragments, promises too heavy to bury. She bent to scoop a stone, smoothed by current, and held it in her palm. It felt like the page she had hidden: ordinary yet weighted with something beyond its shape. She cast it into the current, and ripples widened, colliding, folding, finding new directions. The stone disappeared, but the water remembered.

That night, when the bell tolled to call the town to rest, Leah lay awake, her hand against her throat where the pendant had hung. She felt its absence as she felt the ache of unshed words. She thought of Matthias, his eyes full of conflict. She thought of Elise, whose quiet faith had shielded her. She thought of the sealing of the wall as though it could command silence forever. She thought of the rose window, patient in its watch. She thought of a woman yet unborn who would stand where she stood and know that silence was never absolute.

Leah closed her eyes. The words threaded through her once more, each a promise she could neither deny nor wholly understand: *I will bring you out. I will deliver you. I will redeem you. I will take you to me. I will bring you in.* She repeated them until sleep came, a sleep lined with symbols she could not name but trusted to endure.

. . .

YEARS LATER, when the elders were dust and the chapel had weathered more storms, townsfolk would notice little oddities: a shimmer in the rose window when light struck at angles, a faint echo when the bell rang, a sense that the river carried more than water. They would shrug, laugh, attribute it to weather, to age, to imagination. Only a few would wonder if something once hidden still breathed beneath stone and wood. And in the Adler shop, behind a plank none thought to pry, a page and pendant would wait with the patience of seed in winter. Waiting for the right hands. Waiting for a woman with eyes like Leah's.

1

ARRIVAL AT THE SHOP

The brass key trembled faintly in Miriam Adler's hand as she stood before the narrow wooden door of the metaphysical shop owned by her family for generations. Miriam's late great-aunt had been the last in a long line of family members to keep the shop open for business. The painted letters on the transom window had faded to a ghostly script—*Solace & Sage*—barely visible beneath the layers of dust and weather. For a long moment she let her hand rest on the key, eyes closed, feeling the weight not only of the brass but of everything that had carried her here: the quiet house in the city now empty of her husband's voice, the ache of widowhood that no ritual or condolence could soften, and the strange, unspoken pull that had insisted she come to Cedar Creek.

The town itself smelled of river moss and wood smoke. Early autumn had crisped the air, though sunlight still lingered with warmth. A crow perched on the lamppost nearby, tilting its head as though to witness her hesitation. Miriam inhaled deeply, pressed the key into the lock, and turned. The mechanism groaned in protest before yielding, the door pushing inward to release a sigh of stale air, a mingling of lavender and cedar that carried her back to childhood summers. She remembered standing here as a girl beside her aunt's skirts, tracing the edge of the crystal bowls with fascinated fingers, whispering questions about stones and stars.

She stepped inside. Dust motes swam in the light, disturbed by her presence, as if time itself had been holding its breath and finally exhaled. Shelves crowded the walls—lined with books that bore titles in half-faded gold leaf, jars of herbs sealed with wax, and rows of crystals that winked faintly even under the film of neglect. A table near the center still bore the blue cloth her aunt had favored, embroidered with roses whose petals had thinned to threads. The space felt less abandoned than waiting.

Miriam set her bag on the floor and ran her hand across the counter. The wood was warm beneath the dust, a strange warmth that pulsed as though memory still lived within the grain. She whispered, "Well, Aunt Ruth, here we are," and the sound of her voice startled her. Since David's death she had spoken mostly to herself, her prayers mumbled in kitchens, her questions offered to empty rooms. Now her voice echoed back, soft but firm, as though the shop had answered.

She took off her coat, draping it across the chair by the counter, and walked deeper into the shop. A mirror leaned against the wall near the shelves, its frame carved with ivy. When she caught her reflection, she barely recognized herself—hair darker than memory, streaked now with silver at the temples; eyes that once held laughter, now carrying the burden of questions without answers. At thirty-nine she was not old, not young, but carried in her body the wear of grief and the faint resilience of survival.

"Belonging," she murmured, recalling the word her aunt had written in her last letter. *Cedar Creek is where belonging is found, Miriam. Come home when the time is right.*

The time was now, though it felt less chosen than compelled. Miriam let her fingers wander across the spines of the books. Titles on Kabbalah, metaphysics, herbal healing, and dream interpretation. Some she had read before, others she had never opened. One slim volume fell forward into her palm—*The Thirteenth Petal*. She ran her thumb across its cover, startled by the familiar symbol, and then set it carefully back, her breath tightening.

A sound drew her attention—footsteps scuffing just outside. She turned toward the window and saw two women pausing on the boardwalk. They pressed close to each other, whispering, eyes flicking toward the open door. One pointed discreetly at Miriam, then at the sign above. The other shook her head, lips pursed as though tasting something half bitter, half sweet. Miriam raised a tentative hand in greeting, but they shifted quickly along, their whispers trailing like threads.

The Adler gift. She had heard it murmured all her life, though never plainly defined. Her great-aunt Ruth had been known for her intuitions—knowing when a child was ill before fever broke, sensing quarrels before voices rose, whispering counsel that seemed to draw from some hidden well. Miriam had inherited the sensitivity, though she had spent years tucking it away, focusing instead on family, on ordinary rhythms of marriage and work. But in the last months, since David's absence had hollowed her life, the gift had surged, dreams vivid as prophecy, coincidences too sharp to ignore.

She sat at the counter, allowing herself to feel the strangeness of the moment. Widow. Shopkeeper. Stranger returned to a town that had only half-remembered her. A faint hum lingered in the air—perhaps only her nerves, perhaps something more. She pressed her palms flat to the wood and whispered, "I'm here."

For the first time since her husband's passing, she felt the faint stir of belonging, like the fragile edge of a root pressing into soil.

THE BELL above the door rang out with a surprised jangle later that afternoon, as Miriam dusted the shelves with a rag dampened in lavender oil. She looked up to see a man in a red flannel shirt, his arms thick with years of logging work, his beard flecked with gray.

"Didn't think anyone would open this place again," he said, stepping inside and removing his cap. "Name's Walter Crane. Ruth helped my wife through her childbearing years. Tinctures, teas, prayers—whatever you call it, it worked."

Miriam smiled politely. "I'm Miriam. Ruth was my aunt."

Walter's eyes softened. "Then you've got her look. Folks will be glad to see the lights on here again. This shop's more than herbs and books. It's where we sat when we couldn't sit in church. You understand?"

She nodded, struck by the honesty of his voice. "I hope I can honor what she built."

"Honor it just by being here," he said. He placed a hand on the counter, thick fingers tracing the wood. "Ruth called this a threshold. Said people come in with heavy loads and walk out a little lighter. You'll see soon enough."

As he left, tipping his cap once more, Miriam felt the

weight of responsibility settle more firmly on her shoulders. The shop was not merely inheritance—it was a place that mattered.

By evening, more townsfolk wandered in, drawn by curiosity. A pair of teenagers giggled at the jars of crystals, daring each other to touch the amethyst cluster. An older woman asked shyly if Miriam might still sell chamomile tea the way Ruth had. Even the town baker, Miriam Levine, came by with a loaf wrapped in linen, insisting that no new shopkeeper should start without bread.

As the hours passed, Miriam realized how easily conversation flowed here. The counter became less a barrier than a hearth, gathering stories and laughter. One man recalled how Ruth had taught him to rub rosemary into his hands before fishing for luck. Another admitted she had once left the shop with nothing but a prayer and somehow found her son's fever breaking by morning.

It was not superstition alone—it was community. The shop had been a gathering place where fears could be spoken without ridicule, where loneliness could be eased by tea and quiet counsel. Miriam felt herself stepping into Ruth's role not by effort but by presence, her listening more important than her words.

By the time she closed the door, lanterns glowing along the boardwalk, she sensed the shop was alive again. Dust had receded, replaced by voices. Shelves no longer felt like relics but companions. She whispered her thanks to the room before dousing the lamps, her heart both heavy with exhaustion and lightened with purpose.

THE FOLLOWING MORNING, as she carried a crate of books up

from the cellar, Miriam was stopped on the boardwalk by Mrs. Callahan, a sprightly woman with quick eyes.

"So you're Ruth's niece," Mrs. Callahan said. "We wondered if you'd stay long enough to matter. Cedar Creek doesn't take to transients."

Miriam lifted her chin. "I plan to stay."

"Good," the woman replied, satisfied. Then she leaned closer, lowering her voice. "If you need to know anything about this town's history, you'll find it at the fort museum. Julian Roth keeps the records better than anyone. Knows every family tree, every brick laid in the old chapel. Talks too much, but harmless."

The name lingered in Miriam's mind after the woman walked on. Julian Roth. She tried the syllables quietly, as though testing a charm. She remembered her aunt once mentioning a Roth among the museum staff, someone meticulous, almost stubborn about facts. Miriam felt an unexpected stir of curiosity.

Back in the shop, she set the crate down and brushed her hands. Light streamed through the front window, falling across the book that had slipped out of the crate—*Founding Families of Cedar Creek*. She opened it, tracing the names: Wagner, Dubois, Adler. The page felt oddly alive beneath her fingers, as though its stories were not finished.

From the street outside came the murmur of voices again, drifting into the open door. "The Adler gift," one said. "Maybe it runs true. Maybe not."

Miriam closed the book gently, her resolve hardening. She had not come to Cedar Creek merely to inherit a shop. She had come because the town itself seemed to be waiting, because the past had not finished speaking. And perhaps, as Mrs. Callahan had hinted, she would need the help of this Julian Roth to understand what her aunt had left behind.

For now, though, she stood in the center of the shop, breathing in its mingled scents of cedar and lavender, dust and ink. She was no longer only a widow seeking a place to belong. She was an Adler, keeper of a gift she was only beginning to claim. And somewhere in the weave of Cedar Creek's history, a thirteenth petal waited for her to find it.

2

———

MARKET SQUARE WHISPERS

The morning sun spread slowly over Cedar Creek, softening the outlines of rooftops with a golden haze. Miriam woke to the faint scent of cedar shavings drifting in from a carpenter's shop and the sharper, sweeter note of apples being pressed for cider nearby. When she stepped outside, she followed the hum of voices until the narrow street widened into the town's market square.

It was alive with movement, the square's cobblestones echoing with the hustle and bustle of shoppers and the scuff of boots. Stalls spilled over with pumpkins arranged like glowing embers, bundles of corn tied in sheaves, and jars of jam stacked with the pride of housewives who had boiled and stirred through late-summer nights. Children darted between the stands with wooden whistles, their laughter carrying as brightly as the brass notes from the fiddler posted near the fountain.

The square's fountain itself was a remnant of another age, a rough stone basin carved by early settlers, its water catching sunlight like fractured glass. Old Mrs. Levine had already placed chrysanthemums around it, blooms the color of copper and fire. "For luck," she was saying, her voice rising above the chatter. "A festival without flowers is no festival at all."

Miriam lingered on the edge, her shawl pulled close against the cool air, feeling both drawn in and apart. The town carried a rhythm as familiar as heartbeat to those born into it: the quick gossip traded over crates of pears, the shared laughter that carried a history she had not lived. Yet she could not help but smile at the tapestry of it—how voices wove together like threads in a quilt, different colors and timbres but bound to the same pattern.

She passed a stall where Mr. Crane was hammering nails into a wooden booth, pausing every few strikes to shake his head at the younger man beside him. "No, lad, you've got to drive the nail straight or the whole thing'll lean like a drunk sailor," he muttered. When he caught sight of Miriam, he lifted his cap. "Morning, Miss Adler. You'll be joining us for the Harvest Parade, I trust?"

"I'm still finding my bearings," she admitted. "But it seems I won't be able to escape it."

He chuckled. "Nobody escapes the festival. That's the point. It swallows us all whole, and we're better for it."

At another stall, two sisters bickered over the best way to braid garlic for hanging. Their laughter bubbled through their quarrel, so that anyone listening might think it less argument than music. A fiddler struck a tune nearby, quick as river water over stones, and a young boy danced in clumsy circles until his mother pulled him back by the collar with mock sternness.

Everywhere Miriam turned, she found color and motion: bolts of cloth dyed in autumn shades, honey glinting gold in glass jars, smoked fish laid out on cedar planks. The mingling scents were almost dizzying—cinnamon and pine, cider and cured meats.

It struck her that this was more than a market. It was the pulse of the town, where history and present day collided in the simple acts of barter and laughter. A man sold tin charms shaped like stars, swearing they warded off bad luck. Another displayed wooden toys carved with more patience than profit. In each face Miriam sensed stories, and her heart ached with the awareness that she stood at the edge of them, invited to watch but not yet to belong.

She paused near a stall of quilts, running her hand across the patchwork of one particularly bright piece—blues and golds sewn into a star pattern. The woman behind the stall, heavyset with silver hair pinned back, smiled kindly. "You've Ruth's hands," she said without preamble. "Gentle, deliberate. We wondered when you'd come back."

Miriam swallowed. "I'm not sure I've come back so much as... arrived."

The woman chuckled. "Cedar Creek has a way of deciding for us. You'll see."

As Miriam moved on, the square's chatter seemed to tilt toward her, threads of curiosity weaving in her wake. Whispers traveled quickly here, she realized. The Adler shop open again. The widow returned. The gift passed on. She felt it in the sideways glances, the measured smiles, the too-bright greetings.

And though it unsettled her, she could not deny that part of her longed for it too—the recognition, the place within the weave.

· · ·

THE LONGER SHE LINGERED, the sharper Miriam felt the divide between invitation and distance. For every warm smile there was a hesitation, for every welcome a caution. The townsfolk seemed to be measuring her as much as greeting her, as though she were a piece of fruit to be weighed before purchase.

Near the fountain she overheard two men talking as they loaded hay bales for the parade float. "Adler's girl, back again," one muttered, not quietly enough.

"Carries the same light in her eyes," the other replied, half admiring, half wary. "But light like that can cut both ways."

Miriam kept walking, her chin lifted, though the words pressed against her ribs. Light that could cut—was that what they saw in her? A gift or a wound?

Children clustered near her booth, staring with the unashamed curiosity of the young. "Is it true you can see things?" one girl asked boldly. "Like ghosts?"

"Like secrets," another whispered, wide-eyed.

Their mother shushed them, offering Miriam an apologetic smile before pulling them along. But the words hung in the air, the same whispers she had carried from childhood: the Adler gift.

She paused near the baker's stall where Mrs. Levine was selling warm loaves wrapped in cloth. The older woman regarded her with something between fondness and scrutiny. "You'll have to choose soon," she said, handing a loaf to a customer.

"Choose?" Miriam echoed.

"Whether you belong to this town or only to yourself. Outsiders are tolerated. Belonging requires surrender."

Miriam frowned, unsure what surrender the woman

meant, but before she could ask, Mrs. Levine turned to the next customer.

She walked on, her steps slower now, her senses attuned to the undercurrent beneath the festival bustle. Laughter was plentiful, but it carried shadows. Jokes carried hints of rivalry. Warmth carried conditions. This was no simple welcome; it was a testing.

At one corner, a group of young women stitched banners for the parade. They spoke in low voices, glancing at Miriam, their words muffled by the cloth between their hands. She felt her cheeks flush, though she pretended not to notice.

Her aunt had warned her in letters: Cedar Creek gives itself only when it knows you will stay. Miriam now understood. The town was watching, waiting to see if she would take root or drift again like so many others.

The question pressed harder than she expected: Did she want to belong here? Could she bear to open herself again, to risk both acceptance and rejection? Widowhood had left her adrift, her heart brittle as thin glass. Yet the shop, the market, even the wary glances called to something in her—a longing to be part of a living story again, not just an observer of it.

As the morning deepened, Miriam found herself drawn toward the edge of the square where a cluster of older townsfolk had gathered. Their chairs faced the sun like cats soaking its warmth, and their conversation ebbed and flowed with the rhythm of age.

One of them, a woman with sharp cheekbones and hair plaited tightly around her head, beckoned Miriam closer.

"Ruth's niece," she said, her voice like a gate swinging on rusty hinges. "You'll want to hear this."

Miriam approached cautiously. The woman leaned in, her breath carrying the tang of peppermint. "The chapel's rose window has cracked. You've not seen it yet, have you?"

Miriam shook her head.

"A shame," the woman continued. "It's the pride of Cedar Creek. Twelve petals, shining like the crown of heaven. But last week, during vespers, a hairline crack spread across the glass. No one knows how. Some say age, some say storm. I say otherwise."

"Otherwise?" Miriam asked, her curiosity pricking.

The woman's eyes gleamed. "Windows don't crack without reason. Not windows like that. They reveal what the town tries to hide."

A hush followed her words, the other elders nodding or looking away. Miriam felt a chill that had nothing to do with the autumn air. A memory stirred—her aunt's trembling letter, warning her to seek the thirteenth petal.

Before she could press further, the fiddler struck up a louder tune, and the crowd's attention shifted. The conversation dissolved into laughter and talk of floats and pies. But Miriam's thoughts remained caught on the woman's words: *Twelve petals... cracked... revealing what the town tries to hide.*

She stood at the edge of the square, the sunlight suddenly sharper, the air colder. She felt again that strange hum beneath Cedar Creek's surface, the sense of something waiting. The whispers of the townsfolk no longer sounded like idle chatter but like fragments of a puzzle she had not yet learned to assemble.

As she turned back toward her shop, she glanced once more at the fountain, at the banners, at the laughter and bustle of the market. It was all so ordinary, so vivid with life. And yet, beneath it, she sensed the thrum of mystery, faint but insistent, like a heartbeat beneath a scar.

For the first time since arriving, Miriam felt not just the ache of belonging but the tug of destiny—an inheritance heavier than the shop's key.

And somewhere, not far from where she stood, the rose window waited with its secret.

3

FIRST MEETING WITH JULIAN

The blockhouse of the old fort rose above the river like a stubborn memory, its squared timbers weathered to the color of ash and rain. Morning light slanted between clouds, casting the parade ground in alternating bands of brightness and shadow. Miriam paused at the gate where a brass plaque announced, with understated pride, *Cedar Creek Historical Museum*. She stood for one breath, steadying herself. The market's cheerful noise had receded; here, the air held a hush that felt earned.

Inside the yard, a docent in a knitted vest shepherded a knot of second graders toward a burnished cannon, their chatter ricocheting off the palisade. Beyond them, the main hall breathed cool air and the faint fragrance of old paper. She stepped over the threshold and felt the familiar nervousness of the newcomer—would this be another room where curiosity must be hidden, or one where it might be welcomed?

The front desk sat at an angle to the door. Behind it, a man studied a ledger, pen balanced in his fingers without touching the page, as though the line he was considering did not wish to be hurried. His hair was thick and dark at the crown, cut short in a way that suggested practicality more than vanity; a river of burnt red threaded the sideburns. No ring on his hand. There was, however, a pale band of skin where a ring had once lived. His sleeves were rolled to the forearms, revealing the long, spare muscles of a man who moved books and boxes more often than he lifted weights. He looked up as Miriam approached, and the corners of his mouth tugged into a cautious smile—as if friendliness for him was a door always cracked open, never flung wide.

"Welcome," he said. "You must be Ruth Adler's niece."

The town was quick; news traveled here as fast as weather. Miriam nodded. "I'm Miriam."

"Julian Roth," he replied, standing and offering his hand. "Curator. Archivist. Sometimes janitor. Depends on the day." The handshake was warm and brief, his palm dry, the pressure precise—an academic's handshake, she thought, neither performative nor limp. "I'm sorry for your loss," he added, and the softness in his voice was not performative either.

"Thank you," she said, surprised by the flicker of comfort the words carried. She gestured toward the hall beyond. "I wanted to learn more about the fort—and the chapel."

"Do you have a few hours?" His eyebrows lifted in the self-mockery of a man aware of his own verbosity. "We'll pace ourselves."

He led her into the first gallery. Glass cases held artifacts arranged with a pleasing, almost musical logic: a flintlock pistol beside a child's wooden whistle, a map annotated with a trader's careful hand beside a wedding hankie embroidered with a rose. The juxtapositions felt intentional, as though someone believed history belonged to families as much as to battles. Julian spoke in a register that carried without intruding on the hush, folding dates and names into small stories with the care of a man placing stones to mark a trail.

"Many of the families still in town were here early," he said, nodding toward a faded photograph of three stern couples on church steps, their faces composed into the long exposure. "Some names you'll recognize—Wagner, Dubois, Adler. They braided themselves into a single rope whether they meant to or not."

Miriam smiled. "Braided. That sounds more deliberate than history usually is."

"History's not deliberate," he said. "People are. And then they call whatever happens afterward 'history' and pretend it was inevitable." His mouth curved again, the smallest smile. "If this sounds like a lecture, blame the community college. I try to leave the lecturing there."

"You teach?"

"Survey courses. Pacific Northwest history, historical methods. Tuesdays and Thursdays. The rest of the time I try to keep this place from forgetting more than it remembers."

They paused before an oil sketch of the chapel as it had looked when the paint was new—rooflines sharper, the rose window a blaze of color. The painter had not been talented but had loved the subject. Miriam stepped closer, feeling that now-familiar tug in her chest, a thread drawing her toward an image the way a hand might draw her toward a door left ajar.

"The chapel is why I came today," she said softly. "I've heard the window is... unusual."

Julian's gaze flicked to her face and then back to the

painting, the shift so quick it might have been a trick of light. "It is. In more ways than one. We can look at plans in the archives—if you don't mind dust."

"I don't mind dust," she said. "I mind secrets."

His mouth did that almost-smile again. "In that case, you'll like the archives. They don't keep secrets, exactly. They just tell them slowly."

He gestured on, and she followed, noting as she did the way he moved—not with swagger, not with hesitancy, but with a practiced care that kept his shoulder from brushing glass and his voice from waking the sleeping things that museums tend to shelter. He was handsome, she realized, but the observation felt less like a flare of attraction and more like a fact filed among catalog cards: height, posture, timbre, that pale band at the ring finger. Facts first; meaning later.

THEY CLIMBED a narrow staircase that creaked at honest intervals. The second-floor reading room faced the river; sunlight fell across long tables scarred by the elbows of decades. A board on the far wall listed volunteer hours in neat block letters. Among them, a child's hand had added *Mr. Roth knows all the stories*, the *all* underlined twice. A mug sat near the card catalog with a wedge of lemon floating like a sun. Miriam inhaled and tasted tea and old paper—two scents that, in combination, had always felt to her like a promise.

Julian retrieved a cloth-bound register and a box labeled *CC–Chapel: Plans & Correspondence*. He set them down with reverence, as though both objects had feelings he did not wish to jostle. Miriam slipped into the chair opposite him. The table between them felt less like a barrier than a bridge in mid-construction—planks set down, gaps left on purpose.

"Your aunt used to sit there," he said, nodding at her chair. "Most Thursdays. She'd help us decipher illegible marginalia." His eyes warmed as he spoke; grief, shared in the smallest of ways, softens rooms.

"I didn't realize she came so often."

"She liked to say the archives were a kind of medicine. The dose depended on the day." He slid the register toward her. "Go ahead."

She flattened the cover, and the paper sighed. Names marched across pages in tidy columns: births, donations, repairs to roofs and fences and hearts. She searched for *Adler* and found it again and again—tinctures donated to the infirmary in '28; assistance after the flood of '31; a line item, almost throwaway, *rose pendant, silver, given to chapel—anonymous*. The date was more than a century old. She felt a pulse in her throat and forced herself to turn the page.

"Found something?" Julian asked.

"Only proof that my family liked to put itself where it would be useful." She glanced up. "What about yours?"

"Roths arrived later than the first rope-braid," he said. "Paper-keepers. Notaries. A habit of finding ink wherever truth had slipped out of it."

"Useful," she said.

"Sometimes. Sometimes inconvenient." He opened the box and laid out onion-skin letters weighted at the corners with small lead snakes. "You asked about unusual."

"Mm."

"The chapel's rose window is modeled on a common European template," he began, adopting the careful tone of a teacher who doesn't want to talk down. "Twelve lobes. Twelve is the number a certain kind of builder trusts. Months. Tribes. Apostles." He tapped a blueprint, pale blue deepened to gray by time. "But look here."

She leaned in, and their shoulders nearly brushed; she willed herself not to move away and not to lean closer, choosing a stillness that felt like an agreement. On the plan, the rose's spokes radiated in perfect symmetry. And yet— there, faint as a thought, a penciled curve nested between two petals, an extra line someone had sketched and then erased so lightly it had never fully left.

"Thirteen," she whispered.

He did not startle—perhaps because he had seen it too often to be startled, or because he had been waiting to see if she would. "We don't have any evidence the window was built with thirteen. The glass shows twelve." His voice shaded gentler. "But sometimes plans tell you what a craftsman wished to do before a patron told him otherwise."

"Or before the town told itself otherwise," she murmured.

He studied her. Not suspiciously. Not even inquisitively. Simply with the attention of a man who collects details the way other people collect coins. "You said you mind secrets," he said at last.

"I mind the harm they do."

"Good," he said, as if she had passed an exam he had not intended to administer. He sat back, the chair creaking. "This is where I admit I'm the one who's supposed to be skeptical in this conversation."

"You can be skeptical," she said. "I'll be careful. They can live in the same room."

"They can," he agreed. His mouth warmed. The guarded

door in his face opened an inch, then settled. "It's been a while since I let them try."

Silence laid itself down between them, companionable. From somewhere below came the echo of children's feet and a docent's thin laugh. A floatplane droned low over the river and faded. The lemon in his mug spun once, slow as a second hand. She became aware of the pleasant fact that she was enjoying herself—not as distraction from grief, but as activity that invited a different shape of attention: the kind that builds, not destroys.

He lifted one of the letters, brow furrowing. "Do you see how many gaps there are in the correspondence between 1845 and 1847? We have purchase orders for panes, arguments about labor, budget debates—but very little from the months when the window was actually installed. It's as though the town decided not to write anything down when it mattered."

"Stillness where sound should be," she said. The phrase arrived unbidden; it felt less like rhetoric than like a report from inside her own chest.

Julian slid the letter aside, his gaze tipping to the pale band on his ring finger as if surprised by it anew. "I used to tell my students that archives are the story of what a community can bear to remember. They're also the map of what it can't."

"And the chapel?"

"The chapel is where remembered and unremembered live in the same glass."

She almost laughed with relief. "You do know all the stories."

"That," he said, deadpan, "is slander penned by an eight-year-old on the volunteer board."

"An authority if ever there was one."

He smiled, and this time the door opened half an inch more.

HE LED her from the reading room to a narrower corridor where a locked door bore a polite sign: *Archives—by appointment.* He unlocked it with a key from his belt and stood aside, the small formality suggesting respect rather than chivalry. Inside stretched a cool, long chamber of compact shelves. The air temperature dropped a degree, the air scenting more sharply of lignin and linen tape.

"This is where paper sleeps," he said. "Sometimes we wake it gently. Sometimes it wakes us."

Rows of gray boxes bore tidy labels. He pulled one from a shelf marked *CC–Ecclesiastical Artisans* and set it on a table with a felt mat. The lid lifted to reveal packets tied with cotton ribbon, each tagged in a clerk's tidy hand. He selected one labeled *Glazier: Correspondence/Sketches.* Inside were small squares of paper—thumbnail studies, color trials. Many were mundane. One was not.

It was a fragmentary tracing, perhaps done with a soft pencil from the back of the glass itself. The rose appeared ghostly and reversed, its lobes whorled in negative. There, where twelve petals met, a faint thirteenth line arced shyly, its curve feathered as if drawn in a hurry and smudged by a thumb. In the corner, a notation in French: *essai caché—* hidden attempt.

Miriam did not touch it; even her breath felt like a trespass. Her aunt's letter echoed in the bones of her hand: *seek the thirteenth petal.* The phrase moved through her like a migrating bird, leaving a wake of certainty. "Do you ever," she asked, "get the sense that an object wants to be found?"

"Wants?" He almost laughed, then didn't. "No. But I

believe people do. Whoever made that tracing wanted someone to see what couldn't be seen."

"What if the town didn't want to see?"

"Then we're back to maps of what a community can't bear to remember," he said quietly.

He returned the tracing to its packet with care, and she felt a ridiculous gratitude—as if he had tucked in a child. "What happened last week?" she asked. "I heard the window cracked."

His jaw worked once, a muscle flickering. He looked, she thought, like a man who keeps his own library of unshared reactions and is sparing with loans. "A hairline," he said. "During evening vespers. No storm. No shudder of the ground. People said they heard a sort of... sound. Like a breath caught." He shrugged. "Glass ages. Lead fatigues. But when the entire room inhales at once, it's hard to call it only physics."

"Were you there?"

"I was outside. Too many people, too little space." He smiled, wry, an apology for his own edges. "I'm not always great with crowds."

"Neither am I," she said. "But I'm getting better at standing where I'm meant to stand."

"And where is that?"

"In a shop I barely know how to run. In a town that isn't sure it wants me. In a room with a man who calls paper medicine."

"That seems like a reasonable place," he said, so simply that for a moment it hurt. She steadied herself with a breath.

He closed the box, replaced it, and wrote a neat note on an index card: *Ruth Adler's niece—Miriam—reviewed chapel plans/'essai caché'. Interested in glazier records.* He offered the card for her to read, as if to say: I am writing you into this place. "If you like," he added, "we can set aside some hours. I could use help indexing the chapel correspondence. Only if you don't mind tedium. And only if you sign the forms that say you won't lick your fingers to turn pages."

"I can promise to keep my saliva to myself," she said gravely.

"It's the romantic banter that keeps me in this job," he replied, and then regretted the word *romantic*—she saw the flicker of caution cross his face and let it pass without rescue.

She signed the form, the pen surprisingly heavy. "One condition," she said.

He lifted a brow.

"When we're done, you walk with me to the chapel."

He considered, not because he doubted but because he weighed. "All right," he said. "Not during services. I don't sit well in pews." A beat. "I'm divorced. That often gets asked badly, and this is my way of answering before anyone asks."

"Thank you," she said. "I am widowed." It amazed her that the word could be placed on the table between them without shattering either of them. He nodded, accepting the fact as one accepts a weather report that explains a certain slant of light.

They left the archives the way one steps out of a dim theater into noon, blinking as the living color of the present reasserted itself. On the landing, he paused and looked back at the locked door, as if checking he had truly closed it. "Paper sleeps," he repeated. "But sometimes it dreams loud enough to wake the house."

Outside, the river ran by with the serious playfulness of autumn water—bright at the surface, cold and fast beneath. He walked a few steps with her along the palisade path, keeping a companionable half-pace that allowed space for breath. "There's a town meeting tomorrow night," he said. "Festival business. Also chapel repairs. You'll hear more rumor than plan, but rumor is a kind of plan here."

"Will you be there?"

"Yes." He slid his hands into his pockets and studied the river, then her. "If you want a seat where people talk like you aren't there, sit to the left of the stove."

"I want to hear what they say when they forget to be careful," she said.

"Then left of the stove," he confirmed. "And—if the window calls you to look longer than is polite, let it. Plenty of us have been polite for decades."

They reached the gate. She turned to face him, the air cool enough that her breath showed. "Thank you. For the archives. For not glossing the crack with physics."

"You're welcome." He hesitated, then opened the small door again, as if to let out one last sentence. "When you stand under the window," he said, "try not to search for anything. Just... see. Sometimes attention is less a spotlight than a meadow. Things come out when they feel safe."

She filed the sentence among the day's facts. "All right." Her smile found its courage. "And sometimes things come out when someone scratches a line and calls it an *essai caché*."

"That too." The door in his face opened another fraction. "See you tomorrow, Miriam."

He returned to his post. She walked back toward the square with the careful steps of someone balancing two new things at once: an invitation and a mystery. In her mind's pocket, she carried both—the pale trace of a thirteenth curve and the feeling of a new name written, in tidy museum hand, on a card that would be filed in a drawer where paper dreams.

The river flashed between buildings. Distantly, she heard the bell at the chapel mark the hour with its dignified restraint. It rang true—today. She lifted her face to the sound and, without quite meaning to, imagined the moment it might refuse. Not out of malice. Out of fidelity.

"Left of the stove," she murmured, smiling, and let the town carry her forward.

4

———

THE ROSE WINDOW CRACKS

Vespers drew the town like tidewater. Lamps winked on along the square as dusk settled over Cedar Creek, and the chapel at the crest of the green gathered people with a magnetism Miriam could feel in her bones. She had not planned to attend—too much of church still tasted like absence—but after closing the shop she found her feet taking the path past the fountain and up the steps worn smooth by generations.

Inside, the air held the scent of beeswax and old varnish. The wooden pews were already filling, coats folded along polished rails, whispers braiding through the nave. Candles guttered in iron sconces, and beyond them the rose window glowed with the last light of day—glass catching what the sun surrendered. Miriam slipped into a seat along the side aisle, two rows from the back, where she could see without being seen.

The choir's opening note rose like a held breath. Pastor Elijah stepped to the lectern, his voice steady, his sentences shaped for comfort more than surprise. Miriam let the words pass through her without resistance, a stream flowing around a rock. She had learned not to fight prayers she did not know how to answer. In the stillness that followed a hymn, she found herself gazing upward.

Even shadowed by evening, the window commanded the room. Twelve petals in a wheel—reds and blues, amber at the rim where the glass thinned. The crack described at the market—"a hairline," the elder had said—was not immediately apparent. Miriam's eyes adjusted; she softened her focus the way she did in the shop when letting a symbol reveal itself. A thread appeared—yes, there—running from the central boss toward the lower right, so fine she might have mistaken it for a stray hair on the pane.

A tremor went through her chest. She could not have said if it was fear or recognition. The air near her skin cooled. She blinked and the thread seemed to brighten, not with reflected light but with a glow as intimate as breathing.

Pastor Elijah's tone shifted, some pivot from homily to petition. The congregation lowered their heads. Miriam didn't. The window held her as surely as any prayer.

And then, as if the room itself inhaled, the hairline moved.

It did not snap or splinter; it crept. A clear, almost musical tick—like a fingernail gently tapping glass—rang so softly she could not be sure she heard it. The line inched, a minuscule migration that would have escaped notice if not for the way light gathered at its edge, as though the crack were drawing luminosity to itself. A few pews ahead, a woman stiffened and touched her neighbor's sleeve. Some-where, a child whispered, "Mama—look."

The hairline paused. In that stillness Miriam felt a second tug, not in her chest now but between her eyes, a pressure like the beginning of a headache and the begin-ning of a vision fighting for the same space. She shut her eyes—and in the darkness behind her lids a shape flared: a petal nested between petals, a thirteenth curve where no curve should be, faint as pencil, definite as intention. It wasn't a thing seen so much as a thing *known*, like an answer arriving before the question formed.

She opened her eyes. The window's twelve lobes held their ground, stained colors cooled by night. The hairline glimmered. Along the rim of two adjoining petals something shimmered that no one else seemed to notice—a thread of brightness like dew at dawn. It traced the ghost of an arc she had glimpsed in the archives, the *essai caché* that had smudged her breath when Julian set it on the felt.

Her palms prickled. She gripped the pew-back until the wood pressed a memory into her flesh. The choir resumed —a simple Kyrie—and as the voices rose, the hairline crept another grain-width toward the rim. This time, the chapel reacted. A collective intake. A ripple of alarm disguised as reverence. Pastor Elijah faltered midsyllable, recovered, and quickened the end of his prayer as though outrunning his own surprise.

Miriam did not move. The sensation of being looked *through*—not looked *at*—passed over her. Something in the glass was attending, meeting attention with its own. She felt the same alert tenderness she felt with fragile books: turn the page, but do not break the spine. The shimmer gathered and dimmed, gathered and dimmed, like breath under lamplight.

She lowered her gaze to the people around her, seeking confirmation that what she perceived did not exist only in her. Faces tilted upward. Brows knit. Some lips pursed in the prim way of those who prefer their miracles on schedule. But she saw, too, the other expressions: wonder unpracticed, fear unmasked, a childlike will to believe pulling against the adult will to dismiss. No eyes, though, followed that thin, extra curve of light.

The hymn closed on a chord so clean it made her throat ache. Silence filled the chapel, the reverent kind that is also listening for the next sound. When it came, it was not voice but another soft tick from the rose, the sound a ring might make if struck very gently with a fingernail. The hairline stopped—no longer advancing, but present now, undeniable, a new fact inscribed into the town's most visible symbol.

The service hurried toward benediction, as if speed might reseal what had opened. Miriam stayed seated after the dismissal, hands slack in her lap, until the pews had begun to empty and the mutter of commentary replaced the cadence of psalm. Only then did she rise, drawn aisle-ward as if on a cord.

Up close, the glass was beautiful and flawed in ways that made it more itself—air bubbles imprisoned in color, minute waviness where the pane had cooled. The hairline traced through a blue lobe the shade of deep riverwater; at its edge, where two petals met, the shimmer lingered like a thought unwilling to abandon itself. She lifted a hand, stopping inches from the pane. The chill that rose from the stone felt old. The warmth that rose from the glass felt alive.

A breath near her shoulder. "Miss Adler," Pastor Elijah said, not unkindly. "Best not to touch."

"I wasn't," she answered, and did not add: I was listening.

BY THE TIME Miriam stepped into the evening air, the square had loosened into clusters of conversation. Lanterns swung under eaves; moths threw themselves at flame, persistent in their misunderstandings. Cedar Creek had not the patience to let rumor ripen in silence. It spoke.

"Glass settles," a man insisted near the pump, as though volume equaled authority. "The lead fatigues. That's all it is."

"Fatigues during *vespers?*" his companion said. "It's a sign, I tell you. We were warned."

"Warned by whom?"

"By the ones who came before. People forget—the window was a covenant before it was decoration."

At the foot of the chapel steps two teenagers were conducting an autopsy of the event with the relish of those recently converted to skepticism. "You could hear it though," one said, thrilled by the possibility of evidence. "Like, a tick."

"My aunt said she felt it in her fillings," the other replied, spooked, bragging about being spooked.

Farther along, near the bakery, Mrs. Levine dispensed sweet buns and commentary in equal measure. "There's no need for panic," she announced to a semi-circle of clients who had not asked for a sermon. "But there is need for care. We do not plaster over cracks. We repair them. Properly."

"Is it true the whole window could fall?" a young mother asked, clutching her child's shoulders as if a shower of glass were imminent.

"Only if we lose our nerve before we find our tools," Mrs. Levine said firmly, then caught Miriam's eye and nodded once—as if to say: I saw you stay.

On the boardwalk, Julian emerged from the alley by the palisade path, hair wind-tossed, coat unbuttoned, walking with the precise hurry of a man who wants to appear not to be hurrying. He joined a small knot of committee members near the town hall steps, where a blackboard had been dragged outside and chalked with phrases: *funding, scaffold, glazier?, insurance.* The practicalities of repair asserted themselves like weeds—unromantic, necessary.

Miriam hovered at the edge of a group forming around Walter Crane. "I told you," he was saying, eyes bright with weather reports and memory. "Some things crack when you say a word you shouldn't. Some things crack when you don't say the word you should."

"That's poetry, Walter," someone teased. "The board will want receipts."

Miriam drifted toward the fountain, where the water held the amber of a sky that couldn't decide whether to clear or brood. A familiar sharp-cheekboned elder sat with her hands folded, watching the town as a seamstress watches fabric for the pucker that will tell her where the stitch has gone wrong.

"You saw more than most," the woman said without looking up.

Miriam did not pretend otherwise. "I think the glass wanted to be noticed."

"That's one way to put it." The woman's mouth twitched. "Another is that something we put off saying found a different tongue."

"What is it we've put off?" Miriam asked, though she knew the woman would not answer directly.

"The kind of thing we only tell to people who show up *and* stay," came the reply. "We'll see which one you are."

Miriam let the gentle challenge land. Stay. The word felt like both invitation and test. Perhaps in Cedar Creek they were the same.

Rumor wheeled overhead like the crows at dusk, settling in bursts on whoever would feed it. "A flaw in the glass, that's all," someone declared. "The maker's mistake." "No," another said, "I heard a bride prayed here once and the prayer was denied; the glass has been holding that pain for years." "Hush," a third hissed, "you'll scare the children."

Beside the hall steps, Julian had chalk and a list and the patience of a court clerk. He listened, asked two or three questions for every ten sentences offered, and wrote the answers he wanted rather than the ones he was given. His eyes flicked up and found Miriam across the square. Something like recognition moved between them—not surprise, not even inquiry, but a small nod that said: the thing happened, and we both know it means more than the cost of scaffolding.

Pastor Elijah made his way through the clumps, his smile practiced, his assurances scheduled. "We will consult specialists," he repeated, "and we will pray for wisdom." Miriam could not tell if he was more eager to soothe the town or himself. When his gaze touched her, he hesitated half a beat and then continued on, as if he had almost decided to speak and then remembered her hands lifted near the glass.

At the far end of the boardwalk, adolescents plotted how to turn the crack into a ghost story for visiting cousins. The town would process the event in every register available: physics, finance, folklore. None of them were wrong. None of them were complete.

By the time lanterns burned low, the square had made its decision in the only way small towns do—by not making one. The window was cracked. A committee would convene. A glazier would be consulted. Insurance papers would be exhumed from a drawer and made to answer for a century of quiet. And in kitchens up and down Cedar Creek, the story would slip into murmurs soft enough for children to overhear and misremember.

Miriam walked home under a sky beginning to star. The shop's door unlocked with the same reluctant sigh as the night she first opened it. Inside, the smell of lavender and cedar met her like a palm on a fevered brow. She did not light all the lamps, only the small one on the counter. Its circle of light felt like a vow.

On the worktable, she laid out the day: the tick of glass, the hush after the hymn, the shimmer only she seemed to see. She wrote none of it down. Some things she trusted to ink; others she kept where the body kept truths it wasn't ready to pronounce.

The bell over the door tinkled once—wind—but the sound made her start. She laughed at herself, then stopped laughing when a pulse—no other word fit—rose behind her eyes like the memory of a dream. She pressed thumb and forefinger to the bridge of her nose and waited. It passed.

The town would settle. She would not. Not yet.

MORNING ARGUED its way over the rooftops, pale and insistent. Miriam woke before the carpenters and long before the committee. When she stepped outside to sweep the boardwalk—Ruth had always swept early; the habit seemed part of the deed—Mrs. Callahan was already headed toward the market with a basket.

"You were at vespers," Mrs. Callahan said without preface, as though ticking off attendance. "Saw the whole fuss, I suppose."

"I saw a hairline move," Miriam said. "And a town decide how to talk about it."

The older woman snorted approval. "You watch like an Adler." She leaned in conspiratorially. "The fellowship group will want you to say a blessing over the window tonight. Not a *church* blessing," she added quickly, forestalling objection, "a... *you* blessing. Ruth did that sort of thing. Oils. Words."

Miriam held the broom a little tighter. "What they want is comfort."

"And you don't give comfort?"

"I don't give anything I can't mean."

Mrs. Callahan's eyes sparkled. "Good. Mean it, then."

After she left, a steady stream of visitors found reasons to wander into the shop. Some came for tea, some for chamomile, some to warm their hands above the kettle and deliver a fresh account of the previous night. "I heard the crack spelled out a letter," one woman confided, ashamed of believing her own sentence. "An L. Or a J."

"Letters are what we impose when we're afraid of shapes," Miriam said gently, and the woman looked both hurt and relieved.

By noon, Miriam had heard six explanations and given none. She brewed more tea. Between customers, she stood at the counter and touched the blue cloth whose embroidered roses had thinned to threads. She found herself whispering, not to any person or doctrine, but to the quiet that lived behind the symbols. *If I am meant to see, teach me how to look. If I am meant to speak, teach me how to do no harm.*

Julian arrived just after one, hat in hand, an apology tucked into the set of his shoulders as though he had knocked and not been heard. "I won't stay," he said, though he had already stepped inside. "I'm making a list for the glazier—measurements, photographs, date ranges. I wondered if you'd walk back with me later to look again. Not during services."

She remembered his caution from the day before. "I can

come," she said. "But I won't pretend I only see what can be measured."

"I'm counting on that," he answered, the confession unguarded enough to surprise them both. He glanced at the shelves, as if trying to decipher her the way he would decipher a label. "People are assigning the crack to their favorite culprit—time, neglect, God."

"And you?"

He considered. "I think something that's been wanting to be said found a way to get our attention."

"That's not in the maintenance manual."

"No," he said. "But we can write addenda."

He reached into his coat and produced a small envelope. "Also—this was in the municipal file, misfiled with river permits." He slid it across the counter. Inside lay a fragment of onion-skin paper, brittle at the edges, bearing a diagram of the window and a notation in a hand different from the glazier's: *thirteen not permissible*. The words were slashed through, then written again in a smaller, defiant script: *thirteen belongs*.

Miriam traced the letters without touching them, the way one hovers a hand over heat to measure it. "Who wrote it?"

"No signature. The script doesn't match any of the usual suspects." A half-smile, thin but real. "I thought you'd like it better than the insurance policy."

She did. She liked it in the way a body likes water after salt. It wasn't proof of anything the town would agree to, but it was a companion to her seeing. "Thank you," she said, and it seemed to her the words were bigger than gratitude for a scrap of paper.

After he left, the shop quieted. The clock on the back wall ticked with the nostalgic insistence of clocks, turning the day whether anyone meant to go with it. Miriam tidied, wiped, made a list of herbs to order. She wanted, foolishly, to go sit under the window the way a person sits by a fevered child—keeping the vigil that does nothing and everything. Instead she kept the shop's vigil: hands busy, attention wide.

Toward late afternoon, Pastor Elijah appeared at the door, hat held to his chest, apology rehearsed but not perfected. "Miss Adler," he began, "a few of us are gathering this evening to... to pray over the window." He cleared his throat. "Several members of the fellowship thought perhaps you might offer—something in your tradition."

Miriam's mouth was dry. "In *my* tradition?"

He colored. "In your aunt's," he amended quickly. "I mean—oils. A word. She was known for words that— comforted."

"You already have prayers," she said, not unkindly.

"We have many prayers," he said. "Not all of them know where to put their hands."

The honesty disarmed her. She could refuse. She could guard herself. She could participate and shrink herself to keep others comfortable. All the old options waited, practical as coats on pegs.

"Tonight," she said slowly, "I will come. I won't offer spectacle. I will bring oil, and I will speak in a way that does not ask anyone to pretend they believe what they don't."

He looked relieved. "That is more than enough."

After he left, she stood very still behind the counter, both palms pressed to the wood as if checking whether the tree that had made it still lived. The word *seer* hovered like a moth above a lamp. She did not want the title. She wanted only to help the town look where it had learned not to.

In the quiet that followed, she remembered Leah—she did not know the girl's name, but she knew the feeling of a young woman standing under the same glass, hiding a page where hands that needed it would someday find it. The echo came with no narrative, just a pressure of kinship across time. Whether it was memory, imagination, or something in between no longer mattered. What mattered was the posture it asked of her: a willingness to stand where sight was needed and to speak in the modest voice the truth preferred.

Dusk came earlier, as it does on the days when a town is tired. Miriam closed the shop and took the path up the green again, a small vial of frankincense and myrrh oil in her pocket—a blend her aunt had used when blessing doorways and thresholds. The chapel's lamps burned calmer tonight. The crowd was thinner, the voices softer. Pastor Elijah greeted her with a nod. Mrs. Levine squeezed her hand.

Miriam stood beneath the rose. The hairline held, a new fact in a familiar face. She uncapped the oil, breathed it once to steady herself, and then anointed the stone lintel with the smallest of crosses—not a church's sign but a human one, a way of saying *this is a threshold and we intend to pass through whole*. She spoke quietly, enough for those near to hear.

"May what is cracked teach us to be careful," she said. "May what reveals itself teach us to be honest. May we repair not only glass but promise. May we look without fear and mend without pride."

No one said *amen* at first. Then someone did. Then someone else. The sound that followed was not applause and not the sob people bring to ceremonies for their own sake; it was a sigh like the one the shop had breathed when she first opened the door—relief at being named without being forced.

The oil shone briefly where she had touched the stone. She capped the vial and stepped back. She felt no grand rush of power, no vision loud enough to demand capital letters. Only a quiet acceptance, wary and resolute, like stepping into water you know will be cold, knowing you will warm to it if you don't flee.

Outside, stars ached into visibility. Julian waited at the bottom of the steps, as if he had calculated the end of the gathering by the length of a psalm. He offered no question, only a presence that made questions feel less like tests. "Left of the stove was good advice," she said.

"I have a talent for seating charts," he said softly. "How are you?"

"Cracked," she said. "Not broken."

He nodded, the kind of nod two people can share only after naming their losses. They walked a little way together, saying very little. At the square, they paused with the unspoken acknowledgment that each road belonged to them separately tonight.

"Tomorrow," he said. "We'll measure. And we'll listen."

"We will," she said.

Back in the shop, she wrote, at last: *The crack moves like a conversation more than like damage. Perhaps we are being invited to answer.* She put down the pen and let the sentence stand.

Her reluctant acceptance had not made her suddenly bold; it had, instead, made her precise. She would see. She would speak. She would not perform. She would stand where the town could look through her if it needed to, so long as what came through was something like truth.

She blew out the lamp. In the dark, she could almost feel the window across town, holding its new line the way a body holds a scar—tender, instructive, and alive.

5

COFFEE AND SKEPTICISM

The Riverlight Café kept its windows polished even on gray mornings, a habit that felt like defiance. From the street, Miriam could see the reflection of the square—the fountain, the fluttering banners, the stack of hay bales waiting for the parade float—tilting across the glass like a second town superimposed on the first. Inside, the bell above the door chimed a small, honest note. Cinnamon lived in the air. So did the darker scent of espresso that always reminded her body what it meant to be awake.

She chose a table by the mullioned window because it gave her the illusion of privacy without the risk of loneliness. A server with a diamond stud in his ear and a tattoo of a Blue Jay on his forearm introduced himself as Theo and recommended the cedar-spice latte. Miriam smiled and asked for black coffee—strong, no syrup—and a slice of apple cake if it hadn't run out. It had not. He set the mug down on a clay saucer that looked hand-thrown, the glaze pooled into a small lake at its center.

At the next table, two men leaned over their phones like

conspirators. One wore a carpenter's pencil tucked behind his ear; the other had the scrubbed, permanent sunburn of a roofing contractor. They were not whispering. Some people never learned how.

"—and then she stood up there like a priestess," the roofer said, sawing his toast with unnecessary vigor. "Oil and words. I mean, come on."

"Ruth used to do that sort of thing," the carpenter replied, not unkindly. "Nobody complained when the fevers broke."

"That was Ruth. This is the niece. She barely unpacked and now she's blessing public property."

Miriam kept her face quiet, her gaze on the square. It helped to pretend the words were weather. Pretend long enough and sometimes a storm spent itself against a wall and passed on. She broke the crisp edge of the apple cake with the side of her fork and tasted cinnamon, butter, the tart of fruit. The coffee cut through sweet like a clear sentence.

"The crack is fatigue," the roofer continued. "Glass shifts. Lead sags. You want a blessing? It's called scaffolding and a decent glazier. Not whatever this 'Adler gift' is."

"Maybe both," the carpenter said. "Metal fatigues. So do people."

"You think a prayer rewires physics?"

"I think a town needs to look at what it's afraid to look at," the carpenter said. "Maybe it uses physics to avoid that as much as it uses candles."

Miriam didn't move, but gratitude warmed the back of her neck. The roofer snorted, called the carpenter a poet like it was an insult, and reached for the sugar he had no intention of using.

The door chimed again. She didn't have to look up to

know who it was; some presences have a signature—the cadence of step, the brief pause at thresholds, the careful way a body takes ownership of a room without announcing itself. Julian stood for a beat, letting his eyes adjust to the wider light. He carried a leather folio tucked under his arm and wore an expression that translated to *I am here for tea and facts.* Theo greeted him like a regular. "Green tea?"

"Green tea," Julian confirmed, then added, "and—what passes for lunch?"

"Cheddar scones and a bowl of soup as big as your skepticism."

Julian's mouth tipped. "Tomato, then."

When he turned, his gaze swept the room and caught Miriam's. He looked briefly surprised, then pleased, then—as always—measured. He approached with the embarrassed confidence of a man who knows how to deliver a lecture but is still learning how to sit at a table.

"May I?" he asked.

"Please." She curled her hand around the mug to hide the tremor she only half imagined. "Riverlight is yours by right of green tea."

"Green tea and a permanent line of credit with the napkin dispenser," he said, setting the folio down. "You heard, I assume."

"Physics versus priestess?"

His mouth tightened in apology. "The priestess comment was unkind. I didn't mean for you to have to field that alone. I wasn't here to intercept."

"You're not my bodyguard," she said lightly. "Besides, it's easier to be told you're ridiculous than to be told you're dangerous."

"Both have been said in this town," he answered, not quite smiling.

Theo slid a pot and cup onto the table, then an enormous bowl of soup that steamed like an argument. "You two want to move to the corner table?" he asked, jerking his head toward a nook by the bookshelf. "Less drift from the peanut gallery."

"We're fine," Miriam said. "If I run from drift, I'll never learn how to breathe."

Theo winked and left them to it. The roofer at the next table lowered his voice a shade—enough to feel polite to himself, not enough to change content.

Julian stirred lemon into his tea, then did nothing with it, as though stirring had been the point. The folio sat like a third participant. "I have measurements," he said. "Angles, lead lines, span widths. The glazier in the city wants photographs and a sketch of the crack's path. We can manage the first; the second will require a ladder and the town's patience."

"Two scarce resources," Miriam said.

He took that in, neither agreeing nor arguing, which she had come to recognize as his version of respect. The roofer behind them launched again into scaffolding and insurance, and Miriam watched Julian's jaw work—his instinct to defend the integrity of process braced against his distaste for conversation as blunt instrument.

"You can say it," she offered. "Physics is a friend. I don't mind friends."

"I would never malign physics," he said. Then, after a beat: "I would also never tell you not to listen the way you listen. I just—" He groped for the border between their ways of seeing. "I am allergic to explanations that take a shortcut through mystery to get to spectacle."

"I'm allergic to explanations that stop at matter when something is clearly trying to speak," she said.

He lifted his cup. "Then we are each other's antihistamines."

She laughed, startled by relief. The roofer looked over; Julian's gaze slid past him like water around stone. The tension loosened a notch. They were not arguing about the same thing, she realized. They were negotiating how to stand in the same room without demanding conversion. It felt like learning to dance without music, counting under one's breath.

He opened the folio and drew out the tracing she'd glimpsed yesterday—the ghostly rose, the extra arc, the French note in the corner. He placed it between them, away from coffee rings. The roofer's voice faded into meaningless syllables. The page altered the air.

"*Essai caché*," Julian said softly, as if there were a correct volume for understatement. "Whatever the crack is or isn't, this exists. A hand tried to add a thirteenth curve to the plan. Another hand erased it. A third hand kept the attempt."

"And a fourth hid it in a municipal file," she said. "Your hands found it."

"Paper tells the truth we let it keep," he said. "Which is not the same as the truth."

"Then we keep both kinds," she said. "While lemon steeps."

The roofer coughed the word *superstitious* into his napkin. The carpenter told him to let people have their languages. Outside, a gust lifted the corner of a banner; sunlight struck the square and brightened the fountain's edge like a set stage. Miriam breathed. The café held the town the way the shop did—voices placed close enough to touch, separate enough to choose.

.   .   .

Theo returned with scones and butter that tasted faintly of salt and smoke. "The Riverlight has a new policy," he announced to no one in particular. "If you bring work to the table, you also bring appetite. Otherwise, I confiscate your notes and make you do the crossword."

"Threat duly noted," Julian said, tearing a scone with the seriousness of a man handling fragile ephemera.

"Crossword would reveal character," Miriam observed. "No one wants that on a weekday."

Julian glanced up. "You say that like weekends are safer."

"They're shorter. Less time to be revealed."

"Fair," he conceded, the corner of his mouth tipping. He pushed the butter toward her, habit more than choreography. She spread it thinly, careful at edges. She had not expected eating with another person to feel like consent. It did. Consent to survive a day, to enjoy, to risk.

"So," he prodded, "what did you see last night?"

"A line migrating toward honesty," she said. "A room bracing against it. The shimmer where two petals meet— like dew at dawn."

"You use dew a lot," he said, not unkindly. "In your descriptions."

"I use what the room gives me."

"What did the room give you about the people?"

"Fear that refused to name itself fear," she said. "And kindness that refused to name itself courage."

His eyes acknowledged the accuracy. He spooned soup with the care of a man who mistrusts stains. "You didn't flinch when Pastor Elijah asked you to bless the stone."

"I flinched," she said. "I chose anyway."

"Why?"

"Because rituals—when honest—help people direct their looking. And because refusing would have been about me." She sipped coffee. "I am trying to want the town more than I want my safety."

"That's a dangerous sentence."

"Safety or the town?"

"Wanting anything more than safety."

She nodded. "I know."

They ate quietly for a minute, not an awkward quiet but the kind that registers as belonging. She watched his hands: the way he steadied a page as if preventing wind that wasn't there, the way he caught a drop of soup before it reached the table, the almost invisible pause before he reached for his cup—as if asking permission of the moment to continue it. She knew nothing useful about his favorite books or the shape of his mornings, but she knew his grammar of care. It was a good grammar to share a conversation with.

"Do you ever wonder," he asked, "whether we're the ones the town summoned? That the rose and this crack and the archivist with tea and the woman with oil—"

"—walked into a sentence already partially written," she finished. "Yes."

He looked almost embarrassed at being seen that close to mystery. "If my colleagues heard me, they'd revoke my chalk privileges."

"You can borrow mine. I've never owned any."

His laughter surprised them both, a short, real sound. He hid it in a sip. The roofer glanced over, confused that a man could laugh without permission. The carpenter smiled into his mug.

"You said yesterday you don't sit well in pews," Miriam said. "You stand well at tables."

He studied her, weighing compliment against deflection. "Tables are honest," he said. "They have work to do. Pews ask for posture."

"And staff meetings ask for murder," Theo inserted cheerfully as he dropped a carafe of hot water on their table. "Refills are on the house if you save me from the committee that wants to rename the Riverlight the 'Pioneer's Perch.'"

Julian winced. "We are not renaming an institution after a bird that never learned to look."

"Look at that," Theo said to Miriam. "He has opinions about ornithology now."

"Only about metaphor," Julian replied, playing along.

Miriam leaned back, the chair creaking in a way that sounded like a living body acknowledging weight. "What's your metaphor for divorce?" she asked, not because she hoped to pry, but because she had learned that naming facts early prevented them from becoming landmines.

He didn't startle—he rarely did—but he took a breath that made room. "A bridge that needed weight to be tested," he said finally, "and couldn't take it. That's not a judgment. Just the physics of load."

"Mine for widowhood is a key that still opens a door and nothing behind it," she said. "The key didn't change. The house did."

He nodded, and their eyes didn't break away. Something in the room changed temperature—not warmer or colder, exactly, but more precise. The roofer at the next table had the sense, finally, to keep his critiques to himself. People at other tables moved into their own conversations. Theo turned up the radio two notches and then turned it back down, relieved to discover it hadn't been necessary.

"You know what I like about this room?" Julian asked. "It insists on being ordinary."

"That makes it available for truth," she said.

"Sometimes truth needs a stage," he countered.

"Sometimes it needs a booth and a chipped saucer," she said.

"One day it will need scaffolding."

"Preferably not from the lowest bidder."

Another small truce. Another plank laid across their river.

He leaned in. "There's one thing I will ask you not to do."

"Name it."

"When we go back to the window—and we should—don't help me see what you see by telling me what I ought to see."

"That's easy," she said. "I don't know what you ought to see."

"Many people believe they do."

"Then many people have decided to be lonely," she said.

He studied her again, the steady look that wasn't a challenge so much as a kind of care. "You're going to be very inconvenient," he said.

"For whom?"

"For the story that has kept this town comfortable."

"Then let's be inconvenient together," she said. She reached for the tracing, their fingertips close enough that the hairs along her wrist registered proximity. Neither of them made a show of moving away. Neither made a show of staying. The fact took its place quietly at the table, like a regular who came every Thursday and never stayed too long.

BY MIDAFTERNOON, the Riverlight had settled into its soft, steady tempo: the hiss of milk, a spoon against a ceramic rim, the door-bell's soft chime every twelve or thirteen minutes like a metronome that allowed for human error. A chalkboard above the counter announced *Thursday Open Mic • Friday Pie Night • Saturday Archives Hour (New!)* in Theo's tidy hand.

"What's Archives Hour?" Miriam asked, finishing her coffee.

"Something I invented thirty seconds ago," Theo confessed. "If I put it on the board long enough, the town will assume it was always there. You two talk about paper and glass while people eat pie. Those who prefer skepticism can heckle politely at a distance."

Julian arched a brow. "You are conscripting me."

"I am paying you in scones," Theo said. "And in the civic good of giving rumor a place to sit."

Miriam looked at Julian. "He's not wrong."

"He is not wrong," Julian admitted. He watched the chalkboard, as if expecting the letters to edit themselves. "Saturday afternoon. We can talk about glaziers. And about the line between repair and restoration."

"And about the difference between attention and spectacle," Miriam added.

"And about what records say when they're missing," he said, the archivist's creed.

Theo clapped once, delighted. "See? It's happening already."

At the front window, Mrs. Callahan and Mrs. Levine argued affectionately over whether the café should sell rugelach next to the scones. "If you bake them properly," Mrs. Levine said, "I will provide approval and clientele." "If you stop using 'properly' as a weapon," Mrs. Callahan said, "I will provide apricot jam." The server with the blue jay tattoo whispered to a new hire, "Those two could run a country," and the new hire said, "They already do."

The roofer and the carpenter stood to leave. The carpenter paused by Miriam's table. "For what it's worth," he said, "I've never seen a stone lintel look grateful before. Last night it did."

"Stones are terrible at saying thank you," Miriam said. "We'll take what we can get."

The roofer shifted, chastened more by tone than content. "I didn't mean 'priestess' like—well. You know."

"I do," Miriam said, saving him from further flailing. "And I know scaffolding also blesses a building."

He nodded, grateful to be allowed decency. When they were gone, Julian exhaled as though he had been holding his breath on their behalf.

"You didn't humiliate him," he said.

"I have no spare humiliation to distribute," she said. "I'm hoarding it against my own mistakes."

At the counter, Theo rang up a retired teacher who asked, not as a challenge but as a genuine question, "Will the window fall?" Theo didn't look at Julian for help. He said simply, "We'll catch it before it does." The teacher nodded. Sometimes a café is a church at the precise moment a town needs one.

"Look around," Miriam said. "This room is how Cedar Creek rehearses being kinder than it knows how to be in public."

"We should exploit that," Julian said. "Saturday, yes. And perhaps... Thursdays. After the museum closes, before dinner. Bring a letter or two, a plan drawing, let people touch history with clean hands."

"Clean hands optional," Theo called. "But no licking your fingers."

Miriam smiled into her empty mug. "You're building a

ritual," she told Julian. "Careful, the town may begin to rely on you."

"It already relies on you," he said without inflection, and the lack of flourish made the sentence land truer. She didn't pretend not to hear it. She also didn't pretend to be ready to own it.

A young mother with a stroller approached, tentative. "Ms. Adler? I'm sorry—I don't mean to bother—but my daughter hasn't slept well since the bell… since the window…" She trailed off, embarrassed by her own grammar.

"You aren't bothering," Miriam said. "You are describing something many of us feel with better honesty than we manage to say it."

The mother exhaled. "Do you have—something? Tea? A word?"

"I have both," Miriam said. "Chamomile and cardamom. And a sentence I've been practicing: 'We will mend what can be mended, and we will sit with what cannot until it changes shape.'" She wrote the sentence on the back of a receipt, not because she believed paper had magic but because people often need something to hold when belief is slippery.

"Thank you," the mother said. "Will you—will you be at the chapel tonight? I heard there's another small gathering."

"If I am, it will be to listen," Miriam answered, and the mother nodded as if that were the sweetest offer anyone could make.

When the room thinned and the light turned that late-afternoon color that makes wood look like it remembers trees, Julian closed his folio. "Walk?" he asked. The question was small. It contained no demand.

"Only to the door," she said. "I have orders to fill. And a shelf that wants reorganizing."

"Shelves have opinions," he said, accepting her limit without reading it as rejection. "I can help carry a box later."

"Thank you," she said, letting the word be as big as it needed to be.

At the door, he paused. "Miriam," he said, and when she looked up, he didn't deliver a thesis. He delivered an observation. "You didn't deny what you are. You also didn't perform it."

"I'm practicing," she said. "At both."

He nodded. The bell chimed as he stepped into the square. She watched him cross the cobbles with a measured stride, a man who had chosen to remain in a town that remembered through argument and repair. The fountain threw a little arc of light as if in benediction or mischief. Someone shouted across to someone else about nails and float height. Theo changed the chalkboard to add *Thursdays, 4–5pm: Cedar Creek Paper & Pie* in big optimistic letters.

Miriam returned to the table to gather cups. Her hand brushed the tracing, and the faint, penciled thirteenth curve felt—ridiculous as it was to think—less lonely. She slid the paper into the folio and carried it to the counter for Theo to keep behind the glass until Julian returned. "For the display case?" Theo asked.

"For the room," she said. "It behaves better when watched."

He grinned. "Don't we all."

As she stepped back onto the boardwalk, the café's bell chimed behind her and resolved into the echo of the chapel's more solemn bell. It had rung on the hour, precise and dutiful, as it always did—today. Above the square, a gull cut the sky in a white parenthesis. She thought of bridges and load, keys and doors, rooms that insisted on being ordinary so that truth could quietly take a seat.

The Riverlight's windows caught her reflection as she passed: a woman with a spine like a vow and eyes still learning how to see without demanding to be believed. Inside, tables waited with scones and napkins and the dangerous possibility that people told to face each other might learn a little habit of gentleness that would make meeting under a cracked window easier.

Saturday would bring pie and paper. Tonight would bring oil and quiet. Between them, coffee.

She went back to the shop to brew the teas that could help someone sleep and to write, on a slip of card to tack under the counter, a sentence she wanted to remember when skepticism tried to flatten what she knew: *Attention is not persuasion. It is care.*

And because the town had ears everywhere, the sentence, by evening, would find its way back to the Riverlight, where Theo would chalk it small under the menu as if it had always been there.

6

THE FIRST LETTER

The attic stairs were steeper than Miriam remembered, a ladder disguised as a staircase, its treads polished by generations of cautious feet. She climbed with a box cutter in her pocket and a hand on the wall, tasting the dry sweetness of dust in the air. Afternoon light reached the attic through a small, round window, slanting in a circle that drifted across the floorboards as the sun moved; in the cone of that light, motes drifted like slow snow. The shop below carried on its own heartbeat—doorbell chimes, the soft clink of cup against saucer—but up here the sound came as a memory rather than a noise, muffled by beams and insulation and the stubborn quiet of stored things.

Boxes lined the eaves, labeled in Ruth's careful, looping hand: **LEDGERS 1978–2001, APOTHECARY JARS, HOLIDAY CARDS (MIXED), HERBS—RETIRED.** Some labels had been reinforced with linen tape, the corners neat enough to make Miriam smile; her aunt had practiced care as though it were a craft. Miriam set a folding table under the window, laid out a rag for dust and a thermos of tea, and began with the boxes least likely to topple—always start with the boxes least likely to topple, Ruth had taught her, as if order were more than tidiness, a promise that attention would do no harm.

She cut the first box open and found shelves of amber bottles cushioned in newspaper. **Valerian, calamus, horehound**—labels handwritten in Ruth's small, definitive script. The next box yielded a set of pressed-flower frames, roses faded to tea-colored ghosts. Under those, a tin embossed with a thistle and the word **Scottish** in a font that belonged to biscuits and bridges. Miriam lifted the lid and inhaled a faint sweetness that had outlived its origin. Inside: a handful of postcards, clipped recipes, an envelope addressed to no one—no name, no street—only the words **For when it begins.**

The envelope was yellowed to the color of bones. Miriam turned it over; the flap was sealed with wax. The seal had cracked long ago, but Ruth had pressed the flap back into place as though re-sealing the past by intention alone. Miriam's thumb hesitated at the edge. She imagined opening a private organ, the kind that, once exposed to air, requires decisive action. She breathed, felt the attic's quiet settle around her shoulders like a shawl, and slid a fingernail under the flap.

The paper inside was thin and crisp; it sighed as she unfolded it. Ruth's hand—so familiar it made Miriam's throat ache—filled the page. The letters trembled, not with age but with the kind of fear that steadies itself by writing.

My Miriam,

If you are reading this, the town has asked for what it has put off. You will know the hour by feeling it in your bones before the bell tells you. You will think you are mistaken. You will not be.

When the window speaks (and it will not use words), do not argue with it. Stand where you can see and let it show you what it is ready to show. Others will want you to comfort them. Comfort them only with honesty.

Seek the thirteenth petal.

The sentence carried weight disproportionate to its ink, as if a heavy object had been wrapped in tissue and was now taking shape in air. Miriam's eyes moved to the next line.

Your mother could not, though she tried, and I could not, though I stayed. I do not write this to burden you but to tell you what the shop already knows: you were chosen because you will look without pride and speak without spectacle. Some will call you priestess to punish you. Some will call you fraud to save themselves. Let that pass as weather passes. Do not answer to names not yours.

The attic's silence deepened. Miriam's skin prickled in the draft that found its way along rooflines and under shingles. The letter went on, not long, but with the economy of someone laying out a map that would look like nonsense until the walker reached the right turn.

There is a place in wood that remembers. You will know it by touch. When you find what the wood is keeping, treat it like a living thing that survived winter. Warm it, don't tug. If you open it too fast you will tear it.

Her breath hitched. She could feel Ruth's hand, the light tap of forefinger against the note—**remember**—as if her aunt stood beside her.

Do not do this alone. You will need the man who listens with paper. He will say he is not a believer. Believe him about that and trust him anyway. He will ask good questions and keep poor records from telling you they are the whole truth.

Julian. The name did not appear in the letter, but the

shape of him did, clear as if he had stepped into the attic light and said something about green tea to make the room bearable.

I am afraid, Miriam. Not of the glass or the town. Of our habit, as Adlers, of staying quiet when we ought to say a thing. If the thing is ready to be said in your time, say it. If not, rest beside it until the weather turns. The shop is yours as a door is yours when you have the key. You know what a door requires.

—R.

The initial sat with a finality that undid Miriam's composure more than if Ruth had signed her full name. She set the page down on the folding table and waited for her breath to catch up to itself. *For when it begins.* It had begun last night, under the rose window, with a sound she would have called a tick if the room hadn't inhaled at the same time.

She turned the page over—not from doubt, but because the hand, once attuned to the possibility of message, seeks more. On the back, a single line: **If you need courage, find it in the places where water is blessed and where bread is broken.** A note to look not only in the chapel but in the rooms where the town practiced being a town.

Miriam folded the letter along its old crease and held it to her palm. The attic felt larger now, filled with a presence that wasn't haunting, exactly—more like an invitation that included the right to refuse. She closed her eyes and saw the hairline in the glass, the shimmer where two petals met, the ghost of a thirteenth curve glowing the way dew glows before the sun claims it. She did not say **yes.** She did not say **no.** She did what Ruth had asked: she stood and looked.

· · ·

SHE STAYED with the letter a long time without moving, as if proximity could do part of the work. When she did move, it was to the boxes marked **LEDGERS** and **CORRESPON-DENCE**, a choice that felt like honoring both breath and bone: the living paper of commerce that kept the doors open and the letters that had kept the heart shaped to its use.

The ledger covers were cracked but clean. Ruth had tracked tinctures and teas, nights stayed late with candles to see Mrs. So-and-So through a fever, mornings opened early because the fishermen said the river had turned mean and they needed rosemary and courage. There were entries for herbs and for what herbs could not mend: **Mrs. L. sat an hour. No charge. Walter needed to talk about his boy. Gave tea.** Between the lines, Ruth had lived the quiet, weighted truths the shop absorbed like wood absorbs oil.

At the back of one ledger, a different kind of record began: **THRESHOLDS.** The word sat centered at the top of the page, underlined once. Beneath, a list:

- **Shop door** — *belonging / leaving — amend threshold with oil at seasonal turnings*
- **Market fountain** — *voices rehearse kindness here — bring bread when things are brittle*
- **Fort museum reading room** — *paper breath / teach people to listen to it*
- **Chapel** — *window — do not perform here; let it speak first*
- **River confluence** — *if anything is to be released, release it here — not words, not pages, only what is done with breathing*

Miriam's mouth quirked in an involuntary smile at *paper breath*. The shop, the fountain, the museum, the chapel, the river: Ruth had drawn a pentagon of care around the town. What you inherit, Miriam thought, is not only keys and shelves. You inherit routes.

A cloth packet lay under the ledgers. Inside: a folded map of Cedar Creek hand-drawn by Ruth, not for navigation but for meaning. Small circles inked at the thresholds she had named; beside each, a word: **door, water, paper, light, confluence**. A sixth circle marked the alley behind the shop where deliveries came—a place no one would think symbolic. Beside it Ruth had written: **keeping**.

"Where wood remembers," Miriam murmured, touching the circle with the pad of her finger. She felt, suddenly and absolutely, the shape of the back wall shelves in her palms—not the look of them but their give under pressure, their small, almost imperceptible **sigh** when a hidden nail is eased instead of pried. The image arrived without a story to carry it. She set it down in her mind like an egg set down in a nest.

She opened another box. Old photographs, a stern great-great-grandfather in a stiff collar who looked kind despite the fashion of his era; Elise—her name in pencil—Ruth's aunt, eyes crinkled, hair pulled back in a coil like a thought kept at the ready; a wedding portrait that had been exposed a second too long so that the bride looked as if she were starting to move. In the margin of that photo someone had written a date and one word: **Leah**. The name hummed in Miriam without context, tuning a string she hadn't known was stretched inside her.

Beneath the photographs, a worn envelope: **DEED**. The paper crackled. The deed named the shop, listed property boundaries, assigned taxes, and included a rider in an old-fashioned hand—Elise's?—stating that the shop's **contents** were more than inventory and should be treated **as instruments of trust, to be kept or given as the keeper discerns.** *Instruments of trust.* Miriam sat with those words until they settled into place like a stone in a riverbed.

Ruth had not left her money so much as a position—keeper of thresholds, steward of a route built of places where the town told itself its own story without flinching. A letter that trembled with fear and courage both had hand-delivered the first instruction: **seek the thirteenth petal.** And then there was the line that mattered for living: **Do not do this alone.** She thought of Julian in the museum reading room, hands careful, humor self-conscious. *The man who listens with paper.* She smiled, the smile of a person who realized she had been given permission to enlist help.

Under the map, one more envelope, thin and barely holding together. It contained a pressed rose petal, almost translucent, its veins like writing burned into paper. On the envelope's front Ruth had written: **For courage; do not refuse it because it is fragile.** The petal lay like a blessing and a dare. Miriam did not lift it. She closed her hand over the envelope instead, willing the symbol to do its work through paper as courage often does—quietly, unseen.

She set things to rights with the care she had used to discover them, rewrapping what had been wrapped, aligning corners so the lids would seat properly, labeling what had not been labeled with pencil so that future hands could erase. When she stood to stretch, the round window had shifted its circle of light across the floor; the cone now struck the far wall, illuminating the place where the rafters met. She would need to buy a better lamp up here. She would need to clean. She would need to return soon, and often. The attic had changed from storage to archive in the space of an hour because she had changed from inheritor to steward.

She slid Ruth's letter back into its envelope and tucked it into the inside pocket of her cardigan. The paper's weight felt disproportionate, as though it were wearing more gravity than its size entitled it to. On the way down the stairs she paused on the landing and pressed her fingers to the wall. The plaster was cool; behind it, wood. *You will know it by touch.* The instruction didn't insist; it waited.

In the shop, she brewed tea and set out two cups as if someone were expected. She folded a cloth on the counter for no reason other than the way order calmed her. The bell above the door jingled as Mrs. Callahan stuck her head in with a tin of shortbread and the latest installment of news told as advice. "Bring a sweater tonight," she said. "Chapel drafts out of spite."

"Thank you," Miriam said, and meant it. When the door closed, she took out Ruth's letter again and read the line that had set the room into motion: **Seek the thirteenth petal.** The shop watched, the way rooms watch, with patience that expects being needed.

AT DUSK she locked the front door early and lit only the small lamp on the counter, letting the rest of the shop fall into a comfortable twilight. The day's customers had come for chamomile and conversation, for reassurance without lies, for a place to sit where the town did not require them to pretend stoicism. Miriam had given what she could without promising what she could not. The letter had burned in her pocket all afternoon like a coal one carries to start a fire elsewhere.

Chosen. Ruth had written it as if the word did not belong

to crowds and applause but to chores and routes. Miriam had never wanted a title. She wanted to do her work and—if God could be coaxed into it—belong quietly to something larger than herself. *Chosen* argued with her modesty. It also explained the pressure she had felt since stepping into Cedar Creek, a sense that the town had expected her the way a house expects a certain weather at a certain season.

She washed the tea cups and set them upside down to dry. She wrote one sentence on a card and slid it under the glass at the counter's edge: **Attention is not persuasion; it is care.** A line she could touch when someone demanded that her seeing perform. A line she could look at when her own fear whispered that seeing without spectacle would be ignored.

She took the letter out again, sat on the stool, and read it aloud in a whisper, as though giving the attic's private words their first public hearing. "When the window speaks," she read, "do not argue with it." The instruction felt both impossible and simple. The impulse to argue rises in the exact measure of one's fear of being wrong. She would have to let the town watch her be unsure. That was, perhaps, the cost of being the kind of seer Ruth asked her to be.

The bell tinkled softly; she started and then laughed at herself—only the night air nudging the door. If Julian came, she would show him the map, not the letter—not yet. *Do not do this alone,* Ruth had said. But *alone* and *undiscriminating* were not the same. For now, the letter belonged to the space between them as an unspoken possibility. She imagined saying: *There is a line between the petals the plans tried to hide.* He would say something about hands and erasures and the integrity of evidence. She would say something about wood that remembers and the way a shelf will tell you if it is ready to open. And, if they were careful, neither would need the other to convert.

The thought of the shelf sent a thin current along her fingertips. She stood, set the letter on the counter, crossed the shop, and knelt by the back wall where the oldest shelves lived. The boards were dark with age and oil; Ruth had polished them until they learned to glow. Miriam laid her palm flat and waited, not for magic, but for the familiarity wood offers when it has kept a question and thinks it recognizes the person asking it. She moved her hand an inch at a time, pressing gently along the seam where one board met another. On the third pass, a minute shift—not a give so much as a sigh. *Warm it, don't tug.* She lifted her hand. Not today. The wood had nodded, not opened. Her heart settled. The letter had not asked for haste. It had asked for fidelity.

Back at the counter, she opened her journal and wrote:

- *Ruth left a route disguised as a shop.*
- *The town will want me to be useful more than it wants me to be true. Resist the barter.*
- *"Seek the thirteenth petal" = glass + plan + hand + erasure + the thing that refuses to vanish when erased.*
- *Water and bread = Riverlight + fountain + chapel.*
- *Do not do this alone.*

She paused, then added a sixth line in a smaller hand: *I am afraid, and not only of being wrong. I am afraid of being right where the town prefers to be comfortable. I am afraid of what belonging costs. I am more afraid of not paying it.*

The street outside shifted from commerce to the small sounds of evening: boots on boards, a bicycle bell, laughter that had completed its daytime work and now sought home. In the distance the chapel bell marked the hour. The sound moved through her like a measure.

When she slid the letter back into its envelope, her fingers trembled in eerie sympathy with Ruth's script. It surprised her—the physical echo of fear traveling across time not as story but as sensation. Fear had not disqualified Ruth; it had educated her. Perhaps it would do the same for Miriam. She held the envelope a moment longer, then slid it beneath the counter in the narrow drawer where Ruth had kept matches and a tiny bottle of frankincense—threshold tools, not for display.

She considered walking to the museum to show Julian the map and the ledger's **THRESHOLDS** page. She considered, and chose instead to write him a note: **Saturday— Paper & Pie? Theo conscripted us. Bring the tracing. I have something you'll want to see.** She left the note with Theo, who promised to place it under Julian's mug like a fortune when he came in for green tea.

At the door, Miriam locked up and stood for a moment in the square, breathing cedar and smoke. The Riverlight's windows glowed with companionable light. The fountain murmured. On the hill, the chapel's rose window, invisible at this hour, kept its silent vigil. She could feel it, the way you can feel a person in a dark room even before they speak —presence in the negative.

"Chosen," she said quietly, to test the word's bite. It didn't bite. It sat in her mouth as a vow you make to yourself before you say it aloud to anyone else. Not chosen above others, not set apart for glitter or grief. Chosen the way a key is chosen for a door, which is to say: matched for use.

Back in her small apartment over the shop, she set the letter on her desk, placed a smooth river stone on its corner as if to keep it from flying off in the night, and climbed into bed without turning on the radio or looking for distraction. Sleep came slowly and then in a rush, bringing with it a dream that was less dream than instruction: her hand on wood, warm; a petal drawn where no petal had been; a voice she recognized as her own, saying, without theater, *I will see. I will speak without spectacle. I will stay.*

When morning came, she would make tea for the mother with the restless child, answer Mrs. Callahan's questions with questions of her own, measure the crack with Julian and consent to scaffolding, take the map to the museum and put it beside the tracing so paper could breathe to paper. She would also—quietly, without explaining herself—press her palm again to the seam in the shelf and listen for the sigh. Not to force. To befriend.

The letter lay in its small gravity at the corner of the desk. In the room below, the shelves settled minutely as the night air cooled, as wood that remembers often does—never fully still, never fully loud, keeping what it keeps until hands arrive that have learned how to touch.

7

FESTIVAL PREPARATIONS

Town Hall looked like it had been built to argue in—high ceiling, stern portraits, a potbellied stove that clicked even when it wasn't lit, and folding chairs that punished fidgeters. By the time Miriam slipped in, half the town had beaten her there. She took a seat "left of the stove," as Julian had suggested—where, if you listened, people forgot to edit themselves.

Theo from the Riverlight had brought a carafe of coffee big enough to baptize a skeptic. He moved through the aisle, pouring refills with the dignity of a maître d'. Mrs. Levine had arrived with a basket labeled **FOR BRIBES ONLY**, which, judging by the scent of cinnamon and butter, contained rugelach that would reduce any zoning dispute by half. Mrs. Callahan occupied a front-row seat with a legal pad and three pens clipped to the top like warning flags.

The festival committee chair, a man named Everett Pike who believed "chair" to be a spiritual calling, banged his gavel against the lectern. "Order," he said to a room that would not give it easily. "We're here to finalize parade floats, pie contest rules, and—" he glanced at the agenda, as if surprised by his own handwriting—"risk management for the hayride."

"Risk management," Walter Crane echoed with relish. "That's what they call common sense when insurance overhears."

Laughter loosened shoulders. Pastor Elijah crossed one ankle over the other and looked like a man practicing calm as a discipline. The roofer and the carpenter sat together, temporarily allied by chairs. A cluster of teenagers in the back whispered with the high-drama intensity of those for whom a banner's font is a hill to die on.

Julian entered a few minutes after Miriam, a sheaf of papers tucked under his arm, hair damp as if the river air had decided to decorate him. He nodded to people scattered across the room with the understated familiarity of a person who'd cataloged them already: donors, volunteers, the one who brings too many staplers. He caught Miriam's eye and tilted his head minutely toward the stove. She held up the corner of the agenda in salute.

"First item," Everett intoned, "the parade's lead float." He looked at the front row like a referee daring a whistle. "Proposals?"

A hand shot up. "Salmon," declared a woman with a braid thick enough to coil a tugboat. "Full-scale. We put the children inside so they can wave through the gills."

"The children?" Pastor Elijah repeated, alarmed.

"Not the littlest," she said, mollified. "Just the fearless."

"The salmon must be anatomically correct," a science teacher insisted from three rows back. "We are not raising a town of liars."

"We could dress Geraldine," Mrs. Callahan suggested, to gasps. Geraldine—the town's most opinionated goat—had been known to insert herself into events with a grace inversely proportional to her weight. "A wreath of ivy, a cart of apples, a sign that says **WELCOME, AUTUMN**."

"Geraldine ate three hymnals last Christmas," someone said.

"She prefers the minor keys," Theo added, deadpan.

Miriam watched the room toggle between delight and dread, between the practical mechanics of parade floats and the gentle, ridiculous dignity of insisting that they matter. The market square flickered across her mind: pumpkins like embers, banners stitched with gossip. These meetings were how the town rehearsed itself—arguing over details so that, in the moment, it could act like all of this had always been inevitable.

"The logging float returns," Everett announced, perhaps to regain control. "Scaled down. No chain saws."

"No chain saws," Mrs. Levine repeated, brandishing a wooden spoon as if she had smuggled it in her sleeve. "We are not staging a cautionary tale."

The teenagers in back raised their hands in a bundle. "Skateboard brigade," their spokesperson said. "We learned a routine—interleaving figure eights set to bluegrass."

"Helmets?" the room asked in a single, suspicious voice.

"And knee pads," the girl sighed, already bored by compromise.

A man Miriam didn't know stood to advocate for a "heritage float," which he described as "a tableau of the founding families—Wagner, Dubois, Adler—each represented with dignity." The word *dignity* made every tongue in the room itch.

"As long as we don't put children in bonnets," Mrs. Callahan said. "History can be evoked without requiring heatstroke."

"We could build the chapel window out of crepe paper,"

a teenager suggested, which produced a collective wince. "Too soon," a dozen voices murmured.

Julian cleared his throat and rose, not in objection but like a man stepping into the current to help ferry a log. "We can honor history without replicating it," he said. "A float of symbols, not costumes. A river for the Dubois, a book for the Adlers, a rope for the Wagners—three strands."

"Braided," Miriam said softly, then felt the word recognize its own echo. He glanced at her, the quick, private acknowledgment of an idea successfully handed across a crowd.

"Braided," he agreed. "No bonnets. No chain saws. Children waving through salmon gills to be discussed."

"Seconded," Theo called from the aisle, refilling mugs. "If you keep arguing, I'm instituting scone fines."

The room laughed again. The Riverlight had become Cedar Creek's auxiliary parliament; coffee soothed where rules inflamed. Everett banged the gavel with the exasperated affection of a schoolteacher whose students had decided to be charming instead of obedient.

"Next," he sighed, "pie rules."

The collective inhale was as reverent as prayer.

BY THE TIME they got to pies, the room had unbuttoned its restraint. A whiteboard had been dragged to the front, its surface quickly colonized by categories: **fruit, custard, savory**. Past controversies—canned pumpkin, lattice integrity, whether crumble counted as a legitimate top—were invoked like case law.

"Judge selection," Everett read, as if memorizing his own fate.

"I will not judge again if Walter is allowed to

submit *and* heckle," Mrs. Levine declared, receiving a wounded hand-to-heart from Walter Crane.

"I heckle to improve outcomes," he said.

"Outcomes improved by heckling are not outcomes we can trust," Mrs. Levine replied.

"The judges must not be related to entrants," Pastor Elijah offered, counting cousins in his head. "We should publish the rubric."

"Rubrics are how we pretend fairness," Theo said. "But fine. We'll pretend."

Paper rustled. People proposed judges and un-proposed them. The roofer suggested the science teacher for "objective rigor," the science teacher insisted on a blind tasting to reduce "affective contagion," and the teenagers demanded a youth category with flashing lights. "No flashing lights," three grandmothers chorused, invoking migraines and last year's debacle.

Then, like a weather shift, the meeting's air changed in that subtle way that towns recognize when something older than the agenda slips under the door. Mrs. Mathers—sharp-cheeked, hair braided into a crown, one of the elders who preferred the edges of rooms—rose without being recognized.

"Our pie rules," she said, "might consider our *old family promises*."

A murmur cobbled together curiosity and caution. Everett blinked, off-map. "I'm—sorry?"

"Promesas viejas," she repeated, frowning at the English word. "Before the festival was festival, it was pact. Families promised to feed the town, each in a way. The Wagners provided flour and rope. The Dubois, fish and stories. The Adlers, the bread that is not eaten." Her gaze flicked to

Miriam, then away. "When the window was set, they promised again."

"Bread that is not eaten?" someone asked, amused and wary at once.

"Blessing," Mrs. Levine said gently. "Doorways. Thresholds." She didn't look at Miriam, either, which was its own kind of recognition.

Everett shuffled his agenda as if it had betrayed him. "This is—fascinating," he said with the best smile he could comb across the moment, "and perhaps suitable for Archives Hour?"

Julian stood again, and Miriam could see him make the decision to be bridge instead of guard. "Mrs. Mathers isn't wrong," he said. "We have mentions in early ledgers—families contributing in ways that looked like groceries and, also, like promises. The festival grew out of a harvest gathering that was part feast, part... reaffirmation."

"Of what?" the roofer asked, genuinely.

"Of being a town," Julian said simply. "Of handling what was too big for one house to hold."

"And the window?" someone else ventured, the question carried on a draft.

"The window watched us do it," Mrs. Mathers said before he could answer. "And remembers when we don't."

The room shifted again—the weight of a subject too thin for mockery, too broad for a motion. Miriam felt Ruth's letter against her ribs like a small firm hand. *Seek the thirteenth petal.* She did not speak; she watched, the way Ruth had instructed: *Stand where you can see and let it show you what it is ready to show.*

"We have a crack," Walter said, almost tenderly. "That's a kind of memory too."

"We will repair it," Pastor Elijah put in, voice practiced. "With professional help and with care."

"Care includes appetite," Theo declared, because a meeting can only ride one solemnity wave before capsizing. "Which brings us back to pie."

"Indeed," Everett said, grateful to be returned to script. "Rules."

"A lattice should count only if it is a lattice," Mrs. Callahan insisted. "No performative strips. They must interweave."

"Amen," said three elders.

"We also add rugelach," Mrs. Levine announced, to gasps of theological dissent. "I will make them properly. We will call them *heritage crescents* so that those allergic to Yiddish can enjoy without rash."

"Seconded," Theo sang out.

Miriam found herself smiling. The town, when faced with the undertow of older promises, did what it always did: it made a joke sturdy enough to carry meaning, and then it carried meaning anyway. The kids in the back were designing a *Heritage Crescents* banner on a napkin. Pastor Elijah whispered to Everett about scaffolding bids. The roofer and the carpenter were arguing about lattice metrics with the rigor of mathematicians.

Julian angled over during a lull and slid into the chair beside her without fanfare. "I didn't expect Mrs. Mathers to be the one to say it aloud," he murmured.

"Someone had to," Miriam answered. "The room was getting lonely with the truth in the corner."

He followed her gaze to Mrs. Mathers, who sat down with the satisfaction of a woman who had fulfilled a personal statute. "You're quiet," he said.

"I'm practicing."

"At being quiet?"

"At not making the room do more than it is willing to do."

"That might be harder than repairing glass," he said, the ghost of a smile.

"Glass only breaks in one language," she said. "Rooms break in many."

He tipped his head, conceding. "Paper and pie Saturday," he added, as if reminding both of them that not everything had to be solved on a Tuesday night. "I found another glazier's note, by the way. We'll talk then."

"Bring green tea," she said.

"Threats are unnecessary," he returned.

THE FINAL ITEM on Everett's battered agenda read **Hayride Safety**, which summoned a different kind of liturgy. Out came the stories: the time a bale slid and a toddler floated down the lane like royalty; the year the tractor stalled and Mr. Pike had to haul the wagon with three horses and a grudge; the night Geraldine leapt aboard and discovered the aerodynamic properties of panic.

"No goats on the hayride," Everett said, pounding the gavel like a judge who had discovered a clause he could enforce.

"Define *on*," Mrs. Callahan muttered.

"Define *goat*," Theo said.

"The hay bales must be tied with actual rope, not 'inspired-looking twine,'" the carpenter read, quoting last year's fiasco report.

"Teenagers ride separately from the sound system," Pastor Elijah added, not looking at the teenagers. The teenagers groaned like a Greek chorus. "The sound system rides separately from the generator," the science teacher sighed, under the breath but not enough to escape the record.

"And lights?" the roofer asked, rubbing a forehead that remembered wiring. "We want festive, not seizure."

"Lanterns," Mrs. Levine ruled. "Not candles. I will lend my string of electric stars if the committee signs a waiver pledging to return each one."

"You keep waivers for lights?" Walter marveled.

"I kept this town together with Tupperware and waivers," she said. "Do not challenge me."

Miriam watched people who had grown up together—or had decided to—practice their fondness in the idiom of dispute. It was the kind of arguing you do when you expect to see each other again tomorrow and every tomorrow after. The kind you can't replicate with strangers, because it depends on the knowledge that no one gets to flounce out of the town.

"New business?" Everett asked, brave. A hand rose in the second row—a young mother clutching a pen with the determination of someone determined to be important for fifteen seconds. "Can we have a quiet hour at the festival?" she asked. "For the kids who don't love noise."

"Bless you," Theo said. "Yes. I'll put it on the chalkboard at the café and then it will be law."

"It will be law because we will vote," Everett corrected, but he was smiling. The motion passed by acclamation, which in Cedar Creek meant nodding until your neck learned the habit.

Another hand. "Can we invite the museum to set up a booth with photographs? People would like to see who we were when our hair behaved."

Julian lifted a brochure like a flag of truce. "Already printed," he said. "Archives Hour goes portable."

"Bring the glazier notes," Mrs. Mathers called, then pretended not to have called anything at all.

"We will," he answered. Miriam heard the plural and let it drop anchor somewhere decent inside her.

"Last item," Everett said, holding up a finger like a man begging the wind to cooperate. "Volunteer assignments." The room sighed. Every festival needed people to move chairs and pour cider and remind Geraldine that some fences were not metaphors. Names were matched to chores with the efficiency of people who remembered who had two good shoulders and who baked when they were nervous.

"Ms. Adler," Everett said, consulting his list. "Would you consider—ah—'threshold steward'?"

Miriam blinked. "Define."

"Doorways," Mrs. Levine supplied, amused by fate. "You stand where people enter the square. You smile, you hand them a program, you remind them that kindness is free."

"That last clause is new," Walter said.

"It was implied," Mrs. Levine said. "We are making it explicit."

Miriam glanced at Julian, whose mouth did not move but whose eyes clearly said **there are worse assignments.** She nodded. "I can stand at doors."

"Excellent," Everett said, relieved. "And Mr. Roth—archives booth. Theo—coffee."

"Perpetually," Theo intoned.

"Mrs. Callahan—float permits and general scolding."

"I prefer *gentle correction,*" she said.

"Same spelling, different font," Theo whispered.

The meeting adjourned by the ancient rite of people standing and continuing to talk. Chairs scraped, the stove clicked even though it had never been lit, and the sound of a small town re-threading itself rose like a secular hymn. Miriam was buttoning her coat when the roofer approached and scuffed his boot like a boy.

"Ms. Adler," he said. "About the priestess thing. In the café. I was—"

"You were being a man who likes scaffolding," she said, saving him. "Which the window will also need."

He nodded, grateful. "If you need help with shelves," he blurted, and she realized he meant the literal kind, not the symbolic. "I'm decent with wood."

"I suspect the shelves will prefer you over me," she said. "I'll let you know."

Julian appeared as if conjured by competence. "Walk you out?" he asked. They stepped into the chilly night, Town Hall's door swinging shut behind them like a mouth that had decided to rest. The square was mostly empty; the fountain whispered; the chapel on the rise kept its lampless watch.

"That was a good room," he said. "For what it was."

"It was a human room," she said. "Which is better." She thought of Mrs. Mathers' phrase—*old family promises*—dropping into the agenda like an uninvited ancestor and being allowed to stay.

"Left of the stove worked," he added.

"It did," she said, smiling. "Nearly as well as green tea."

They paused where the boardwalk turned toward the Riverlight. Theo had already updated his chalkboard: **QUIET HOUR SUNDAY 2–3** underlined twice, **Paper & Pie SAT 4** in hopeful capitals. Someone had drawn a goat wearing a laurel wreath. Geraldine, Miriam thought, was a fact you either planned for or repented.

"Threshold steward," Julian said, with the affectionate irony of a title that had found its rightful wearer.

"It was either that or goat wrangler," she said. "This felt more consonant with my training."

He grinned, and in the grin was relief that the town could be funny about itself even when the window could not. "Saturday," he said, "bring your map."

"I will," she said. "Bring your tracing."

They parted with the unromantic comfort of people who expect to see each other again soon and do not need to extract a promise. At the shop door, Miriam paused and looked up the hill. The chapel's rose window was dark, but she could feel its shape, the way you feel a sentence in your mouth before you find the words. *Old family promises,* Mrs. Mathers had said. The room had nodded, nervous and honest. Disputes about lattice crust and hay bales had kept everyone human-sized, which is the only size in which promises can be kept.

Inside, she lit the small lamp and set the **FOR BRIBES ONLY** basket on the counter, rescuing two rugelach from their day. She wrote on a card and tucked it near the register for herself and whatever nerves wandered in before the festival: **Rules are how we remember we belong to each other. Promises are how we agree to keep belonging when the rules aren't enough.** Then she locked up, listened to the shelves exhale as the shop settled, and allowed herself one unguarded thought before sleep: the town was making itself ready—not only with floats and pies and goat strategy, but with a memory that had begun, at last, to speak in a room with good light.

8

THE JOURNAL FRAGMENT

The attic had become Miriam's nightly threshold. She swept the shop floor, put away the herbs and oils, locked the front door, and then climbed the narrow staircase with a lamp balanced in her hand as if she were apprenticed to the dark. The boxes that Ruth had stacked decades ago seemed to shift in personality depending on the hour—at noon they were practical, at dusk they were heavy with history, and by nightfall they became something closer to companions, waiting for her to choose which one would speak.

She had left one shelf half-cleared the day before, its surface bare except for a crooked row of apothecary jars and a single ledger whose spine had split like an old scar. When she slid the ledger forward, her fingers brushed the back panel of the shelf. It didn't feel quite flush. Wood met skin with the resistance of something that had been pressed too long against secrecy.

Miriam leaned closer, moving the lamp until the glow caught a ragged slip of paper wedged behind the shelf. Not folded—tucked. She slid it free with the delicacy of someone pulling a thorn from fabric. The page was brittle, its edges singed with time, the ink browned to the color of dried roses. Across the top, in a hand that belonged unmistakably to another century, a line trembled:

September 1846 — The pact, and the silence it requires.

The breath left her chest. She lowered herself onto the stool, lamp angled so the words might reveal themselves without crumbling. The voice that lived in the handwriting was undeniably feminine: not Ruth's careful loops, not the stern script of Elise in the photographs, but a flowing, urgent hand, the kind of writing one does when the heart races faster than the pen.

"We stood in the chapel beneath the glass, and the families said their promises aloud. My vows were not mine to speak, yet they left my mouth. I have married into a silence, and I do not know if it will kill me or only haunt me. The petals show twelve, but I saw the thirteenth before the men pressed their will upon the glazier. If ever another should read this, know that the pact was not unanimous. Some of us wished to choose truth, and some of us wished only to belong."

Miriam swallowed. The bride's words echoed Ruth's warning almost perfectly, as if time were less a river and more a looped refrain. A rose, twelve petals shown, thirteen hidden. A silence pressed into place like mortar. She could feel the presence of that unnamed bride sitting across from her, candle guttering, pen shaking, aware that what she was writing might never be read.

She whispered the year aloud. "Eighteen forty-six." The date of the chapel's completion. The year Cedar Creek declared itself not only a settlement but a town. The year, Julian had said, where records went missing.

Her hand trembled, not from fear of the paper, but from

the uncanny certainty that this page had been waiting for her. That Ruth had known she would find it—not by sight but by touch. That the wood itself had conspired to keep the page safe until the right hand came along.

She copied the words onto a card in her own hand, letter for letter, so that if the fragment disintegrated she would still have its content. Then she pressed the page back between layers of acid-free tissue she had brought from the museum gift shop, careful as a conservator, as though the bride's voice were fragile but alive.

When she finally descended to the shop, lamp balanced against her hip, the square outside had gone quiet. She locked the door, leaned her forehead against the glass, and whispered, "I will not let you stay buried."

THE NEXT MORNING she carried the tissue-wrapped fragment to the fort museum in a cloth pouch, her pulse quick with the combination of secrecy and urgency. The museum was nearly empty, the docent corralling a pair of visiting cousins through the weaponry exhibit. Miriam found Julian in the reading room, his sleeves rolled, a pencil balanced in his hand over a map of the town circa 1850.

"Do you have a minute?" she asked, trying to keep her voice casual.

His head lifted. Even before she withdrew the pouch, something in her expression had alerted him. He pushed the map aside and motioned to the chair across from him. "What have you found?"

She unwrapped the fragment with the reverence of liturgy. The paper, luminous in morning light, seemed almost too fragile to show. Julian leaned forward, elbows braced on the table, but didn't touch. His eyes scanned the lines once, then again, narrowing as he translated the trembling script.

"'The pact and the silence,'" he read aloud softly. He glanced at her, as though confirming that she too understood the gravity of the phrase. "Miriam—this is... this is precisely the period where we lose half the town's records. And you're telling me this came from your attic shelf?"

"Yes. Tucked behind the wood."

He pinched the bridge of his nose. "This can't be coincidence. The word 'pact'... the chapel consecration was in '46. We know three families bore the cost of the window: Wagner, Dubois, Adler." His hand hovered above the page but did not land. "And a bride writing—married into silence."

"You see it too," Miriam whispered, relief softening her shoulders. "The window wasn't just decoration. It was witness."

He leaned back, pacing his breath. Skepticism warred with the archivist in him. "I have to be careful here," he said finally. "Fragments without provenance are dangerous. People want them to mean more than they can support."

"This one already means more," she said. "It's not asking permission."

His eyes flicked to her, caught by the intensity in hers. For a moment, the guarded historian disappeared, replaced by the man who had told her archives are maps of what a community can't bear to remember. "You're not wrong," he said. "But if this is genuine—and my gut says it is—it's dynamite. The pact she names... it isn't recorded anywhere else."

Silence stretched between them, charged. Miriam could feel the pull—Julian being drawn into her orbit not because she asked but because the evidence itself demanded it. He reached for a magnifying lens, adjusted the light, and examined the ink. His voice softened. "Brown iron gall. Period appropriate. The hand matches a few marriage certificates I've seen from that decade—though I'd have to compare more closely."

"You want to," she said.

"Yes," he admitted. "I do."

He looked up, and their eyes locked—hers fierce with conviction, his cautious but compelled. The tension between them, usually shaped by their opposing instincts, tilted into alliance. He had crossed the line from skeptic observing her to scholar partnering with her.

"Let me keep it here," he said at last. "For analysis. I'll return it in better housing than tissue paper."

Miriam hesitated. Trust was not something she granted easily—not after months of feeling her life unmoored. But Ruth's letter had warned her: *Do not do this alone. You will need the man who listens with paper.* She exhaled. "On one condition. I stay while you work."

"Done," he said, a hint of surprise flickering through his tone. He adjusted his chair closer to hers, the distance across the table shrinking in more ways than one.

THEY SPENT hours bent over the fragment, Julian carefully sketching the handwriting, Miriam whispering the bride's words aloud as though repetition might anchor them deeper into the present. When he compared the script to an 1846 marriage record for Leah, his brow furrowed.

"Look here," he said, pointing. "The loops of the 's,' the way she closes her 'e'—they're nearly identical. If this was Leah's hand—"

"She would have been a bride that year," Miriam finished. "One of the families named in the pact."

"The Wagners," Julian said. He sat back, visibly shaken. "Which means the pact wasn't simply economic. It was marital. Interwoven families sealing promises not only with money but with unions."

"And silence," Miriam added. The word felt heavy in her mouth, like metal.

He nodded slowly. "If this fragment is hers, then we've uncovered not just a personal lament but a record of dissent. At least one member of a founding family didn't consent freely." He tapped the page, then stopped himself, catching his instinct to touch what shouldn't be touched. "And if so, every descendant of these families still in Cedar Creek is tied to the pact. By blood, by silence, by inheritance."

Miriam thought of Mrs. Mathers at the meeting, muttering about old family promises. Of Mrs. Callahan's warnings wrapped in humor. Of Pastor Elijah's insistence that some truths should remain buried. The whole town, she realized, was an orchard grown from rootstock they hadn't chosen, carrying fruit they might not wish to eat.

"Do you see now why Ruth warned me?" Miriam asked. "Why she said to seek the thirteenth petal?"

Julian looked at her, his skepticism breaking under the weight of evidence and her conviction. "I see why she trusted you," he said quietly. "And why this won't be easy."

They sat in silence, listening to the ticking of the clock on the reading room wall, the scrape of children's shoes downstairs, the murmur of the docent's tour. The ordinary life of Cedar Creek hummed on while, upstairs, two people stared at a page that threatened to reorder the town's history.

Miriam pressed her fingers against the desk, grounding herself. "The pact spans families still here," she said. "If silence was demanded then, it may still be enforced now.

That means what we've uncovered isn't just memory. It's danger."

Julian exhaled, a sound that was half agreement, half dread. "Then we'd better decide what kind of danger we're willing to live with."

She looked at him, and in his eyes she saw not only caution but commitment—the reluctant acceptance of a man who had been pulled into her orbit and now knew he could not leave without betraying both her and himself.

The fragment lay between them, fragile and unassuming, yet pulsing with more power than any relic had the right to. The bride's voice had survived a century and a half of silence. It had chosen them as its witnesses. And Cedar Creek, whether it liked it or not, would have to listen.

9

SUSPICIONS IN THE SQUARE

The morning after the fragment, the square wore a light as thin as eggshell. The fountain's lip shone; the banners Theo had re-chalked at dawn ruffled like ideas that hadn't made up their minds yet. Miriam crossed the cobbles with the cloth pouch in her shoulder bag—empty now, because the fragment sat under a conservator's weight at the museum—but heavier for the decision it implied. She headed, instinctively, to the bakery.

The bell over the door chimed with the merry good sense of kitchens. Warmth rolled toward her, cinnamon and butter breathing together like old friends. Miriam Levine—Cedar Creek's kindly baker and namesake twin—stood at the counter transferring rugelach from sheet to tray with the expertise of someone who had turned repetition into art. Her hair was pinned back; her hands moved with an economy that made Miriam crave competence.

"Ah, Miriam," Mrs. Levine said, and the double name still amused them both. "You look as if the town has told you a secret and then asked you to keep it alone."

"That's too accurate," Miriam admitted. "Do you have coffee strong enough to stand up for itself?"

Mrs. Levine poured from a battered steel pot into a thick mug, slid it across as if passing a token between allies, and waited with that serious, patient attention Miriam had already come to trust. The bakery was half full—parents with strollers, an older man wrestling a crossword, two teenagers with their heads together over a single cinnamon roll like conspirators in mercy. Miriam leaned in.

"I found something last night," she said. "Behind a shelf in the attic. A page from a bride's journal—nineteenth century—she uses the words *pact* and *silence*. Julian thinks the hand matches Leah's marriage record."

The baker didn't gasp; she didn't even blink at the names. She set the spatula down and steadied both palms on the counter, grounding herself and Miriam at once. "And you were always going to find something," she said softly, not as prophecy but as consent. "Your aunt left that shop full of small doors only your hand could open."

Miriam wrapped her fingers around the mug, letting heat put courage back in them. "Part of me wants to take the page and knock on every door in this town until someone admits what they did," she said. "Another part of me hears your voice in my head saying, 'Not everything that wants to be shouted should be shouted.'"

"Good," Mrs. Levine said. "Keep at least one of my voices in there. But—tell me the rest."

Miriam recited the line that had crushed her heart so gently it left it shaped rather than broken: *I have married into a silence, and I do not know if it will kill me or only haunt me.* The baker's face changed in the particular way older faces change when they recognize a hurt they survived without language.

"People forget the cost," Mrs. Levine murmured. "We build festivals on top of promises and pretend the ground doesn't shift." She glanced toward the window, where two women paused outside, whispering low, eyes on the bakery door. "You know why people fear old stories, don't you?"

"Because they make the present accountable," Miriam said.

"Because they make the present complicated," the baker corrected gently. "Accountable comes later."

A child at the corner table dropped a spoon, startled, then giggled; the room relaxed. "You think I should keep quiet," Miriam guessed, not because she wanted to, but because habit had trained her to test every impulse against somebody else's better sense.

"I think," Mrs. Levine said, "you should keep careful. There is a difference. Our town has always preferred to bury what won't stand still. If you dig abruptly, the ground collapses and swallows you along with the bone you're after. If you loosen the earth, one handful at a time, people can bear the sight of what you lift."

"And if someone kicks dirt back in?"

"Then we employ the Riverlight's scone fines," she said dryly, then softened. "Miriam, listen to me. There are names on that page that still live in this square—on mailboxes, in recipes, in those poor teenagers' ears. If families made a pact of silence, they taught their grandchildren a grammar for not seeing. You will be tinkering with the town's sentences. People will take it personally because silence is a family heirloom here."

Miriam stared down into the dark coffee. The fragment's words had felt like a flint striking tinder. The baker's counsel felt like water finding a path. "Do you want me to stop?" she asked, and the question surprised her with its childishness.

"I want you to do it like bread," Mrs. Levine said. "Time and heat in the right order. Knead, rest, rise, bake. You rush any of it and you get a brick you can't feed to a goat."

"Geraldine eats hymnals," Miriam said. "She'd manage a brick."

"Even goats have limits." The baker breathed out. She reached into the case, cracked a warm rugelach in half, and pushed one piece toward Miriam. "I'm not telling you to keep the town comfortable. I'm telling you to keep it from breaking the teeth it will need later to chew the truth."

Outside, the square's traffic eddied. Everett strode past in a hurry, skirting the fountain like a man dodging civility. Walter balanced a coil of rope on his shoulder and a story on his tongue, stopping two different people to offer each separately. Theo wiped his chalkboard and added a small line at the bottom: **QUIET HOUR SUN 2–3 (no goats).** Across the way, Mrs. Mathers sat on the bench and watched the town the way a sparrow watches a hawk—alert, unsurprised.

Miriam finished the rugelach and let the sugar lay a small courage on her tongue. "The fear is thick today," she said.

"That's because people can feel something rising," Mrs. Levine answered. "They don't know its name yet. Call it memory. Call it debt. Call it a crack that wants to be mended honestly." She reached across the counter and touched Miriam's wrist with two fingers, a blessing disguised as emphasis. "You were not chosen to be popular. You were chosen to be precise."

Something in Miriam unclenched. She didn't need permission so much as a witness. The bakery gave her both. She paid, refused change, and stood a moment on the threshold—Ruth's favorite word—letting the warm air of the room argue against the cool outside. The bell chimed behind her as she stepped into the square, carrying the baker's counsel like a recipe written on a scrap of bag.

SHE COULD PRACTICALLY MAP Cedar Creek by where people gathered to say what they meant: the café for arguments wrapped in jokes, the fountain for confessions disguised as errands, the museum for facts slow enough to be trusted, Town Hall for rules that wanted to be loved. Today each enclave broadcast its weather.

At the Riverlight, Theo polished glasses and announced to anyone with ears that "Paper & Pie" would feature "safe handling of nineteenth-century outrage." It drew eye-rolls and RSVPs in equal measure.

"Is it true," asked a woman with a cardigan like armor, "that Ms. Adler is poking around in other people's business?"

"It's the town's business," the carpenter said mildly from the corner table. "That's why it never got finished."

"You're all ready to make a spectacle," the roofer muttered, stirring coffee like it had insulted him.

"We're ready to make a record," Julian said, appearing at Miriam's shoulder with the disconcerting ease of a man who had learned her orbit without trespassing. He carried a small archival box and smelled faintly of lemon and old paper. "Morning."

"Morning," she returned. Their eyes met—just long enough to exchange the day's brief: still in, still careful. The roofer looked from one to the other and decided against the conversation he'd been preparing to enjoy.

Outside, Mrs. Callahan and a pair of cousins were measuring the square with a frayed tape, arguing about parade spacing with the exact volume of sisters who planned to forgive each other later. "If Geraldine walks, we add three feet," Mrs. Callahan said. "She requires room for commentary."

Miriam crossed to the fountain where the science teacher—Elena Ruiz, thin and quick—was conferring with a teen whose skateboard stuck out of his backpack like a plea. Elena nodded respectfully at Miriam; her eyes were curious, not aggressive. "People are nervous," she said, low. "It's measurable—faster speech, shorter sentences, more declarations disguised as questions."

"That last one is a town specialty," the teen said.

"Supporters?" Miriam asked.

Elena ticked names on her fingers like variables in an equation. "Levine. Theo. Walter, in his poetic way. The carpenter. The quiet mother with twins—what's her— Nadia. She cried at vespers and then told me she was relieved someone else had seen something." She looked toward the chapel, where the rose window was invisible at noon but felt like an eye behind a door. "Skeptics include half the committee, one-quarter of the pews, and anyone who's had to repair a window with their own money."

"Pastor Elijah?" Miriam asked.

"Worried more about the church's ability to hold everyone than about theology," Elena said. "Not the worst worry, not the best compass. He wants quiet. Quiet isn't the same as peace."

"And the families?" Miriam asked, because it had to be spoken aloud to shed some of its power. "The Wagners. Dubois. Adlers."

Elena's mouth quirked. "You *are* the Adlers," she said gently. "Welcome to the problem set." She sobered. "Old names carry long shadows. The Wagner grandson is decent

—Mack—works at the hardware store. But his father? He still believes the town owes the family a reputation. The Dubois branch is complicated—some of them want to teach the past, some want to sell it to tourists. You know your side better than I do."

Miriam thought of Ruth's letter, of the maps and threshold notes; she thought of Leah's slanted script. "I know that the name I carry is an invitation and an impediment."

"Which is what a good variable always is," Elena said. "You can still solve for x."

Miriam thanked her, trusting Elena's equations as much as she trusted Theo's chalk. They turned when the Riverlight's door banged open. Julian stepped out with the archival box under one arm, motioning for Miriam. "A minute?" he asked. "I want your say before I show *Paper & Pie* our work."

They stood in the alcove between café and bookstore where the wind forgot to be sharp. He set the box on a table and lifted out the fragment, now housed in a rigid Mylar sleeve that framed it like a small window. "Safer," he said.

She bent over the page as if it could still hear her read it. The bride's ink seemed darker in the new enclosure; Leah's tremor of fear and resolve looked less like fragility and more like insistence. "Better," Miriam murmured. In the glass of the sleeve her face and Julian's appeared, not quite overlapping, as if the fragment had put them into the same frame.

"You know this pulls me past my comfort," Julian said, not wheedling for praise, merely documenting a state change. "There's a difference between presenting context and presenting a complaint the town doesn't want filed."

"Then let's not file it," Miriam said. "Let's hold it up. If people see themselves in it, fine. If they don't, fine. Both are a kind of information."

"You make restraint sound like action," he said.

"It is," she said. "Ask any baker."

He laughed, short and grateful. Over his shoulder, the roofer watched them with narrowed calculation, as if their not-quite-touching proximity were, itself, evidence of plot. Beside him, Mrs. Mathers made no effort to hide her notice; she registered the scene like a court stenographer who planned to keep her own copy.

Back at the fountain, Walter was telling a story he had told seventeen times—about the year the hayride hit a rut and spilled them all like apples—and people were choosing to laugh because laughing keeps a day breathable. Allies gathered loosely but not secretively: Elena with her math, Theo with his chalk and jokes, Mrs. Levine with her stern kindness, the carpenter with his laconic decency, Nadia with twins and honest tears. Skeptics clustered in their chosen shade: the roofer, who liked physics as a shield, Everett, who liked agendas the way sailors like charts, Pastor Elijah, who wanted, urgently, not to lose anyone.

Miriam felt the line between those groups as a cord pulled taut. To step too far in either direction would risk allegiance at the expense of truth. She stayed in the middle of the square because thresholds had become her obligation.

"Ms. Adler," said a voice at her elbow. Mack Wagner—Elena was right; his face was earnest in the particular way of men who fix things and wish that fixing were sufficient. "Look, I don't know all the history. My dad... he has feelings, you know? But I think what you're doing might help the window get fixed properly. If that's what it is—helping, not accusing."

"I don't have enemies on my list," Miriam said. "Just repairs."

He nodded in relief, then in worry. "Some folks don't draw that line," he said. "Careful is good. Careful will be the only way you get through the door with most folks."

"Then careful it is," she said, grateful for his undecorated warning.

The square, viewed from the bakery's stoop an hour later, looked like an amphitheater readying itself for a play half the actors refused to admit they'd been cast in. Miriam could feel the town dividing the way water divides around a stone—no malice, exactly, but no ignorance either. She had allies. She had skeptics. She had her own doubt and the stubborn fragment that would not be denied. She had the baker's sentence about kneading and resting. She had the feeling of a shelf under her hand, warming slowly to a yes.

By late afternoon the light turned flatter, the kind that makes faces look more honest than people prefer. Miriam stocked the shop, wiped the counter, and tacked a small card beneath the register where only she could see it: **Do not mistake appetite for permission.** The bell chimed and drifted without bringing bodies; people had decided today to buy bread and coffee in places where they could overhear others rather than oil and chamomile where they might have to overhear themselves.

She brewed tea anyway and carried a mug to the door, standing on the threshold with its view of the square's small theater. Across the way, the roofer bent toward Everett, and their conversation had the conspiratorial hunch of men about to claim responsibility for the town's safety. Pastor Elijah moved in his pastoral orbit, smoothing what could be smoothed, delaying what could be delayed. Theo drew a small rose—thirteen petals this time—at the bottom of the chalkboard so tiny no one would notice unless they were standing close with their eyes already tuned to it. The gesture felt like a hand pressed briefly to Miriam's back: I see it too, even if we don't say so out loud.

A woman Miriam did not know—fifties, careful haircut, a coat whose neatness translated to a life whose lines had been repeatedly enforced—stopped on the boardwalk. "Ms. Adler," she said, smiling with the kind of smile that forgot its teeth. "I heard you are... involved with the museum now."

"With the archives," Miriam said, because it mattered to put the word *paper* in the world.

"Hmm." The woman's eyes did the small, tidy scan of Miriam's body and belongings that some people call friendliness and some call inventory. "Our town has always valued discretion," she said. "I do hope you remember that not every story benefits from light."

"Some light is kinder than some dark," Miriam said, not angry, not sweet.

The woman's mouth tightened. "If you stir what should stay settled, you will lose the patience of people who've been very patient with you."

"Thank you for telling me your boundary," Miriam said, and the woman blinked in confusion at the tone which held neither apology nor surrender.

After she left, Miriam realized her shoulders had lifted; she unclenched them with an exhale. Being an outsider had advantages—permission to notice, to ask—but also costs measured in small, daily abrasions. She had walked onto a stage halfway through the play and spoken a line that altered the plot; some actors would never forgive that. She did not require their forgiveness. She required only to keep her own balance.

She locked the shop early, left a sign in the window—**Back at 4 for Paper & Pie**—and carried the pouch (empty again) back to the museum. She and Julian stood together at the reading room table as if it were an altar. He had printed a one-page handout: *Rose Window: Design Notes & Gaps, 1845–1847*. It was an honest document that neither pandered nor dared. He handed her the stack to proof; she read it twice and added one sentence at the bottom: **This conversation asks for care. Thank you for choosing it.** He nodded, accepted the addition without comment, and placed it on the pile.

"People will demand an answer," he said.

"Then we will give them an invitation," she said.

He leaned one hip against the table and rubbed his thumb over the Mylar sleeve's edge. "You're being watched," he added, as if she didn't know. "By people who want you to fail loudly and by people who hope you succeed so quietly they won't have to admit they helped."

"That's a lot of people," she said.

"That's a town," he said, mouth tipping. He hesitated. "Be careful walking home."

"I will," she said. Neither of them pretended the warning was dramatic. It was ordinary, like telling someone to bring a sweater. It landed that way, too.

Back in the square, the wind tumbled a loose poster—*FESTIVAL SATURDAY*—so that it flapped like a fish trying to decide whether to breathe. Teenagers practiced their figure eights while a grandmother counted beats under her breath; Walter trailed a story behind him like a kite string. Mrs. Levine leaned in her doorway, arms crossed, as if to both guard and bless the afternoon. Miriam lifted a hand;

the baker lifted hers back and then pointed—subtle—toward the chapel on the hill.

Miriam followed the line of the gesture. Even in daylight the rose window made itself felt, the way a truth makes itself felt in a room that has not been told it yet. She imagined Leah's hand writing at a narrow table: *I have married into a silence.* She imagined Elise's coil of hair; Ruth's neat lists; the unknown glazier tracing a thirteenth arc and then erasing it because someone told him to. The present carried all of that like the body carries scars: not healed over so much as integrated.

The outsider tension clarified, not as a wound to be nursed but as a function to be used. Outsiders see angles insiders forget. Insiders hold keys outsiders can't cut alone. Miriam understood that she would have to stand with a foot on each side of the line long enough for the town to redraw it. It would punish her for the posture. It would also, eventually, learn from it.

On her way back to the shop she passed the Riverlight. Theo had added another note under his minuscule rose: **Attention is care.** She knocked on the window; he saluted with a dish towel like a sailor lowering flags. The carpenter stepped out and tipped his cap in a not-joking, not-flirting way that men use when they're acknowledging that a person has taken on work the town needed done.

Night came on cleanly, a wash of indigo that made the chapel's hill look nearer. The bell tolled the hour with its habitual dignity. Miriam lingered on the boardwalk in front of her door, letting the sound settle. Fear moved through the square like weather, as Mrs. Levine had said; you dressed for it, or you built a shelter, or you learned how to walk anyway.

Upstairs she lit the lamp, set the pouch on the desk, and wrote three names on a card: **Wagner. Dubois. Adler.** Then she drew a small circle around them and wrote **we**. The pronoun felt presumptuous and correct at once. Another card: **Promise ≠ silence.** She propped both where she would see them in the tired hours when doubt argues best.

Before sleep, she stood a minute by the window with its view of the quiet square. A single gull crossed in a white parenthesis. Somewhere, a door closed the way truth does, softly, after it has looked in the room to be sure everyone is decent. She thought of the fragment resting in its sleeve, of Julian's careful handout, of the baker's recipe for time. She closed her eyes and made, without saying it aloud, the smallest vow a person can make and keep every day: to continue, precisely, tomorrow.

10

ANCESTRAL RECORDS

The fort museum opened with its usual reluctance, the front door drafting yesterday into the room as if history didn't care for punctuality. Miriam arrived with her cardigan pockets full of pencils and patience; Julian arrived with green tea and the key to the locked stacks. They exchanged the sort of good morning that meant both *we slept little* and *we intend to be kind anyway*, and then they began the day's ritual.

Gloves first. Soft nitrile that dulled fingerprints to suggestion. Then the cart: gray boxes stacked in the order Julian trusted—**Selectmen's Minutes, Vestry Proceedings, Marriage & Baptismal Register (1840–1850), The Cedar Creek Observer on microfilm, Glazier & Mason Accounts, Shipping Manifests.** He set the cart brake with the decisiveness of a man who had learned that one small discipline saves a thousand apologies.

"We'll work chronologically," he said, and then corrected himself with a half-smile. "As chronologically as Cedar Creek allows."

They moved into the reading room where sunlight made

rectangles on the long tables and dust settled like punctuation. The clock on the wall announced the hour; afterward, the only time was theirs to arrange.

Selectmen's Minutes, 1845–1847 gave them handwriting the color of weak tea—names and motions marching with bureaucratic virtue. In April '46: *Authorization to disburse funds to sacred works.* In June: *Discussion of iron nails and stained glass shipping.* Then, abruptly, in August: *Meeting adjourned to executive session.* No appended notes, no clerk's summary, only a faint mark in the margin where a page had once been sewn and then lifted. Julian traced that empty stitch with his eyes.

"Missing leaf," he said. "Clean lift. Not water or flame."

"Choice," Miriam said.

He made a note on an index card: **Selectmen—Aug '46 —leaf excised.**

Vestry Proceedings offered more hope. Early entries spoke in the hushed arguments of practical piety—candles too dear, hymnal bindings cracking, shingles blown. Then, midsummer: *Glazier's second invoice received. Petition from three parishioners to review design of rose.* The next page should have carried the petition; instead it carried a summary copied a year later in a different hand: *Private petition on matters of ornament reviewed and resolved.* No names. No arguments. A new heading began as if conversations never left shadows.

Julian sighed. "Someone recopied the book."

"How can you tell?" Miriam asked, leaning over his shoulder to find the difference his eye saw by instinct.

"Ink tone, letterforms, page stock—but look: here the clerk writes with an impatient 's'—and here, months later, the 's' is schoolhouse-perfect. Either he found religion in penmanship, or somebody rewrote."

Miriam's jaw tightened. "You can't repair memory by transcribing it prettier."

He smiled without joy. "Tell that to a century of town clerks."

He pulled **Marriage & Baptismal Register** from the cart with the care of a man retrieving a sleeping child. The names slid past: Wagner, Dubois, Reeves, Adler—pastors' hands blessing what the river and the road had conspired to bring together. On September 20, 1846, he stopped. *Wagner, Matthias, to Leah…* The surname trailed off in a flourish where the ink blotted. No maiden name recorded, as if the writer had run out of room or nerve. On the line below: *Witnesses: H. Dubois; E. Adler.*

"Leah," Miriam whispered. Not proof, not yet. But a seam.

They made more notes. They turned more pages. **The Cedar Creek Observer** on microfilm promised to be tedious and proved itself with fidelity. Headlines about salmon runs and schoolhouse debates flickered in negative, the film reader humming as Miriam cranked carefully past July. August '46: a flood that tore logs from the riverbank. September: a block of issues missing, the microfilm counting them as if to discipline absent days. October: an editorial praising *a new spirit of unity* that read like a scold.

"At least five issues gone," Julian murmured. "If they were ever printed."

"Or if they were printed and then put politely to sleep," Miriam added.

"Polite towns have violent archives," he said, almost under his breath.

Glazier & Mason Accounts—a hand-bound ledger that mixed numbers with little apologies—proved unexpectedly eloquent. In June '46: *Advance for imported glass, twelve lobes* *complete.* In August: *Setback. Patron requests amendment. Additional time.* In September: a terse note: *Work withheld pending 'adjustments'; balance to be paid upon delivery of satisfied design.* And then, one line written more lightly than the rest, as if the clerk had tried not to press: *Private contribution anonymous (rose pendant).*

Miriam's breath hitched. "Rose pendant," she said. "Ruth noted it in her ledger too. Anonymous then. Unanonymous now."

He met her gaze. "Thirteen belongs," he had said to her days ago of the scrawl they'd found; now the ledger supplied its own, quieter sentence: *Anonymous belongs.*

They mapped dates against names, hours against habits. They ate at the table with the guilty pleasure of people who refuse to leave when the work is good, Theo appearing at some point with scones and an injunction to blink. **Shipping Manifests** made a cameo: *Crate: stained glass; mark—CC—delivered to chapel; one pane chipped.* The kind of detail that made a scholar's heart glad because accidents tell the truth when people cannot.

They were not discovering a story; they were discovering its hollows. Whole weeks in late summer '46 covered over with a layer of civic frosting as neat as any bakery's. Where intensity ought to have made ink, there was white space; where debate should have left phrases, there were summaries. What remained left a shape like a body you can't quite see in fog: tall enough to be human, too deliberate to be natural.

"You see it," Julian said without looking up.

"I feel it," Miriam said, palms flat against the table's edge. "Like standing in a room that remembers a fight."

He nodded. "We have absences that line up. Three independent records go silent in the same month: the selectmen, the vestry, the paper. That's not misfortune; that's policy."

He wrote another card and pushed it between them like a treaty: **Aug–Sep '46: coordinated quiet.**

Afternoon sank its weight into the windows; the river glinted on the far side of the palisade. They had a list of what was not there and a handful of threads tied to what was. When they finally wheeled the cart—emptier now, the boxes obediently put to bed—both were flush with a tiredness that felt like a promise rather than a cost.

"Tomorrow," Julian said, turning the key to the archive room as if he were closing a chapel, "we pull the private papers."

"Whose?"

"The families'," he said, and didn't bother to hide the way the word worked in his mouth. "If they'll let us."

THEY DID NOT LEAVE the fort; they followed their fatigue down the back stair to the stoop where the museum's shadow made a small pocket of weather. Theo, prophet of well-timed comfort, had left a paper bag with their names on it. Inside: two sandwiches, a slice of lemon pie, a note: *For stamina and stubbornness. —T.*

They ate like people who knew conversation can break more than it builds when blood sugar is low. The river made its articulate sound. Across the yard a child's laugh pinged off wood like a coin off glass.

"Protective is not a word I admire in myself," Julian said at last, eyes on the palisade so he wouldn't be tempted to watch her too closely. "But I feel it. Toward you."

Miriam set down the crust she'd been worrying with unnecessary care. The admission landed with the delicate weight of something that wanted to be put down gently. "Because I'm unwise?"

"Because you are precisely wise," he said. "And because the town can be cruel when it thinks it's being prudent. I am used to shepherding paper. I didn't expect to want to shepherd a person."

She smiled without deflecting. "I don't need rescue."

"I know," he said. "You need margin."

"That," she admitted, "I'll take."

He didn't move closer; he didn't make it an oath. He simply set his hand flat on the step between them for a moment, a small geography of care. Then he pulled it back as if remembering to make room for choice.

"May I say something back that you might not admire?" she asked.

"Please."

"Your doubt has been useful to me," she said. "It keeps me from turning a shimmer into a proclamation. But if you use it to hide how much you care, you'll do poor science."

He laughed once, helplessly. "Betrayed by my own method."

"Not betrayed," she said. "Invited."

They went upstairs again because that is what people do who have chosen a shared sentence: they return to it. Back in the reading room, they arranged their tools as if instruments on a tray. Julian brought out his private index of donors and their deposits—the file he didn't show to tourists because it interrupted the cleaner story of *we have always kept good records.*

"Families endowed the fort," he said, flipping to **W**. "Wagner has a wing in the basement you can't see unless you ask. Dubois loaned river charts and reclaimed them when they didn't like how we labeled the story of the flood.

Adler supplied household ledgers and certain... threshold notes."

"Threshold," Miriam repeated. The word returned to her like a bird used to being fed. She drew Ruth's little town map from her bag—the one marked with circles labeled **door, water, paper, light, confluence, keeping**—and slid it across. "My aunt drew this. She considered the shop and the fort and the fountain and the chapel to be a route, not a collection. She marked a sixth point: *keeping*."

He studied the map. "The alley behind your shop," he said. "Of course. I've received three anonymous donations through that alley. A bag hung on the hook by the back gate. No note. Each time the contents were... inconvenient truths."

Miriam choked on an unearned laugh. "You're telling me Cedar Creek has a dead drop."

"Has had for at least a generation," he said, not even trying to disguise his reluctant pride. "It makes us both ridiculous and serious. I keep a box under my desk labeled **Lost & Found**. It contains letters that didn't want to admit they were letters."

The intimacy of such a confession tightened the room. He had given her a key, not his house. There's a difference. She accepted it as one accepts an heirloom someone hasn't decided to give you yet—by promising yourself not to break it before it's yours.

They moved to the microfilm again because paper sometimes hides its truths in light. **The Cedar Creek Observer** in negative threw their faces together in the glass of the reader, the two of them superimposed on early October. Headline after headline about harvests and road grading. Then an item, small: *Special service of thanksgiving for unity and settle-*

ment of disputes. No disputes named. No thanks recited except the sort the nervous tell themselves.

"Unity is the word people use when they've negotiated someone else's silence," Miriam said.

"Sometimes," he allowed. "Sometimes it's the word they use because they don't possess a better one." He tapped the column. "But this... this has the smell of ceremony about it."

He leaned closer to the reader, his shoulder almost touching hers, and then—remembering himself—sat back. She felt the absence of contact the way you notice that a draft has stopped. She turned a page.

In **Vestry Proceedings** they found a note pinned to an ordinary entry with an ordinary pin: a small square in a different ink, added years later. *Minutes recast in 1892 by consent of officers and families.* Beneath, four initials and a pastor's long flourish. The initials aligned too neatly to be coincidence: **M.W., H.D., E.A., N.P.** Matthias Wagner. Henri Dubois. Elise Adler. Nathaniel Pierce (a pastor whose portrait hung in the hall, his jaw set like a doorframe).

Julian's voice lowered. "They retrofitted the memory."

Miriam touched the pinhole, not the note. "To match the story they liked."

He nodded. "As late as 1892, long after the glass was set."

He took off his glasses and pressed his eyes. "Forgive me," he said without flourish, "if I am not entirely professional, but this makes me want to stand in the square and read names until someone says *stop*."

"Then you would be me," she said. "And I am trying not to be me at full volume."

His laugh was small and grateful and went away quickly. "Thank you," he said after a breath, "for letting me care and not requiring me to announce it as faith."

"Thank you," she returned, "for letting me believe without making me apologize for loving evidence."

The day tilted. The reading room settled. Their sentences braided in the quiet way rope does—no ceremony, just fibers choosing to hold.

IN THE LATE hour when handwriting and eyesight begin to fail the optimistic, Julian wheeled out a narrow, unlabeled drawer from the back of the locked stacks. "Forgive the drama," he said. "This isn't a holy of holies. It's a place where the museum hides its own errors."

Inside lay an assortment of small embarrassments: tags that had fallen off, a minute book with the wrong cover, a folder misfiled under **MISC.** He extracted a slim, calfbound volume whose title had been scraped away. He opened it and smiled a scholar's rare dangerous smile.

"Town Meeting Abstracts," he announced, "compiled 1879. It summarizes early deliberations when the originals had become 'inconvenient to consult.' Which is to say: moldy, ragged, opinionated. And—if we're fortunate—less edited than the recopying we saw."

He set it on the table between them. The entries were brief, as promised, but the compiler had been lazy about laundering. Under **Sept. 1846:**

—*Subscription complete for chapel rose; three families assume balance.*

—*Motion to amend decorative program due to "objection of conscience" by unnamed party; carried to executive session; resolution satisfactory to contributors.*

—*Vote to seal Appendix C of vestry minutes "for the peace of households" until the year 1900; key held by officers; copy sealed with them.*

Miriam's finger hovered above the line about "peace of households." "That is not an accident of phrasing," she said. "That is an intent."

"And it worked," Julian said. "At least until 1900. Perhaps longer."

He flipped forward to **1892** and found the clerk's neat acknowledgment: *Proceedings of 1846 recast per resolution; Appendix C status unchanged.* Beneath, the four initials again. The same hand as the pinned note.

"That's our proof of deliberate omission," he said quietly, the way one says *we have located the source of the fire.* "It isn't just water or time. They made decisions to remove and reseal."

He pulled **Appendix Register** from the same drawer—a logbook that only cataloged the existence of appendices, not their content. A clerk with a fondness for flourishes had written: *Appendix C—concerning window design, spousal counsel, and admonitions to discretion—sealed by key, copy noted to be placed with Pastor; also, note of a cedar reliquary placed within south wall, vestral side.*

"Cedar reliquary," Miriam breathed. She could smell the faint ghost of the wood through the years. She could see— without knowing how she knew—the shape of a small box in a wall. The words from Ruth's letter rose, unbidden: *There is a place in wood that remembers.*

Julian looked at her so quickly it might have been a flinch. "You knew?"

"I felt," she corrected. "But now I know."

He closed the register carefully, like a person closing a door someone is sleeping behind. "We have a motive and a method," he said. "Families who paid for the window and then guaranteed a version of the story. A dissenting bride. A sealed appendix. A reliquary in a wall. And a century of clerks asked to be complicit with nicer hand-writing."

"Which means," Miriam said, "that if we open the wrong door too loudly, we are not only embarrassing the dead. We are making the living feel accused."

"The living," Julian said, "who wear their names like uniforms."

He slid another folder onto the table, its label newer: **Loan Agreements, Private Collections.** Several sheets listed temporary loans from town families of items "pertaining to the early chapel." Three agreements had the same clause, written in the same legal hand: *Exhibitable at the museum only with explicit family consent; reproductions prohibited.* The signatures ran like a genealogy: Wagner, Dubois, Adler. The dates were clustered around 1978 and 1994—moments when the museum had tried to show more than its donors would bear.

"They're still managing the frame," he said.

"And they think the content belongs to them," Miriam said. It wasn't anger, exactly. It was the exhaustion of someone who has watched a door barred for so long that the shape of the bar has become part of the architecture.

He stood, paced once between table and window, and then stopped as if he didn't trust his feet not to walk him straight into a fight. "I'm supposed to be neutral," he said.

"You're supposed to be accurate," she said. "Neutrality is a lovely word when nothing is at stake."

He scrubbed his hand through his hair, leaving it more disordered than the museum liked. "Then let me be accurate. The founding families hid deliberate omissions, and they maintained them across generations. They paid for the glass and the silence in the same coin."

Miriam exhaled. There it was, said aloud in a room that

kept faith with paper. Saying it did not make it easier. It made it real.

He sat again, took the Mylar sleeve with Leah's fragment, and placed it atop the **Abstracts** and the **Register** like a person completing an altar with its necessary object. "This is the dissent that won't stay sealed," he said.

"And we," Miriam said, "are the keepers who won't keep it for them."

He glanced up sharply at *we* and then let the pronoun soften the line of his mouth. "We," he agreed.

Evening pressed its hands against the windows. Somewhere downstairs a docent locked a case; somewhere across the square Theo chalked **PAPER & PIE • 4PM** with optimism that felt like faith's less anxious cousin. In the archive room, Miriam and Julian gathered cards and notes and the tender, stubborn sheet with its 1846 tremor. They did not know yet how to open a sealed appendix ethically. They did not know whose anger would arrive first. They only knew that a path had clarified: from *keeping* to *door* to *light*. Ruth's map had not been sentimental cartography. It had been a route for a day like this.

At the door, Julian hesitated. "If people—if my donors— if they pressure me to shut this down—"

"You won't," she said, not as command but as confidence.

"I won't," he said, surprised to hear it sounded true.

He opened the door for her, a courtesy untheatrical enough not to insult either of them, and they stepped into the corridor that smelled of sawdust and old varnish. The fort had not changed. Their seeing had. On the landing he touched the railing and then—aware of his fingers—tucked his hand back into his pocket.

"Walk you home?" he asked.

"Yes," she said. "But take the alley."

"Keeping," he said, and even in the dim hall the word carried a small light.

They walked out into the square where the chapel rose with its dark rose and its known crack and its unknown reliquary. The town was, as ever, doing the ordinary work of making a life—sweeping, arguing, forgiving in miniature. Above it, the window held its count of twelve and its ghost of thirteen. Inside the fort, a piece of paper refused to be alone.

11

———

CONFLICT AT THE CHAPEL

The chapel door was heavier than Miriam expected. She pushed against oak that had swollen in the damp and slipped into a space that still smelled of beeswax and stone dust. The air was hushed, as though the congregation's breath had been stored from last Sunday and was still waiting to be released. The rose window loomed overhead, its fractured geometry catching the afternoon light in subdued, uneven flames. The crack ran like a river vein across two petals, subtle but undeniable. From the nave, no one else seemed to notice the faint shimmer Miriam saw — the ghost of a thirteenth petal still insisting on its presence.

She had come without intention of spectacle. She wanted only to sit, to breathe where Leah had breathed, where the town had pressed its pact into silence. She slid into the pew beneath the window, folded her hands on her lap, and closed her eyes. The echo of Ruth's letter stirred: *When the window speaks, do not argue with it.*

For several minutes she stayed in that posture — open, waiting. The light shifted. She could hear the creak of the timbers, the slow settling of old wood. Beneath those sounds, another: the faintest hum, a vibration too slight to call music yet not ordinary silence. Her chest tightened, not with fear but with recognition. She whispered aloud, half-prayer, half-invocation: "Wholeness."

The word startled her with its own clarity. She opened her eyes — and saw the shimmer again, like dew struck by an invisible dawn. Her breath caught. She leaned forward, willing herself not to doubt what she had seen.

That was when the footsteps sounded. Deliberate. Weighted. She turned.

Pastor Elijah stood in the aisle, his dark coat buttoned high despite the warm day, his Bible tucked under one arm. His presence filled the nave not with menace but with the kind of authority that leaves no space for alternative readings. His expression was not anger; it was something worse — disappointment that had already judged itself righteous.

"Ms. Adler," he said, his voice neither raised nor lowered, but carrying the acoustics of habit. "The chapel is open for prayer, but not for... experiments."

Miriam straightened. She felt the fragment of Leah's journal folded in her bag like a heartbeat. "I wasn't experimenting," she said quietly. "I was listening."

His eyes lifted to the window, then back to her. "That window is glass. It bears no message except the one we bring in ourselves. What you are doing—what people say you are doing—confuses the congregation. They come here for stillness, not spectacle."

Her cheeks warmed. She wanted to insist she had made no spectacle, but she knew how gossip traveled faster than footsteps in Cedar Creek. If one person saw her looking up at the shimmer too long, or whispering in a pew, the story would arrive at Town Hall before she had finished her tea.

"Elijah," she said softly, dropping the formality because it felt truer, "if you believe it is only glass, why fear me listening?"

His jaw tightened. "Because I do not fear you. I fear what people will do with their interpretations. A crack has appeared, and some already wish to give it meaning. It is my duty to remind them that not all cracks are prophecies."

The word *duty* landed like a stone. Miriam felt the pew press against her back. She wanted to yield, to let his certainty cover her like the hymns he sang on Sundays. But Leah's handwriting rose before her eyes: *I have married into a silence, and I do not know if it will kill me or only haunt me.*

Elijah took a step closer. "Truth is not always medicine, Ms. Adler. Sometimes it is poison. The families built this chapel to shelter us from storms of division. If you stir those storms again, the walls will not hold."

Miriam's heart pounded. His words were not threat, not exactly. They were worse: a plea disguised as warning, designed to make her believe that silence was virtue. She realized in that moment that Elijah, too, was an inheritor of the pact — not by blood, perhaps, but by role. He was its steward, the keeper of quiet.

She looked up at the fractured rose. Light passed through the crack, making a faint prism of colors across the pews. For her, the thirteenth shimmer glowed again. And she knew that to deny it, here and now, would be to betray not only Leah but herself.

"I RESPECT YOUR CALLING," Miriam said, her voice steadier than she felt. "But if truth is poison, it is because someone made it so. Silence does not heal. It festers."

Elijah's mouth set into a line. "I have walked this town

through grief and famine. I have buried its children and comforted its widows. Do you think I am naive about festering? I know it well. That is why I tell you: some wounds close better if we do not pick at them."

Her chest ached with the temptation to agree. He was kind. He was weary. His eyes carried decades of holding people together with nothing but faith and borrowed strength. But she also knew that Ruth had asked her not to do this alone. And she was not alone — Julian, Theo, Mrs. Levine, even Leah's trembling hand across time stood beside her.

"Then let me ask," she said softly. "What is this window hiding that makes silence more sacred than honesty?"

For a long moment he said nothing. His hand tightened on the Bible's spine. "The founders made decisions," he said at last. "They gave us a town, a church, a place to bury our dead. They sacrificed so that we could belong. Do you truly wish to dishonor their gift by unearthing their quarrels?"

The logic cut sharp: loyalty dressed as gratitude, duty shaped into debt. She thought of the sealed appendix, the excised pages, the deliberate omissions. She thought of Ruth's maps with circles marked *keeping* and *light*. The families had not merely quarreled; they had buried dissent alive.

"Elijah," she said, and her voice cracked with the weight of it, "I am not dishonoring their gift. I am trying to honor the bride who left her voice in the wall because no one else would hear it. Leah saw thirteen petals. She saw the truth, and she was told to silence herself. How many more have carried that silence? How many still carry it?"

His eyes flashed — not anger, but grief so old it looked like anger. "If you speak her name, you will divide households," he said. "Is that what you want? For the Wagners and Dubois to take sides again? For Adlers to be branded troublemakers a second time?"

The words hit her in the gut. She was an Adler. She bore the inheritance. The name alone could be used to paint her as biased, unstable, dangerous. But she also knew that being quiet would not save her from those labels; it would only confirm them.

"I want wholeness," she whispered.

"Wholeness?" He gave a dry laugh. "Wholeness comes from forgiveness, not from digging through graves."

She stood, her knees trembling but her posture unbroken. "Wholeness comes from truth. And forgiveness can't live without it."

They stared at each other, two stewards of different vows. One bound to protect peace by keeping silence. The other called — against her will but not against her heart — to lift silence so peace could be made honestly.

Elijah's shoulders sagged. He looked at her as one might look at a storm cloud: inevitable, unyielding. "You will not stop," he said.

"No," she answered. "I cannot."

THE CONFRONTATION ENDED NOT with triumph but with clarity. Elijah inclined his head, a gesture of reluctant respect mixed with resignation. He turned and walked down the aisle, his steps echoing as though each one were sealing a chamber he could not keep shut. At the door he paused, his hand on the iron latch. "When the town turns against you, remember that I tried to spare you," he said quietly. Then he was gone.

Miriam sank back into the pew. Her pulse still beat against her ribs like a drum calling soldiers to arms. She felt neither victorious nor defeated. She felt the heavy mantle of choice — the knowledge that she had crossed a threshold she could never uncross.

She closed her eyes again, letting the silence wash over her. But it was no longer Elijah's silence, nor the pact's silence. It was the silence of listening. Slowly, gently, the shimmer returned — the thirteenth petal glowing in defiance of erasure. She reached out her hand, palm upward, as though to receive it.

In that moment she knew: Ruth had not chosen her for courage she already had. Ruth had chosen her so she would learn it. Courage was not the absence of fear; it was the decision to act while fear argued for retreat.

She rose and walked to the front of the chapel. Standing beneath the cracked glass, she whispered Leah's words into the empty space: *I have married into a silence.* Her voice trembled, but it did not falter. "I hear you," she added, aloud. "And I will not keep you buried."

Light shifted, just so, through the broken line in the window. It fell across her face, warm as breath. She felt not absolution but recognition. And that was enough.

As she left the chapel, the square below bustled with festival preparations — banners raised, floats half-built, pies cooling on windowsills. The town was rehearsing joy, unaware that history was rehearsing itself in shadow. Miriam stepped onto the path with her fear intact but her direction chosen. She would carry the truth, even if the town preferred the weight of silence.

The bell tolled overhead. Its sound rolled down the hill, across the cobbles, through every doorway. Miriam walked toward it, toward the noise, toward the inevitable storm. She had chosen courage over fear. And the thirteenth petal shimmered, waiting for her to speak again.

12

THE ROSE PENDANT

The drawer stuck the way old drawers do when they've learned patience. Miriam worked it gently, fingers curled under the lip, coaxing wood that had swelled and relaxed with a hundred winters. This was Ruth's dresser in the small back room above the shop, the one that smelled of lavender sachets and camphor, the one Miriam had avoided because it felt like rifling a prayer. Tonight the room held the last light of day, shallow and honey-colored, and the quiet certainty that some objects ask to be found only when your hands are ready.

Handkerchiefs greeted her first—linen with a pale blue border, one corner embroidered with the tidy **R** Ruth had used on everything from labels to recipe cards. Beneath them, a flat book of stamps; a velvet ribbon curled like a tame snake; a tin of buttons heavy enough to bruise a palm. Miriam lifted the layer of folded cloth and felt it before she saw it: a change in weight, the thinnest hollow in the drawer's base. She tapped lightly and heard a different thud.

She breathed, remembering Ruth's warning—*Warm it, don't tug*—and slid her fingers along the thin seam at the back. The panel gave, reluctant but not stubborn, and lifted like the lid of a secret well. Inside lay a small pouch of faded velvet, the ribbon still neatly tied. The pouch carried a scent she could not name: metal, rosewater, a ghost of smoke. For a moment she simply held it, palms open, letting the object announce itself.

When she tipped the pouch, the pendant slipped into her hand with a soft sound—silver on skin. A circle no bigger than a walnut, slightly irregular as if hammered by a hand not a machine, its face engraved with a rose. Not the tidy dozen of the chapel's visible glass. Thirteen petals chased the rim, each line cut with care, the thirteenth nested between two others with the stealth of a compromise the maker refused to accept. Even tarnished, it carried its own light.

On the back, near the edge, a tiny stamp—too small to read without a lens—shone where the silver had been burnished thinner by touch. Opposite it, a notch—no more than a shallow crescent—broke the circle as if meant to register into some unseen groove. The chain, simple and long, looked new by comparison. Ruth must have replaced it. Or perhaps the chain had been added when the pendant changed roles—from offering to inheritance.

Miriam set it on her palm and felt the weight resolve— substantial, not heavy; a thing that knew how to sit in a hand. The sight of the thirteenth petal sent a warmth rising that felt like recognition more than belief. She thought of the ledger entry she and Julian had found—*rose pendant, silver, given to chapel—anonymous*—and of the anonymous that had threaded themselves through every page. Anony- mous had a face now. It sat in her hand and shone without apology.

A folded scrap of paper lay at the bottom of the cavity.

She smoothed it open. A hand—not Ruth's, older—had written three lines:

For the door that does not open with a key.

Wear when you must be seen by what remembers.

Thirteen belongs.

The last sentence was written twice, the second time more lightly, as if the writer had learned to say the words without breaking them.

Miriam lifted the pendant by its chain and held it up. The fading sun licked it once and left, laying a bright oval on the dresser's scarred top. She brought it closer to her face until the lines of the petals blurred into suggestion. The thirteenth curl held its own geometry, modest and insistent. *Essai caché*, the glazier had written. Hidden attempt. Or not so hidden, if someone had worn the attempt as a body's declaration.

She slipped the chain over her head. The pendant settled against her sternum, cool at first, then warmer, the way some symbols learn your pulse before you learn theirs. In the mirror, the silver lay at the hollow of her throat like punctuation—neither ornament nor proclamation, but something between.

She wanted to run to the museum, to show Julian like a child breaking curfew with joy. She wanted, also, to sit with the pendant alone until she had calmed the part of her that worried this was theater. The room, wise to both impulses, suggested tea. She made it, and while the water argued with the kettle she wrote a note to slip under Theo's counter: **Found something. If you see Julian before I do, send him over? —M.** Halfway through the sentence she added, **Not for display. For seeing.**

By the time she stepped onto the stair, the square held that particular evening energy that made Cedar Creek feel like a choreographed accident: voices folding and unfolding, the fountain catching what light the day surrendered, the chapel looking larger because the hill had grown shadow. She tucked the pendant under her sweater, its weight a quiet anchor. If Ruth had intended this as armor, she had chosen the right material—it did not guard; it reminded.

An hour later, as if summoned by something less theatrical than a phone and more reliable than rumor, the Riverlight's bell chimed and Julian pushed through the shop door. He took in her face and the set of the room the way he took in manuscripts—trained to notice what didn't announce itself. "Theo said you'd found—" He stopped. There are objects that adjust a room's grammar simply by being in it. His eyes had already found the silver.

"Ruth's drawer," Miriam said. "False bottom."

He came forward slowly, as if noise might be disrespect. She drew the pendant out and let it lie on her palm. The shop's small lamp caught the engraving and made it breathe.

"Thirteen," he said, not quite a question.

"Thirteen," she answered, and felt the word seat itself between them like a plank laid exactly where it needed to be.

HE DID NOT REACH for it. He leaned in, hands braced on the counter as if he were looking over a parapet into a city he had been told did not exist. "May I?" he asked after a beat, and when she nodded he lifted the pendant by its edge with the same pressure he used on onion-skin letters.

He turned it to the light. The thirteenth petal sat precisely where the erased line on the tracing had whis-pered it might: nestled between the lower-right lobes, not appended, not haughty—correct, in that quiet way craft recognizes. "This is not a whim," he said. "No amateur would choose to complicate a circle here unless he knew the template by heart."

"The glazier," Miriam said. "Or someone who loved his attempt enough to wear it."

He flipped the pendant and frowned gently. "There's a stamp. Too small." He reached into his coat for a jeweler's loupe—of course he kept one—slipped it in front of his eye, and bent. "A star? Or a bee. The lines are soft." He shifted the angle. "Not a federal hallmark. A maker's personal mark, perhaps."

"Local?" she asked.

"Could be," he said. "Or a journeyman who learned here and returned to his own town, keeping his hands' habits and his heart's trouble." He looked up. "The notch?"

She showed him the shallow crescent on the edge. He traced the air near it without touching metal. "Registration notch," he murmured. "Makes sense if someone intended it to seat into something—wood or stone. Or glass." He seemed to hear himself and shook his head once, as if to dislodge a superstition. "Not glass."

"Not glass," she agreed, though she felt the chapel listening.

He set the pendant down and opened his leather folio. From a long envelope he drew the tracing—*essai caché*—they had nearly memorized. He laid the Mylar over it the way conservators teach you to—confidently, without dragging. He aligned the roses by eye, not instrument. The pendant's thirteenth arc sat like a missing syllable over the penciled ghost.

He exhaled. Not a sigh, exactly—more like a small collapse of skepticism into a chair it had been eyeing. "Do you know how much I hate the word *sign*?" he asked, watching the alignment hold.

"Enough to discover we need another," she said.

"Artifact," he said, firmly, as if retraining his mouth.

He took the pendant in his hand again, then put it down, then took it again. Doubt and duty wrestled in his face. "The ledger," he said. "June and September entries. *Private contribution anonymous (rose pendant).* I assumed—" He winced. "I assumed that was a votive to be melted or set. But if it was kept—if it was *withheld*—then someone decided the chapel couldn't bear it and made sure the symbol lived elsewhere."

"Not the chapel's then," Miriam said. "The town's."

He nodded, reluctantly converted by his own discipline. "This changes the type of conversation we're having," he said. "It moves us from story to evidence—and the town will forgive a story faster than it will forgive evidence."

"You're saying *be careful*," she said.

"I am saying—" He stopped. Honesty flickered. "I am saying I was wrong to assume you were craning your neck at shadows. You have been looking at a design."

The admission landed between them without fanfare, as generous as it was hard-won. It softened something in Miriam that had nothing to do with victory; it felt like watching a friend put down a certain shield. He took the loupe to the back again and angled it, searching for a letter that might betray a maker. He found, instead, the faintest incised line, almost an afterthought, invisible without the magnification. He steadied his hand, read it, blinked, read it again.

"What does it say?" Miriam asked.

He lifted the pendant for her to see through the loupe. The script was small and imperfect, the letters crowded. The language wasn't Latin or English. Miriam sounded it in her mouth and tasted adolescent French—*à celle qui voit*—to the one who sees. The phrase carried no flourish, no sermon. It was a note one artisan might scratch for a friend, or a bride for her future. It was also a dare.

Julian made a small, disbelieving sound that wasn't quite a laugh. He removed the loupe, rubbed his eyebrow with his thumb as if his skepticism had left a mark. "This pendant has been waiting for you," he said, and then, hearing himself, flushed as if he had said too much. "I mean—waiting for someone who would know how to… read it."

"Ruth knew," Miriam said. "She kept it until she decided to give it away."

"The drawer," he said, nodding. "The false bottom." He glanced at the scrap she had found with it and read the lines about the door that does not open with a key. "This is either the worst kind of theater," he said, "or the best kind of proof."

"Or both," she said. "The truth likes a good stage."

His mouth tilted. "I will lose my chalk privileges for saying this, but—this feels like the town wrote itself a note and hid it where only the right hand could lift it."

He took a breath and let it out slowly. When he spoke again, the cadence had changed. "Tomorrow," he said, "we'll photograph, measure, and note. We'll look for matches in any carving—pew ends, baluster tracery, the sacristy chest. The notch is a clue. And we… will not parade this."

"We'll let it breathe," she said.

His skepticism was not gone. It had simply moved aside for awe.

SHE REACHED to lift the pendant and their hands collided, not the awkward bump of strangers but the collision you don't correct because the contact brings steadiness. He stilled; she did too. For a heartbeat the shop held them the way some rooms hold a low note—vibration without sound. Beneath her palm she felt the cool circle of silver and the warmth of his fingers gathered around its edge.

"Sorry," he said, but didn't move.

"Don't be," she answered, and didn't, either.

They let go at the same time and laughed—quietly, because anything louder would have felt like breaking the thing they had just set down gently. He turned to reach for the folio, and when he did the cuff of his sleeve brushed the back of her hand in a soft, accidental sweep that made the small hairs there register weather. She busied herself with a cloth, as if polishing could disguise steadying.

He set the pendant on the counter again, but closer to her side than before, and then—without thinking—touched the hollow at his own throat, mirroring where it lay on hers. The gesture embarrassed him as soon as he finished it; he chuckled softly at himself and let his hand fall.

"It suits you," he said, and meant the pendant, and perhaps the sentence that had begun to attach itself to her —not *seer* in the town's punishing pronunciation, but *the one who sees* in the artisan's small hand.

She slipped the chain over her head again and the silver found its place. It lay there not like a medal but like a reminder. The thirteenth petal rested against her, a curved and careful insistence. She looked up to thank him for the care of his seeing and found him already looking at her— not with scrutiny, not with hunger, but with that complicated kindness that knows the cost of being looked at and chooses to pay it.

Outside, the square began its evening song: Theo dragging in a sandwich board with an invented law written in chalk; the science teacher telling a teenager to count figure-eight beats out loud; the fountain providing its own steady argument for persistence. The chapel on the hill gathered the last scraps of light, turning them into a dusky geometry. In that geometry, Miriam could almost see where a small cedar reliquary might hide; she could almost see the niche that the pendant's notch might recognize.

"Come with me," she said, surprising herself with the sentence's urgency. "Not now—tonight would be performance. But tomorrow morning, before everyone arrives. The south wall, vestral side." She didn't say *Appendix C*; the pendant said it for her.

"I'll bring a soft brush and a headlamp," he said, which was the scholar's version of *yes*. "And Theo's lemon pie. He seems to think it's fuel."

She reached for the tracing, the two of them each holding one corner, and their fingers found the same edge. They didn't retreat from the contact. It felt less like accident and more like agreement. He folded the paper with care and slid it back into its sleeve.

"Not to spoil the moment," he said, smiling, "but when the town sees that around your neck..."

"It won't," she said. "Not until it's ready. Today it's between us and the wood that remembers."

"That narrows the audience to the two most stubborn entities in Cedar Creek," he said.

"I'm counting on it."

He looked at her mouth as if the next sentence would require precision to land well, then chose a safer gesture: he reached across the counter and closed his fingers lightly over hers—a second, no more—and then let go. It was as eloquent as any confession. Syllables of warmth traveled up her forearm, ordinary as heat and complicated as meaning.

"Walk you home?" he asked.

"You're already here," she said, and they both smiled because the answer was true in more ways than one.

They locked the shop together—he turned the key, she lifted the latch—and stepped into the indigo evening. The pendant lay warm and steady against her throat. The chapel's bell tolled once, a small rehearsal for the hour to come. They took the long way around the square, past the fountain and the chalkboard and the bench where Mrs. Mathers had left a bundle of knitting like an encoded warning. Neither of them talked about the families or the sealed appendix or the way Pastor Elijah's eyes would narrow when the next piece of evidence reached daylight. Neither of them said *we are becoming a we*. They didn't have to. The pendant said it for them in a language both of them could read.

At her door, he paused without the fuss of uncertainty. "Tomorrow," he said. "Before the town decides what we've done."

"Before the town has to decide," she corrected gently.

He nodded, and the nod, like most of his offerings, contained much more than motion. He turned to go, then stopped and faced her again as if he had remembered an errand he wanted to add to the list. "Miriam," he said. "I know you don't need it, but I'm going to say it anyway: I'm with you."

She let the sentence do its work. "I know," she said. "I'm with you, too."

When he left, she stood in the doorway a moment longer, the pendant a bright pulse at her throat. Inside, the shop exhaled in the way old rooms do when they've been asked to keep one more secret for one more night. She went to the counter, lifted the scrap with its three lines, and set it beside the register. *For the door that does not open with a key.*

Wear when you must be seen by what remembers. Thirteen belongs. She traced the words with a fingertip and felt, with the clarity of cool air on a warm face, that the door was nearer than it had been—so near she could almost hear wood deciding to say yes.

In bed, the silver rested against her skin and warmed to her. Sleep, when it came, brought a single image: a small cedar box letting go of its stubborn silence with a sound like breath, and a flood of fine dust that smelled like the inside of a violin. In her dream she turned the pendant in that new air, and the thirteenth petal caught dawn. She woke with the feeling you get when a room has recognized you. Tomorrow would ask for steadier hands. Tonight, she wore the answer.

13

FESTIVAL DISRUPTION

The festival morning arrived with the square dressed in colors brighter than its conversations. Ribbons curled from lampposts; banners in orange and crimson snapped above the bakery roof; the fountain had been crowned with garlands of wheat. On the surface Cedar Creek looked like a town rehearsing joy, but Miriam, standing in her shop's doorway, could feel the strain underneath. The air held the thin crackle of words whispered too quickly, alliances drawn too visibly, and eyes that lingered on her pendant though she kept it tucked beneath her blouse.

She joined the flow of neighbors moving toward Main Street where the parade would wind past. The floats were lined along the curb, their wheels chalked against rolling. Each bore the signature of a guild or family: the carpenters had built a miniature fort palisade out of cedar, the bakers stacked pies in dizzying towers, and the schoolchildren had crafted papier-mâché salmon leaping through painted river arcs. It was charming, it was proud, and it was brittle.

Rumors already whispered like drafts between the floats.

Miriam caught a snippet near the Wagner wagon—"They've taken too much space, again"—and another by the Dubois cousins—"We won't march behind them, not this year." She recognized the tones; they were not arguments about parade order, but about inheritance dressed as logistics.

Theo, chalk dust still on his fingers from the café board, appeared at her side. "Festivals bring out the best and worst of us," he murmured. "Sometimes at the same time." He nodded toward Everett, who was trying to command float placement like a general with too few troops. Everett's voice rose above the chatter, authoritative but frayed. The Wagner hayride had been assigned first position, the Dubois float second. The Adler cousins—distant, polite—had been placed third. Everyone else arranged around them like satellites around a reluctant sun.

Miriam felt the weight of the order. First, second, third: the founding families paraded at the head, as though 1846 still decided today. She saw Julian across the crowd, camera slung around his neck, notebook peeking from his coat. He caught her eye briefly, and in that glance she read the same recognition: this was not parade design, this was hierarchy rehearsed.

The brass band struck its opening note, too loud for the space, and the floats began their slow crawl forward. Children tossed petals from baskets; the carpenters swung hammers rhythmically on their float for show; Mrs. Callahan waved pies aloft like banners of goodwill. Laughter rose, but it had an edge. Behind the cheers, murmurs threaded: "They never yield," "Always first place," "Old debts don't vanish."

As the Wagner float rolled past the fountain, one of its axles groaned, loudly enough to hush part of the crowd. The structure shuddered but steadied. Miriam saw Mack

Wagner at the reins, his face set, jaw tight. He waved, dutiful, but his eyes were narrowed, scanning the wheel as though he expected more trouble.

Behind him, the Dubois float followed—painted with river scenes, oars rising in pattern. Elise Dubois's granddaughter stood at the bow, smiling with practiced grace. Children on the curb shouted for candy; she tossed wrapped sweets with a precision that suggested rehearsal.

The Adler float creaked into view next, a simpler design —wooden books stacked to represent knowledge, painted roses curling at their base. Miriam's throat tightened at the sight of those roses. Twelve petals each, bright red, but one —at the back corner, half-hidden—carried a thirteenth stroke of paint. The brush had faltered, the line not fully curved, but it was there. She made a note in her mind, even as the crowd pressed in.

Conflict wasn't loud yet, but it simmered. The parade was supposed to celebrate the town's wholeness. Instead, it was replaying an old script. Miriam could feel the page turning toward something heavier.

THE PARADE ROUNDED the square and climbed toward the chapel's hill. Miriam followed along the boardwalk, weaving between families and vendors hawking cider. Julian caught up, notebook in hand, his brow furrowed.

"Did you see the axle?" he asked low.

"Yes," she answered. "Too deliberate to be accident?"

He hesitated. "I'd call it poor maintenance—except I overheard two men near the carpenters' float joking about how 'the Wagners deserve a stumble this year.' Jokes with teeth."

They reached the corner just as the Wagner float

lurched again. This time the front wheel buckled and the side rail cracked, spilling hay bales onto the street. Mack shouted, pulling hard on the reins to halt the team. The crowd gasped. Children scattered. For a moment chaos hung suspended—the kind that might dissolve into laughter if handled gently, or into fury if stoked.

Everett rushed forward, arms raised. "Stay back! Stay back!" But his voice carried more command than calm, and the townsfolk bristled. Some muttered about Wagner pride; others snickered that the mighty had fallen. The Dubois float, halted behind, stood in uneasy stillness.

Miriam pushed through until she reached Mack. He was already hauling hay aside, sweat on his brow. "Deliberate?" she asked softly.

His eyes flicked to her, startled. Then he looked away, jaw tight. "Bolt was loosened," he muttered. "Not by me."

She helped him drag the broken rail clear. Around them, the murmurs sharpened. "Typical Wagner craftsmanship." "They think they own the town but can't hold a wheel together." "Old debts, old curses."

Julian arrived, crouched to inspect the axle. "Tool marks," he whispered to Miriam. "Fresh. Someone turned this out within days."

Mack heard and cursed under his breath. "Of course," he said bitterly. "Sabotage, and now the whole square will take it as fate." He slammed the hay aside, stood tall, and lifted his voice. "We'll walk it from here. Wagners don't quit."

The crowd cheered reflexively, but the cheer had a split tone—half admiration, half mockery. The float rolled again, slower, pulled by townsfolk now rather than horses. The Dubois float followed, its participants smiling too brightly, as if secretly pleased by the stumble.

Miriam walked with Julian along the edge. She felt history breathing through the street, the same quarrels Leah's fragment had hinted at, the same grudges Ruth had mapped in her coded circles. Sabotage was not about a float. It was about reminding everyone of what silence had never healed.

Theo, balancing a tray of cider, murmured as she passed, "The past keeps showing up uninvited, doesn't it?" He offered her a cup. She shook her head, her throat too tight.

The parade tried to recover. The band played louder, drowning the whispers. But the damage was done. A float collapse wasn't just spectacle—it was metaphor, and Cedar Creek knew how to read metaphors even when it pretended not to.

THE PARADE WOUND back into the square for its final circuit. Miriam tried to steady her breath, telling herself the incident would be dismissed as accident. But her eyes were drawn to the Adler float again. The roses painted along its side gleamed in the afternoon light. She counted them one by one: twelve bright petals each—except the one in the back corner.

She edged through the crowd until she stood where she could see it clearly. The thirteenth stroke wasn't neat; it curved imperfectly, like a hand that had added it quickly before paint dried. But it was intentional. Someone had marked the design with knowledge. The crowd, absorbed in chatter, hadn't noticed. But Miriam's intuition pressed like a thumb against her ribs: this was no accident. It was message.

Julian followed her gaze. "What is it?"

She pointed subtly. "Look. Thirteen."

He squinted, then inhaled. "Good Lord," he whispered. "It matches the pendant."

Her pendant warmed against her chest as if in answer. The thirteenth petal wasn't hiding anymore; it was parading, albeit shyly, before the entire town. Miriam's heart raced. Who painted it? Why? Was it a quiet ally, someone remembering Leah's dissent? Or a taunt, daring her to notice while others stayed blind?

She traced the brushstroke in the air, her fingers trembling. The pendant seemed heavier now, its chain pulling her toward recognition. She could almost hear Leah's voice —*If ever another should read this, know that the pact was not unanimous.*

"Miriam," Julian said quietly, leaning close. "You understand what this means, don't you? Someone alive, today, knows. They're keeping the symbol alive."

She nodded, throat dry. Around them the square erupted in laughter as the bakers' pie tower wobbled dangerously. But Miriam heard it differently. Not humor— warning. The town was laughing at accidents because it feared what was deliberate.

She took Julian's arm, steadying herself. "The rose hasn't gone silent. It's still speaking."

He glanced at her, his skepticism thinner than ever, awe mingling with worry. "Then we'd better be ready to listen."

The parade concluded with the brass band circling the fountain, their final notes triumphant on the surface but trembling underneath. Floats rolled to a stop. Children scattered to chase candy wrappers. Adults clapped each other on the shoulders with the false brightness of people determined to call the day a success.

But Miriam saw what most did not. The Wagners' broken axle. The Dubois too-perfect smiles. The thirteenth petal hidden on the Adler float. All fragments of the same truth: the pact's silence was cracking, and the town was choosing sides even when it claimed to celebrate unity.

As the crowd thinned, Miriam reached for the pendant under her sweater. Her fingers closed around the silver, tracing its engraved petals. She whispered so softly only the pendant could hear: "Thirteen belongs."

The words steadied her, though the air still bristled with unease. Tomorrow, the square would tell itself the float collapse was mishap, nothing more. Tomorrow, the painted rose would fade beneath other decorations. But tonight Miriam knew differently. Symbols don't disappear. They wait. And Cedar Creek had just revealed another.

The bell on the hill rang vespers. Its sound rolled over the square, settling on rooftops and river alike. Miriam lifted her eyes to the chapel's cracked window. The shimmer glowed faint, as if echoing the thirteenth stroke she had seen. She met Julian's gaze, and in it she read what she felt in herself: awe, dread, and the stubborn thread of hope.

The parade was over. The festival would continue. But Cedar Creek was already moving toward its next fracture. And Miriam, with the pendant at her throat and the thirteenth petal in her sight, knew she would have to walk straight into it.

14
____

CONFRONTING THE FAMILIES

The Dubois house sat close enough to the river that you could hear a change in its voice when the tide turned. Miriam and Julian climbed the slate steps at dusk with a bottle of Theo's cordial tucked under Julian's arm like a diplomatic offering, and the pendant—a cool certainty—resting beneath Miriam's collar. Lanterns burned along the veranda, their glass chimneys smudged by moths. On the far edge of the lawn, children looped figure eights with sparklers, their light sketching symbols that dissolved before they could be read.

Vivian Dubois opened the door with the theatrical ease of a woman who'd grown up greeting rooms. Early fifties, fine-boned, auburn hair pulled back and anchored with a tortoiseshell clip, she wore a dress the color of late summer peaches and a smile you could mistake for welcome if you were new to Cedar Creek. Miriam wasn't new anymore.

"Ms. Adler," Vivian sang, turning to include Julian. "And Mr. Roth. Come in, before the river steals all the conversation."

The foyer smelled of beeswax and something spicier—

cardamom, maybe. Photographs lined the wall: Dubois boats on a fast river; a trio of women on a dock, skirts held like sails; a man standing in front of the chapel, hat in hand, the rose window a stain of light above him. The frames had been recently dusted. Miriam could see the streaks of effort where the house had been made ready to stage its version of the past.

The dining room had been set as if for a painting: long table, white linen, an arrangement of river grasses and small white roses in a low bowl, twelve plates aligned with familial precision. A thirteenth place had been added at the corner—a side chair with a knife and spoon laid exactly parallel, as if someone had argued for the extra seat and someone else had conceded only the minimum.

Graham Wagner rose when they entered, a tall man whose age was measured not in years but in rigidity. His hair had retreated in a disciplined arc; his wrist bones showed under the cuff like opinions. Mack, his son, stood beside him looking already exhausted by the effort of being fair in a room that had never practiced it. On the other side, Mara Adler, Miriam's cousin twice removed—their only real blood in this assembly—sat with her hands wrapped around a water glass. She and Miriam had only met twice. The last time, Mara had delivered soup to the shop and a sentence Miriam had kept: *You don't need our permission to be an Adler.*

Other faces sorted themselves quietly: Leonard Pike— Everett's brother—broad-shouldered, eyes watchful; Mrs. Mathers, hair braided and pinned, occupying a chair she had not asked permission to take; Pastor Elijah at the far end of the table, kept at a distance that was both courtesy and quarantine; Elise Dubois granddaughter—Claire—with the same mouth as the woman in the dockside photo.

"Thank you for coming," Vivian said, gesturing Miriam and Julian toward the added chairs. "It seemed... sensible, after the events of the parade, to break bread together."

"Breaking things has become a motif," Walter Crane muttered from the sideboard where he was not supposed to be. Vivian chose not to hear him, which in this town was a choice that passed for piety.

Glasses clinked. Vivian lifted hers—something clear with citrus and a sprig of mint. "To the festival," she said, all brightness. "To Cedar Creek's tradition of unity."

A ripple of polite applause. Julian's fingers found the edge of his napkin and folded it once, then again; Miriam felt the familiar tug to reach over and still his hands. She didn't. This dinner required their restraint to be visible.

Soup arrived—salmon chowder, of course, because some traditions prefer to be on the tongue while announcing themselves from the river. Conversation held its breath in the first minutes while people pretended the soup was more interesting than what had happened to the Wagner float.

Graham broke first, politely. "I'm told," he began, aiming for neutral and hitting something just sharper, "that bolts loosen themselves when parades turn uphill. Gravity, you see."

"Gravity usually tightens," Elena Ruiz said from two seats down, not a founding family but invited for her science and the town's instinct that quarrels require witnesses. "Slope puts load on threads." She dabbed her lip with her napkin. "Unless the threads are reversed."

Mack's spoon paused. "Dad found tool marks," he said to the table, not to his father. "Fresh."

"People have been known to misinterpret what they

wish to see," Graham said smoothly. "Especially when humiliation comes dressed as physics."

"Humiliation doesn't wear physics," Walter said. "It wears old suits and newer grudges."

Vivian's smile tightened. "Let's not litigate parades," she said. "We're here to discuss—" she chose a word with surgical care—"tone. The town's tone. And to assure Ms. Adler that rumors, however... energetic... will not find purchase in this room."

Miriam folded her hands in her lap to keep them from reaching for the pendant. She could feel it, warm and steady against her skin. Rumors. She thought of the painted rose with thirteen on the Adler float, the deliberate turn of a wrench, the way the crowd had cheered and mocked at the same time. Rumors weren't their problem. History was.

Julian thanked Vivian for the invitation with a conservator's diplomacy. "We're grateful," he said, "for any room willing to talk in full sentences."

Graham's glance flicked to Julian's folio, as if paper might be a weapon. "We've always appreciated the museum's role," he said. "Context matters." He said context the way some people say *leash*.

"Context matters," Miriam agreed softly. "So does content."

"Which is where conscience keeps its counsel," Pastor Elijah added, trying to warm the air with pastoral damp. The words were correct; the temperature stayed cold.

First course plates scraped. A hush moved down the table, the kind that announces the entrance of the true subject. Vivian laid her spoon gently on the saucer. "About the window," she said.

The word settled like a stone in shallow water—too heavy to pretend you hadn't heard the splash. Miriam's eyes tipped upward briefly as if she could see the rose from here; she could not, but the shimmer still lived behind her eyelids. She kept her voice even. "Yes. About the window."

Vivian's smile returned, thinner. "Many in town feel... unsettled by speculation."

"Many in town feel relieved it's being named," Mara Adler said, quietly. Heads turned. Vivian's eyes softened, then corrected themselves. "Of course," she said, "people differ. The purpose of this table is to calibrate."

"Calibration," Walter said, unable to help himself, "is just consensus with a ruler."

No one laughed, but Miriam watched three mouths pretend not to.

It turned out the meal had been designed as an act of biography. Each course carried a declaration none of the hosts would risk saying out loud. After the soup came a river trout, roasted with lemon and rosemary, laid on cedar planks. Dubois pride, dressed as hospitality. Graham sliced his filet with small, exact motions, as if demonstrating that precision could tame the smell of judgment.

Graham Wagner: a man whose inheritance had stiffened into posture. He wore a signet ring with the family crest—rope across an anchor—and touched it when he spoke, thumb catching the ridge as if to steady his sentence. He called Miriam *Ms. Adler* with the courtesy of someone who declines intimacy on principle. He called Julian *Professor*, though everyone knew Julian taught by the river more than the classroom now. He wanted order, but his order had calcified into a theology: history is safe if you keep it on the mantel.

Across from him, Vivian Dubois curated the evening

with those peach-colored sleeves and a warmth that could be turned up or down. She had a talent for the dangerous middle—soothing the room while guiding it where she wanted it to go. Her laugh came easily, but her eyes counted everything and decided whether to keep it. In her youth she might have been called charming; now the word that fit better was *capable.* You could hand her a crisis and she would fold it like linen and put it in a cabinet marked *Later.* She would be a good friend and a formidable enemy. She served the next course—dark bread, uncut.

"Bread for the table," Mrs. Mathers said dryly. "Not to be sliced." She met Miriam's eyes. Miriam saw the flash: *bread that is not eaten.* A pact folded into a loaf.

Claire Dubois, the granddaughter, wore a delicate chain with a tiny oar charm and corrected her grandmother's dates with affectionate precision. She had a laugh like a bell and the habit of glancing toward Mack when tempers warmed, which told Miriam more than Claire would have admitted. When the float collapse was mentioned obliquely, Claire's mouth tightened. He's decent, her face said, leave him be. She was young enough to want fairness and old enough to suspect she would have to settle for decorum.

Mack—sleeves pushed up, clean fingernails, a band of grease behind his left ear he hadn't noticed—listened more than he spoke. When pressed, he answered with civility, then braced himself for the punishment civility earns in rooms that prefer loyalty. He loved his father and suffered him; he disliked the show of legacy and was trapped in its script.

Mara Adler kept to the edge of the table's center, neither ceding nor pleading. She had Ruth's long fingers and kept smoothing her napkin as if the linen might tell her which sentence would do least harm. Her voice was steady when she used it, and her silences felt like full cups she'd learned not to offer in rooms that spilled.

Pastor Elijah occupied the chair like a man sitting out a storm in his own church, sure the walls would hold if he didn't breathe too loudly. He asked after children, after illnesses, after pie contests. He avoided direct sentences about the window the way one avoids a cracked step: by placing weight elsewhere as if elsewhere would bear more.

There were others who mattered: Leonard Pike, who said little and watched much, the kind of man whose vote makes and unmakes committees; Nadia Reeves at Elena's side, who refilled water glasses when conversation went thin, whose eyes told Miriam she'd slipped bread into the pockets of women who had forgotten to eat while they were busy keeping everyone from breaking; and Mrs. Mathers, whose hairpins held like testimony and who had the habit of inserting a single phrase into a paragraph that would ruin it for the liar.

"I suppose," Graham said, wiping at an invisible crumb, "we should state the obvious. The museum intends an event tomorrow—" he glanced at Julian, then at Vivian "—Paper and Pie, I believe?"

Julian kept his voice gentle. "A chance to look together. To touch paper with clean hands. That's all."

"Touching," Graham said, "is precisely what concerns me."

"We can wear gloves," Elena offered.

Vivian interceded. "We all want the same thing: for Cedar Creek to be... intact."

"Wholeness," Miriam said softly, unable not to say it. The word felt like a key she carried in her mouth.

Vivian turned sharply toward her, then softened the movement into another smile. "Of course. And wholeness sometimes asks us not to—" she chose carefully—"pry open old boxes."

At this, Mrs. Mathers reached for the bread. "Boxes that are meant to be opened have hinges," she said, tearing a piece off with neat ferocity. She held it up. "And some boxes tell you so by smell. Cedar keeps secrets, yes. It also releases them when the weather changes."

Graham's fork paused. "You speak as though you've stood in that wall."

"In a manner of speaking," Mrs. Mathers said, and refused to elaborate. Her eyes found Miriam's, then Julian's. Miriam felt the recognition pass like a coin pressed into a palm: *I know you know.*

Dessert arrived—apple tarts and an uncut loaf placed again in the center, a second reminder that some breads were not for eating. When Vivian poured coffee, she did it herself, not trusting hands that might jostle. Her posture did not slump, but fatigue showed up in the angle of her wrist.

"I worry," she said, finally dropping courtesy's pitch, "that we are about to make the town choose when it is not ready."

"The town already chose," Mara said quietly. "In 1846."

"And again in 1892," Julian added before he could stop himself. He caught the glance from Graham and didn't look away. "You all signed the recasting."

Claire's spoon dinged gently against her saucer. "Grandfather said those discussions were... necessary."

"They were," Mrs. Mathers said. "To the families."

The room cooled a degree. Vivian's eyes surveyed the table, then settled on Miriam. "I think it's time we asked you to say what you intend, Ms. Adler."

What do you intend—spoken as if intent were a threat. Miriam sat with the question a breath longer than comfort allowed. She felt the pendant against her, the notch's little crescent. She inhaled. "To tell the truth," she said. "And to keep the town from hurting itself with its own silence."

"And if the truth hurts," Graham said.

"Then we will have named what has been hurting us all along," she answered.

"And if it divides households?" Pastor Elijah's voice was quiet and frayed.

"Households divided by a lie are already divided," Miriam said. "They simply speak softly."

A long quiet. The river made its steady sound. Somewhere on the veranda a glass chimed as a moth found it. The room rearranged itself around what had been said. Julian's hand rested on the table, palm down, as if anchoring paper that wasn't there. He didn't touch her. He didn't have to.

AFTER COFFEE, the conversation fractured into smaller currents, the way rivers do when they meet a tangle of roots. People rose, drifted toward the veranda or the sideboard, paired off for what looked like politeness and felt like strategizing. The lanterns outside had burned down to a steadier glow. Miriam excused herself and stepped into the hum of the evening. The air smelled of water and apples. From the river came a soft slap of something wooden against a dock— an oar not tied tight enough, a history not fastened.

She felt more than heard Julian arrive at her shoulder. He didn't report on the room; he tilted his head toward the garden, a silent question. She nodded. They walked down the steps and stood near a row of rosemary shrubs that had been clipped too obediently. The house's windows framed the dinner like a triptych: in one panel, Vivian poured more coffee for Claire; in another, Graham spoke too close to Mack's face; in the third, Mrs. Mathers sat alone, looking at a slice of bread as though reading it.

"Feel it?" Julian asked.

"Guilt," Miriam said. "Not everywhere. Enough."

"Where?"

"Vivian's wrists," she said. "The way she poured coffee for Claire—careful enough to keep her granddaughter from taking on weight she doesn't owe. That's not cruelty. That's a woman who carried something and would rather it die with her than live in someone softer."

"And Graham?"

"His ring," she said. "He touches it before any sentence that sounds like duty. He thinks the ring is the duty. He can't separate them. I don't smell guilt on him. I smell fear of losing the shape that has kept him from feeling it."

Julian nodded, not in agreement, but in the way of someone who recognized the accuracy even if he didn't want it. "Mack?"

"He is tired of paying the bill," she said. "And he knows the bill is larger than the cost of an axle." She turned her face toward the river. "There's guilt in the house. It's not one person. It's a seam that runs under the flooring."

Wind lifted a corner of a linen that had been left on the table outside. It fluttered like a page. Miriam thought of the sealed appendix, of the phrase that had followed them from ledger to ledger—*for the peace of households*. She heard it again, not as justification but as confession.

Behind them, voices rose and fell. Vivian's tone when she said "we did what we had to" contained something stripped of its varnish. Claire's reply was a whisper Miriam couldn't catch. Graham's voice carried, its edges showing:

"We're not revisiting this." Mack's was cool, practiced: "We already are."

Mara appeared at the garden's edge like a useful apparition. "If you're measuring guilt," she said, "you'll need a better unit than teaspoons."

"We were improvising," Julian said.

Mara's smile was tired. "My grandmother used to say the Dubois built houses that kept secrets in the vents," she said. "When winter came, the rooms smelled of whatever hadn't been confessed." She looked over Miriam's shoulder at the windows. "It smells like cedar in there tonight."

"Cedar keeps and releases," Miriam said. "Mrs. Mathers reminded us."

Mara nodded. "She would know. Half of Mrs. Mathers is Dubois. The other half is Mathers." She drew a breath as if to embark on a story and then stopped herself. "You should know two things." She held up a finger. "First, it wasn't just the founders. In 1892 the wives were asked to sign something." Another finger. "Second, the thing they signed mentioned the phrase 'households' three separate times."

"Plural," Julian said quietly.

"Always plural," Mara said. "So no single house had to carry blame. Or truth."

Vivian's voice floated through the open window, soft and flinty: "We are not going to parade our dead." Mrs. Mathers, from the same window but nearer: "They've been walking in the street all day."

Graham stepped outside then, surprised to find them in the garden, recalibrating his expression to politeness. "Ms. Adler," he said. "A word."

Miriam nodded. He led her two paces away, to the edge of the lawn where the ground dipped toward the river path. He clasped his hands behind his back, a schoolmaster's posture. "I recognize," he began, "that you believe you are doing a service."

"I am trying," she said.

He cut a small line in the air with his fingers. "Be careful where your trying lands. A town is a house, and a house holds people who didn't choose each other." He looked toward the windows, toward Vivian's managing light. "There are women in there who signed things to hold this place together. They are dead now. They deserve—"

"Relief," Miriam said. She let the word be gentler than her temper. "And the living deserve not to be held hostage by what someone signed for them a hundred and thirty years ago."

His jaw worked. "We did what we had to do," he said, as if reciting an oath he had been given rather than written. "You will not understand until you have spent a lifetime keeping other people's dignity from shattering."

She thought of Walter leaving pies on porches, of Theo writing rules in chalk, of Elena counting beats for a teenager so he wouldn't trip. "I am trying to keep dignity from being confused with secrecy," she said. "I may fail. But I won't fail by pretending."

He held her gaze, and this time there was something like respect in it—reluctant, wary, real. "Your aunt," he said, "was a decent woman."

"My aunt," she said, "was a precise woman."

"Which is what made her decent," he said, and the admission landed between them like a rung on a ladder neither had wanted to climb.

He turned back toward the house without dismissal. Miriam watched him go with the complicated pity one reserves for people whose choices hardened into walls around them.

Julian returned to her side, not asking what had been said. He didn't need the transcript to read the temperature. Behind him, Claire slipped out and touched Mack's shoulder. "I'm sorry," she said, and meant it for more than the axle.

The evening thinned. Vivian called people back to the table for coffee, for photographs, for closing phrases that would pretend the room had arrived at a shared conclusion. Before Miriam followed, Mrs. Mathers intercepted her with a folded napkin. Inside, wrapped like a contraband, lay a sprig of cedar, a thin shaving of wood, and a phrase written in Mrs. Mathers' careful hand: **South wall, vestral side — listen for hollow.** It was not news; it was permission.

Miriam slipped the napkin into her pocket and felt, with a mix of dread and relief, the near-future tilt. Guilt hummed in the house like a note someone had struck and held too long; people had learned to talk over it, but the tone remained. She touched the pendant through her blouse—habit, comfort, vow.

On their way out, Vivian pressed a small parcel into Miriam's hands—"A token," she said. "No strings." Once outside, under the river's breath and the first scatter of stars, Miriam unwrapped it. A small loaf, unsliced. The gesture might have been grace or warning or both.

"Bread that is not eaten," Julian murmured.

"Promises that are," she said.

They walked down the steps without speaking, hearing the conversation continue behind them in waves. At the bottom, Miriam stopped, turned to look back. In the upstairs window she could see Mrs. Mathers' profile, still, the way women sit when they've decided to spend the last of their currency on a truth.

"You were right," Julian said, matching her pause. "Guilt's in there."

"It's in the bread," she said. "And the vents. And the way a man touches his ring. It's in the word *households*, plural." She lifted the cedar shaving from the napkin and held it to her nose; it had the clean, resinous scent of a door frame waiting for a hinge.

"Tomorrow?" he asked.

"Before the town wakes," she said. "South wall. We'll listen for hollow."

The river shifted its voice—the tide turning—like a sentence changing tense. They started across the lawn, two figures with a loaf they wouldn't eat, a sprig of cedar tucked out of sight, and the certainty that the next door would not open with a key but with the willingness to hear what remembered them.

15

THE FALSE TRAIL

The letter arrived the way certain kinds of trouble prefer to arrive—early, anonymous, and wrapped in the language of relief. Julian found it waiting on the museum's back stoop just after dawn, slid under the door like a truce flag. Cream paper, a tidy hand on the outside: **For Mr. Roth — to spare the town a spectacle.** No return, no flourish. He stood there a beat, hat still on, breath fogging the glass. Then he picked it up as if rescuing a bird that might be alive or only pretending.

Miriam was already at the reading room table when he brought it in, the pendant a cool, flat certainty under her sweater. She'd come in early to gather brushes and a head-lamp for what they still planned: south wall, vestral side. The cedar shaving Mrs. Mathers had wrapped in a napkin lay beside her notes like a compass point. When Julian held up the envelope, she read the temperature in his face. Hope never wrapped itself like that.

He set the thing down and slit it with his pocketknife. Inside: a single sheet folded twice, the fold crisp as something done in this century, not the last. He removed it carefully and placed it beneath the table lamp, not touching the ink.

October 1846, the heading announced in the flourished hand of someone imitating an era. Below that, the body in a feminine script designed to look fragile and brave:

To whom it may concern,

One must confess when fancy has overstepped propriety. The rose window was always twelve. In the fervor of a wedding season I imagined a thirteenth. No pact binds us but charity. Please do not disturb what peace remains.

— Leah

Miriam didn't breathe until she reached the initials. Her ribs felt braced with a metal she had not ordered. Leah— exactly the signature a forger would lift from a marriage register when inventing remorse. The letter bore a faint aureole of brown around the ink strokes as if the writer had tried to simulate iron gall's habit of eating paper. It was neat, careful, plausible the way counterfeit bills are plausible— convincing from a distance, wrong in the hand.

Julian didn't touch the page. He circled it with the lamp's light and the sort of silence that listens, then crouched and drew his folio from the bag's mouth. "If this is real, someone has spared us both years of work," he said flatly. "If it's not, someone is hoping to spare the town the truth."

He fetched the loupe. Miriam watched his face tilt, listened to the soft clicks of the lamp's neck adjusting, watched a scholar seek footing on a slope greased with good intentions. He leaned back after a minute and exhaled through his nose. "It wants to be believed," he said. "That's the first strike against it."

"Tell me the others," Miriam said, forcing her throat to open.

He set the loupe down. "Ink bloom is theatrical—more

halo than creep. The paper fibers…" He lifted a corner with a bamboo skewer, angled the light. "Wood pulp, not rag. You can see the shorter fibers where the tear begins. Rag would be smoother." His voice steadied itself on the facts. "Rag dominated mid-century. Wood pulp arrives later; Cedar Creek's paper mill didn't run pulp through until the 1880s. Also: the watermark. There." He pointed to a faint oval. "It's faint, but it's *Eaton's*. Turn-of-the-century brand."

Miriam felt relief rise—and fall. "Someone could have written a confession years later."

"They could," he said, unwilling to let his own skepticism do all the work for her. "A late-life correction. But then the language." He tapped the sentence with the skewer's tip, not touching ink. "*Myth* doesn't appear—thankfully—but *propriety* and *charity* together in this usage?" He shook his head. "It rings as a pastiche of piety. And the date line—'October 1846'—no day, no place. The person who forged this knows just enough to avoid tripping, and trips anyway."

"Enough to steady a town that wants to be steadied," Miriam said. The page's existence worked on her at a level below evidence: it appealed to the part of any decent person that hopes the painful story isn't necessary after all.

Before they could decide whether to quarantine or parade it, the bell at the front desk tinkled. Everett, punctual as guilt, stood there with a copy of the agenda for Paper & Pie, eyebrows already braced. He saw the envelope, the solemn arrangement of lamp and tools, and his face brightened the way a man's face brightens when invited to believe a problem has solved itself in his absence.

"News?" he asked, the cheeriness a warning.

"We received a letter," Julian said.

Everett's hand closed around the paper before either of them consented. He skimmed, humming that administrative little hum towns teach themselves. "Well," he said, exhaling satisfaction. "That simplifies."

"It doesn't," Miriam said, too quickly.

"Ms. Adler..." Everett's tone softened into patience. "We are responsible for tone, as Vivian so wisely reminded us. If this good woman—Leah—repented a nervous fancy, surely we ought to accept her correction. No need to stir households."

Miriam thought: *households,* again, plural, the word used as a firebreak. She also thought of the pendant's notch and the way cedar smells when it remembers. Julian said nothing. He looked at Everett a long second and then extended his hand. Everett hesitated, surprised; Julian waited. The paper came back, a small victory written in the grammar of custody.

Elijah arrived within the hour, a pastoral breeze where Everett had been a policy front. The letter made its laps— Vivian must have been called, for Claire appeared at the door with a face made careful by heredity; Graham lingered in the hall like a principle. Each read, each performed relief according to habit: Elijah with sorrow that sounds like mercy; Everett with civics; Graham with absolution shaped like dismissal. The room, always so faithful to paper, felt for a time like a court that takes comfort as evidence.

By noon, the letter had done its first job. It had given the town something to point at when declining complexity. Miriam watched the story shift around her like furniture being moved in a house that pretends nothing is changing. *To spare the town a spectacle,* the envelope had said. It was a sentence written by someone who understood Cedar Creek—its appetite for tidy closure, the narcotic of being spared.

When the stream of officials and donors thinned, Julian

slid the letter into a Mylar sleeve and locked it in a drawer labeled **In Dispute**. He didn't look at Miriam until the key turned. When he did, he didn't veil what was in his eyes: worry for the work, and for her.

"Red herring," he said, not triumphantly. "But good bait."

She nodded, and then she didn't. Everything inside her had been tuned the last weeks to the pitch of more. A counterfeit like this could crack a tuning fork. She felt, suddenly, very tired.

THE TOWN DID the thing it always did when a false peace beckoned: it tried it on for size. Theo wrote **EVIDENCE ≠ RUMOR** on his chalkboard and drew a small fish labeled **HERRING** with an arrow through it, which helped those inclined to laugh. Others preferred the phrase Elijah offered—*let us not disturb what peace remains*—and wore it like a shawl. By late afternoon, scraps of the letter's phrasing drifted across the square like pollen. *Fancy overstepping propriety. Charity. Please do not disturb.*

Miriam felt those phrases land on her skin and itch. She also felt the other thing, the thing she learned about herself in grief and in restless nights above the shop: when the town turns its head, the body that keeps looking is briefly lonelier than it knows how to survive.

She returned to the shop to brew tea for no one. The pendant lay against her sternum with the weight of an instruction she suddenly resented. She took it off and set it on the counter to see if she felt less bound; she felt instead as if she had put down an instrument mid-song. She stood at the threshold and watched people pass, waving, nodding, practicing normal. The bakery door chimed. Mrs. Levine's silhouette crossed and recrossed like a metronome. Miriam's hands shook—anger and fatigue and a drop of doubt that embarrassed her with its eagerness.

What if Leah had wanted to be done with this? The thought came uninvited. It made experimental sense: one woman in 1846, pressed by a town's appetites, might have decided—in one exhausted hour—to retract what she saw. The forger's letter mimicked precisely that human weakness. It offered a way out. It was cruel exactly because it was plausible.

She took the cedar shaving from her pocket and held it to her nose. Resin steadied her a little, the way river smell steadies people who have never learned to name weather. She lifted the pendant back onto her neck and said (to the air, to Ruth, to Leah), "Be with me or be still, but don't be coy." Then she laughed once, sharp at herself, because nothing in her experience suggested the dead were coy.

The bell over the door jingled. Julian stepped in quietly, no performance in his entrance, a paper bag from the Riverlight catching on his wrist. He didn't ask how she was; his eyes had already assessed the shape of it. He set the bag down and slid her a lemon bar cut in a triangle. "This is not evidence," he said, "but it's also not counterfeit."

She ate because he told her to without telling her. He leaned on the counter and talked shop the way you talk to someone in a storm about boats, not weather. "Three tests we can do without a lab," he said. "One, fibers—we'll tease a corner under magnification; rag vs. pulp is a century apart. Two, watermarks. You saw *Eaton's*—we can date that to a run the Wagner mill did in 1901 when they tried to do respectable paper. Three, language. I'll pull usage examples —*propriety+ charity* in that coupling is late Victorian. The 1840s would say *neighborhood peace, good order, the peace of households*." He paused. "Four, the hand—letterforms, dot of the i, cross of the t. I'll overlay it against Leah's marriage record. If it matches too perfectly, it's a tracing. If it matches improperly, the forgery's lazy. Either way, the line of the wrist betrays."

"And if it's real?" she asked, because doubt asks to be fed even when it spoils appetite.

"Then we hold both truths," he said, and the scientist's tenderness in that sentence pushed tears to her eyes. "Leah saw and then recanted. The town is still responsible for what it did with both." He gestured toward her desk. "But we don't cede a century to an anonymous note slid under a door."

She wiped her cheek with the back of her hand and laughed a single breath. "You sound like a man who's argued with his own doubt in a tent by the river."

"I carry a tent for that purpose," he said. "For what it's worth, I don't think this is Leah. I think it's someone who needs Leah to be a person they can live with."

They were quiet a moment, sharing the silence that's allowed when you've refused the wrong rescue. Outside, Everett strode by, already practicing phrases he would float at the council. Nadia crossed with the twins in their pram, gave Miriam a look that said *I don't care what paper says; I believe bodies.* Theo lifted a hand from the café door, deliberately erased **HERRING** and wrote **LISTEN**. It landed like a small prayer.

"Walk?" Julian asked.

"South wall," Miriam answered.

They didn't take the alley—they took the square, because retreat teaches the wrong lesson to people who prefer misinterpretation. The chapel hill rose, the bell tower browning toward evening. Elijah was already there on the steps, as if summoned by any sentence that threatened to wake the building. He held the letter in his hand; word had traveled through channels that always worked faster for those who preferred quiet.

"I hoped you'd read it," he said, almost pleading. "I hoped it would... spare you."

"I read it," Miriam said, and surprised herself by keeping her voice soft. "It spares no one."

He looked at Julian for help; Julian kept his eyes on the stone. "We're going to listen for hollow," he said. "Nothing in that letter prevents listening."

Elijah stepped aside—not permission, not welcome. As they passed, he added, "Please, do not wedge open a door the town cannot bear."

"They wedged it," Julian said gently. "In 1846."

Inside, they stayed at the back until their eyes adjusted. The window's crack ran its fine river across colored light. The south wall, vestral side, stood in the half-dark, its cedar beadboard paneling repaired more than once, its seams painted over by volunteer hands for decades. Miriam put her palm against it and waited. At first: wood, cool, indifferent. Then, a note under the surface—sub-bass, almost breath.

Julian knelt, headlamp on. He traced the joints with the soft brush, bristles whispering like grass. He tapped lightly with the butt of the brush—solid, solid, then a slightly different timbre, as if the wood there held air behind it. He glanced up. Miriam nodded. The world that wanted the letter's ease receded a few steps.

They didn't pry. They marked the seam with the smallest pencil dot at knee height—an agreement between future and present. "Tomorrow," Julian said. "With the right tools and the vestry's consent."

"We'll get neither," she said.

"Then we'll get consent from the thing itself," he said, grinning despite himself. "If the wood remembers, we can ask."

Back in the square, the air had cooled, and the chorus of false peace had softened. Miriam found her breath in her chest again. She would still have to walk the gauntlet of Everett's tone and Elijah's sorrow and Vivian's capability and Graham's ring. But the wall had answered, if only with a chord. That was enough to unlatch the small door inside her doubt.

THEY SAT on the museum stoop with the paper bag of lemon bars between them and the forged letter locked ten yards away like an oath someone hoped they'd take. The river's voice in twilight had its grammar: clauses of current, a punctuation of stones. Cedars kept their scents. Farther down the square, Mrs. Levine was pulling in her chalkboard sign; she'd written **KNEAD — REST — RISE** in big letters that looked more like instruction than pun.

"You almost gave up," Julian said, not accusing.

"I almost rested in a lie," Miriam answered. "Which is a kind of sleep."

He nodded. "Then we both did our jobs. You refused to nap. I refused to let you perform exhaustion as proof."

She smiled sidelong at him, startled by how precisely seen she felt. "Does this happen to you? The thing where certainty blinks? You've always looked so sure in the reading room."

"Of my methods," he said. "Not of my hunches. I have woken in the middle of a sentence and realized the verb was wrong. It's not dramatic. It's humbling. It makes you careful in a way that people mistake for cold." He touched the stoop with two fingers. "I am not cold. I am trying not to light fires I can't put out."

"You lit one today," she said.

"I lit a lantern," he corrected. "Enough to keep our feet."

The pause between them had texture, not emptiness. For the first time since the letter, Miriam's body stopped bracing and started registering smaller weather again: the place where her sleeve brushed his wrist; the reflected gold of the café window in his glasses; the half-moon balanced on the steeple as if the town had been pinned to the sky.

He reached into his coat and produced a small sheaf of index cards. "I wrote myself a note after you left the museum the first time," he said. He handed her the top card. In his tidy hand: **Attention is not persuasion; it is care.** He had copied her counter note and kept it, the way some men keep saints.

"I'm borrowing from you shamelessly," he said. "I don't want to spend this season arguing. I want to spend it attending. People think attention is weak. It is not."

She folded the card and tucked it into her pocket beside the cedar shaving. "Your donors will be furious," she said, not as threat, as weather report.

"They were going to be, no matter what," he said. "It's helpful to select the reason."

She laughed, surprised joy rising through the sediment. He turned to look fully at her then, not with the careful archivist gaze he used on fragile things, but with the steady regard he saved for weathered ones. "You didn't put the pendant back in the drawer," he said.

"I tried," she said. "Thirty seconds. It felt like taking out a compass mid-crossing."

"Then keep it on," he said. He hesitated, reached a hand halfway and then, with a decision, completed the gesture.

He touched the pendant lightly where it lay against her sweater, not proprietary, not a claim. A simple touch to silver to acknowledge what it had done for both of them. The contact vibrated through chain and skin and up into her throat where her voice lived. Not romantic in the way novels teach you; romantic in the way men and women choose courage together—by touch, by witness, by naming the few things that matter aloud.

"Tomorrow," he said. "We go with tools that do not wound wood. We ask permission with our hands."

"And if the vestry says no?"

"We go with Mrs. Mathers," he said. "She outranks them in ways that don't require a vote."

They sat there until the square thinned and the night air lay down across the cobbles. When they finally rose, he did the uninteresting chivalrous things that mattered—took her empty cup, turned off the reading room lamp, checked the lock twice. At her door he didn't ask to come up; she didn't invite him. Both their faces said *we are already upstairs in the place that counts.*

"Sleep," he said. "Do not let a counterfeit letter spend your body's currency."

She lifted a hand in a small salute, the kind you give a fellow traveler at the mouth of a narrow pass. "You too," she said. Then, because the world is not generous enough to withhold certain gifts when you've earned them, she stepped forward and touched his sleeve, near the wrist, with two fingers. The gesture was as old as villages and as new as what they were becoming.

After he left, she wrote two cards and slid them under the glass at the register.

- Counterfeits arrive early to be believed. Truth arrives on its own time and asks to be carried.
- We will not be spared. We will be precise.

She placed the cedar shaving beside them and turned out the light. In bed, the pendant cooled against her skin like moonlit metal, then warmed again to her. Sleep came not because the path had cleared, but because she and Julian had agreed to walk it even with fog. In her last waking image—the mind's way of staging hope—she and Julian stood with Mrs. Mathers at the south wall, and the wood, remembering itself, made the small releasing sound old things make when held rightly: the sigh of a hinge that has been waiting for the exact pressure of a careful hand.

16

A WHISPER IN THE NIGHT

The dream began the way wind starts—without edges. Miriam was on the shop's stair with her palm against the wall, counting thresholds as Ruth had taught her, when the numbers thinned into breath and the breath thinned into a word that wasn't a word at all but a pressure. She woke with that pressure over her sternum and the pendant warm against it, as if silver had learned to hold a pulse and was reluctant to give it back.

Midnight had made the square quiet enough to hear water wearing stone. The chapel's hill was dark except for the faintest wash where the rose window was not—no lamp inside, no moon bright enough to pick out color—and yet she felt light where no light was. She stood at the window and waited for the rational explanation that would send her back to bed. It didn't come. The pendant grew warmer, which is not how metal behaves, but then the last month had reshaped what behaved and what didn't.

She dressed in the quiet way people dress when they are making a small treaty with themselves: sweater, boots, the coat that had held cedar smell since last night at the

Dubois. She took nothing sharp and everything steady—Ruth's little notebook, the cedar shaving Mrs. Mathers had pressed into her hand, the sentence she and Julian had promised to obey: **Tools that do not wound wood.** She left the shop dark; she did not leave a note. The square knows when people intend to be missed; she intended not to be, not yet.

Outside, fog lay along the cobbles like a cat, indifferent until you noticed it. Miriam walked through it and felt it brush her calves. The river spoke in clauses; somewhere a gull wrote a parenthesis against the sky. When she reached the foot of the hill, she stopped because that is what you do when a building you love asks you whether you are ready. The chapel kept its questions in stone. She answered by climbing.

On the landing, she heard them. Not voices precisely—too thin for that, too braided. A sibilant convergence like the sound paper makes when it's been lined up and tapped into neatness. A word rose from the breaths or fell into them—she couldn't tell which. **Whole.** Then another, skimming her ear as if embarrassed to be overheard. **Below.**

"Not the wall," she said aloud, not to contradict but to confirm. She had come to listen to the south wall; she had expected the cedar's reply. But the pressure drew downward, toward the foundation where stone and earth met, the place where buildings keep what they can't admit on their altars.

She tried the door anyway, because habit remains a habit even when a dream leads the way. Unlocked, as Pastor Elijah liked it to be, so that insomnia could be mistaken for prayer. Inside, the nave smelled of faint old wax and the washed-cotton smell of pews that have surrendered human heat for the night. She stood under the rose. Even unlit, it had a presence, like a person dozing but listening. If the crack spoke, it did so in a frequency that bypassed ears and went straight to bones.

Whole, the breath-pressure said again. **Below.**

"Are you Leah?" Miriam asked, not because she thought Leah was a ghost that answered to its name, but because names are how we practice respect for the past. No answer, unless the fading of breath can be called an answer. She touched the back of the pew ahead and felt, as she had before, not haunting but recognition. If the chapel was awake, it was awake the way old bodies are: in the places that anchor them, not in the ornaments.

She went out again, around the nave's shadow to the south wall. Here the fog had pulled up like a skirt and the stone went black where it met earth. The chapel had been built in a style that aimed at virtue more than elegance—fieldstone faced where funds were thin, dressed blocks where pride demanded. She ran her fingers along the lower courses until her hand refused a seam and then found one. Her skin told her something her eyes could not: a hairline of looseness, a small misalignment where a mason with a conscience might have placed a secret with a prayer to be found only when a right hand learned how to ask.

The pendant pressed insistently against her. She put her palm flat to the cold and waited. That was the discipline Ruth had trained into her: when you are asked to find, stand still. Let the thing be found first.

Night rearranged itself around her—owl downriver, a bottle rolling in a bin on the square, a laugh too loud inside Theo's shuttered café that could only be Walter. The fog thinned the moon, or the moon thinned the fog. She crouched. The pressure shifted as unmistakably as a tide. **Here,** the not-voice said, which is the most dangerous instruction if you mistake it for permission.

"Tomorrow," she whispered to the stone, embarrassed and honest. "With help." And yet she didn't stand. She put her ear close enough to the foundation to hear a different kind of silence beyond it—air, not solid—the kind old cedar makes when you put a palm against a chest and ask a sleeper if they're still there. The cedar shaving in her pocket released its scent like agreement.

Below, said the pressure again. It felt less like insistence now and more like courtesy. Not *hurry*. Not *claim*. Just the small direction given when two people carry a heavy thing and must turn the same way to keep from dropping it.

She sat back on her heels. "I hear you," she said, and under her skin, under the meeting of stone and earth, something like a hinge sighed once, as if to prove wholeness and below are not opposites.

MIRIAM FETCHED the small flashlight from her coat and covered the lens with her hand to nurse its brightness. She did not want to announce herself to the square. She wanted to understand which stone wanted to be moved.

The south wall had three dressed blocks at the lowest course, then fieldstone, then another patched rectangle where some earlier repair had admitted defeat. Midway along the vestral side a block sat half a finger's breadth proud of its neighbors, a humility anyone else would miss and a confession anyone trained by paper would recognize. She pressed again. It answered with that soft hollowness to the fingertips that tells a person when a drawer has been shut on something thin. Breathing shallow to keep her ear from amplifying her own ribs, she slid her hand along the bottom edge. Mortar chipped under her nail— old lime and sand, not modern. The kind your grandmother makes if you give her a summer and a wheelbarrow.

"Forgive me," she said to the wall, which is not as silly as it sounds if you live in a town where cedar and stone are unembarrassed to remember. She tested the bottom edge with the pad of her finger, the way a safecracker tests tumblers. The block wobbled—once. Her heart tripped. She stopped. To prove your patience, you must interrupt your triumph.

She could feel the next three moves as clearly as if someone had drawn them on the fog: loosen two thumbprint-sized mortar bites, tilt, brace, lift. She also felt the whole town behind her like a hand on her shoulders: Mack's rigid father, Vivian's careful kindness, Pastor Elijah's plea, Mrs. Mathers' napkin with its elegant instruction. **Tools that do not wound wood.** Stone wants less bluntness than wood but more honesty.

She took out the bluntest thing she had—a wooden tongue depressor from Ruth's old tincture kit—and worked it under the block. Wood against stone squeaked faintly and then learned the groove. She levered just enough to test load, then let the stone settle again. Powder rose like a blessing or a warning; it smelled of lime and old rain. Beneath—she felt it—air. Not the large air of a crawlspace. The sincere, close air of a purpose-built cavity waiting under breath-holding.

Her hand went deeper under the block and found what fingers hope for and fear in equal measure: the unmistakable press of something soft and fibrous protected by something stiff and thin. Cloth around paper. It was too tight for her to pinch, and the brush of her skin against it made a sound so small it registered as guilt more than noise.

"Not tonight," she told herself, science and superstition

holding hands for once. She withdrew carefully, so carefully she could feel her own nectar pulse in her fingertips. She let the block kiss its seat and then leaned her head against it as if to apologize for being a person who can be asked things like this at midnight.

That was when the whisper changed. Not louder—sharper. As if the breath had learned a new word. **Watch.**

Footsteps on the hill path, hidden poorly. Not deer—the rhythm was too irregular and the weight carried wrong. A person trying to be quiet is a loud animal. She shoved the flashlight into her pocket, stood, and stepped into the chapel's shadow where her black coat was indistinguishable from stone. The pendant was suddenly cold. Adrenaline has its own weather.

The footsteps paused at the lip of the landing, resumed, paused again. Miriam didn't move. Patience has saved more lives in rivers and in archives than agility has. A silhouette separated itself from the fog at the top of the steps—short brimmed hat, coat too rigid for utility. Graham? Everett? Pastor Elijah? The figure stopped a few paces from the door and looked not at the door but toward the south wall, as if checking whether the building had behaved. Then the figure did the most suspicious thing you can do when attempting to be innocent: they turned their head too slowly to search.

Watch, said the breath.

Miriam watched. The person lifted a hand and touched the wall with fingertips that didn't know how to ask. She willed her body to keep even smaller than it was. The hand hovered, moved on. The figure took one step toward the foundation, then reconsidered, then retreated. You can learn much about a person by which cowardice they choose. They took the stairs again, softer now, away.

Miriam didn't follow. She counted to sixty of whatever measure time uses when you're borrowing it and then counted to thirty more because fear sometimes miscounts. When she crouched again at the block, her throat burned with the taste fear leaves behind: old coins and unfairness. She slid two fingers into the seam—not to pull, only to confirm the cloth and the stiff whisper that meant paper. Her skin told her what her nose had confirmed: cedar. She withdrew again before the muscle memory of curiosity could override her discipline. Tomorrow had been the plan. A plan is a kindness you do for your future self when your present self is strong enough to make it.

Something small that was not an animal moved in the chancel, inside. She stood fast, spine pressed to cold. Then the chapel door swung inward and a wedge of light cut the aisle like new ink.

"Miriam?" Julian's voice—quiet, urgent, human. "Don't be angry. Theo told me you crossed the square with no hat. We had an agreement about hats."

Relief made her knees absurd. She stepped out of shadow because men who care enough to scold about hats deserve not to be terrified. "Here," she said, and her voice carried all the fog's damp that she had refused to let into her body. He swung the light toward her and then down, polite enough to turn it aside when it found her face.

"You scared me," he said, which was small for what she'd done to him and also exactly right. He took three quick steps and then stopped just shy of contact—his constant, practiced courtesy. It felt like living near a stove when you've learned the line between warmth and burn.

"What did you find?" he asked, and knelt without waiting for permission, as if his knees would forgive him later for touching cold stone without a cushion.

. . .

SHE KNELT beside him and felt the pendulum swing from dream logic to method. "Hollow," she said, hand indicating the proud block. "Cloth. Beneath. I haven't moved it."

He put the headlamp on his brow; the light made a tender halo of dust. His hands—wonderfully predictable hands—did what hands do when they've vowed to be careful: they hovered first, mapping with air; they touched only where they could help. He tapped the mortar with the butt of the brush—solid, then a softer tone. He tilted his head and listened, the way doctors listen to children who can't put pain into adult words.

"Tomorrow," he said. "Before we touch it. With Mrs. Mathers and a vestry key, or at least with Mrs. Mathers and a story so good the vestry can't say no out loud."

"Someone was just here," Miriam murmured. "Hat, coat. Walked like their conscience had knees."

He turned off the lamp and let dark settle long enough for their eyes to learn it again. "Which means we'll be met," he said. "Either by a man who wants to help because he's tired of guarding, or by a man who wants to stop us because he's tired of being reminded what he guarded."

She found his sleeve in the dark and pinched it once, a shorthand that said *I'm here* and *don't go* and *don't let me go too far*. He didn't move, which is sometimes the bravest thing to do in the presence of someone who is frightened.

"Tell me the dream," he said. "Or the not-dream."

She did. The pressure and the word that wasn't a word, the sense of *below* that refused to be melodrama. He listened without correction, his attention making even the stranger parts useful. When she finished, he said, "Wholeness below makes theological sense," as if that were a perfectly normal sentence to say on a hill at midnight. "You don't put reliquaries on roofs. You put them where gravity can keep secrets."

The pendant cooled again; the fog had climbed her sleeves. He noticed the small shiver she would have denied. "Take my coat," he said, already undoing the buttons.

"It's your coat," she protested reflexively.

"It has a long, exciting life of keeping people I care about warm," he said. "Let it do its job."

He put it around her shoulders and did not, to his credit and her relief, pull it closed for her. She pulled it closed for herself and felt something like a bell settle in her ribs.

"Come inside," he said. "If we're to wait half a night to practice virtue, we might as well be out of the fog's appetite."

They took the side door and slid into the nave. He left the headlamp off, using the small flashlight pointed at the floor so as not to wake pews that had earned their rest. They sat beneath the rose, not speaking for a minute, as if not speaking were part of the permission they planned to ask the wall at dawn. The crack carried moon in a narrow line, laying a soft blade on the aisle. Miriam watched the blade thin and thicken with passing cloud and thought about how truth gets narrower before it opens.

"Who do you think it was?" she asked at last.

"Tonight?" he said. "Consciences with knees narrows it to five. Everett doesn't come alone in fog. Elijah announces himself. Graham doesn't approach a building he hasn't paid for without witnesses. Leonard Pike prefers corners. My money says a man who had to see with his own eyes if his grandfather's courage had made it as far as the foundation."

"Mack," she said.

"Perhaps." He tilted his head. "Or a grandson from any

house where women have recently started telling stories at dinner."

She smiled in spite of everything. The smile broke what fear had set in plaster. She opened her hand without planning to and found his there—open too. They didn't lace fingers; they let palms meet and rest, an honest contact you could translate into any language as **stay**.

"You keep finding me when I am between brave and foolish," she said.

"I keep hoping to move you an inch toward the former," he said. "And to move myself an inch away from the latter."

A sound downstairs—the soft complaint of an old hinge protest-welcoming night air—brought them back to the practical. He squeezed her hand once and let go. "If we're followed, we will be followed from outside," he said. "No one who loves propriety climbs through sacristy windows."

She laughed again, quietly. He stood, and the movement sent a ripple of dust through the headlamp's breath. He caught her elbow to steady her because the floor crosses itself at the threshold and people trip when they're thinking about truth. The touch was for balance, but bodies don't always file touches correctly; hers stored it under **amounting to more.**

They stepped out to the south wall again when the fog thinned, the hill resetting itself into a geometry of dark and seam. He crouched, took out a pencil, and made the smallest mark against stone—a dot that would be mistaken for nothing else by anyone who didn't know what it was for. "An index," he said. "So we don't donate our discovery to the person who comes earlier by half an hour."

Miriam bent beside him and, feeling suddenly stubborn about having been called out of bed by a breath, slid the pendant free of her sweater. "It told me to wear it when I must be seen by what remembers," she said, not sure whether she was joking or begging. She pressed the silver briefly against the proud edge of the block. The notch found nothing obvious—no groove machined, no clever keyhole— but the cool of the metal coming away felt like a kiss on a coin that had been in a pocket too long. She tucked the pendant back and told herself she had not made that up.

When she straightened, he was closer than courtesy strictly required, and neither of them corrected it. Fog does that to people—it persuades them that distance is a convention for daylight. He scanned her face for wreckage and seemed content with what he saw—tired, not broken; chilled, not discouraged. "I'll walk you down," he said.

"You came up like a man who intends to stay," she said.

"I came up like a man who mislaid his caution and found a person instead," he said, then coughed because even for him that was naked. "And also because Theo texted, *She's out without a hat,* which as we both know constitutes a municipal emergency."

"Bless Theo," she said.

"Constantly," he answered.

They made their way down the steps with the care of thieves and the hearts of citizens. At the bottom, he stopped and looked back up, the way you look back at a house where you have left a sleeping child. "If someone comes first," he said, "we will know by the mark. But also by the smell. Cedar tattles."

"Cedar releases," she said.

He walked her across the square and left her at the shop door with a promise that didn't require a signature: **Dawn.** Inside, she lit the small lamp and sat a minute because sitting is how you shepherd adrenaline back into its stall. She wrote one sentence on a card and tucked it behind the register glass beside the others: **Below is not under—it is within.** Then she turned out the light, lay down without taking off her coat, and slept like a person who had been called and had answered to the extent decency allowed before daylight.

On the hill, fog moved like a choir under a cloak. The south wall held its breath. Beneath the proud stone, cedar waited without impatience, as wood does when the thing it is keeping is heavier than the person who will lift it. In the square, a chalkboard ghost wrote **LISTEN** and **WHOLE** in a hand that wasn't Theo's but might as well have been. And the rose window—a geometry built to stare without blinking—registered moon on its broken vein, a thin, quiet glimmer that looked, if you wanted it to, like a thirteenth petal slipping its shape into the night.

17

THE HIDDEN JOURNAL

They met just before dawn when the square still belonged to fog and bakers. Mrs. Mathers arrived first in her dark coat and practical shoes, hair braided into its usual crown, a ring of keys in her palm that had not been seen at a vestry meeting in twenty years. Julian came next with a canvas satchel that clicked softly—bone folder, bamboo skewer, hog-hair brushes, nitrile gloves, unbleached muslin, Mylar sleeves, a dental mirror, patience. Miriam walked up the hill between them, the pendant warm at her throat as if it recognized the day.

Pastor Elijah was already on the chapel steps, jaw set with the kind of stubbornness that calls itself care. "You'll keep reverence," he said—not a threat, an invocation.

"We brought reverence," Mrs. Mathers replied, holding up the keys. "We can borrow your lock as well."

Inside, they didn't head for the rose—no one even tilted a gaze toward the crack whose thin geometry had reordered the town's appetite. They moved to the south wall, vestral side, where Miriam had found the proud stone and the breath-pressure of *below*. Julian crouched, clipped on his headlamp, and touched his brush to the seam. Dust lifted and hung in the slanting early light like a memory made visible.

"Tools that do not wound wood," he said, a little under his breath, as if reciting a psalm.

"And hands that ask permission," Miriam answered.

The block answered with that tiny, unmistakable hollow that isn't absence so much as readiness. Miriam slid her fingers into the seam again and felt the cloth she'd felt in the night: a whisper of fiber, a promise pressed against stone. She drew her hand back and nodded. Even in this practical light the instruction from the dark held: *Here.*

They worked slowly. Julian eased a wooden wedge—tongue depressor sanded into a kind of shy pry—beneath the block. He levered a fraction of an inch. The mortar at the corners flaked like old snow. Mrs. Mathers held the dustpan like a midwife and accepted what time released. "This wall," she said softly, "is built on women's patience."

"Then let it unbuild the same way," Miriam said.

With a final, careful lift the stone rocked—and came free. The sound it made set the hairs on Miriam's forearms upright: a sigh more than a scrape, as if the chapel had leaned away to give them room. Beneath, cedar. A mortised cavity, lined with boards rubbed thin at their edges where someone's fingers had pressed often. Julian took the dental mirror and angled light into the dark. The cavity's dimensions declared intention, not accident.

"I can see cloth," he said. "Not moldy. Tight." He slid the mirror farther. "And... a seam."

Mrs. Mathers bent with a small, involuntary noise in her throat, the sound some women make when they're about to hear a child take a first breath or a secret finally stop pretending. "God grant you steadiness," she told their hands.

The cloth resisted the first touch and then yielded, the way linen does when it was folded by someone who expected to be obeyed. Julian teased an edge free with the bamboo skewer and Miriam, gloved now, pinched what the skewer offered. The bundle lifted into morning air, lighter than she had feared, heavier than she had hoped. Cedary breath rose, resin and time. The cloth was old but intact, tied with a faded ribbon whose dye had bled its color into the fibers like a memory that won't keep to its room.

Julian set the bundle on the unbleached muslin he'd spread. He cut the ribbon not with his knife but with his breath—one small huff of disbelief—and then with the duller, kinder blade he kept for twine. He folded the linen back. Inside lay a small book the color of winter bark, boards wrapped in calfskin worn slick by a hand that had worried its corners in prayer or dread. A rose faintly stamped in the leather had once been bright; now it was suggestion. The book's spine had given up years before, so that the text block sat in the cover like a child in a borrowed coat.

He didn't touch it. No one spoke. They stood a moment as three witnesses and a pastor, a square in which faith did not argue with evidence but held the bowl while evidence poured.

"Now," Mrs. Mathers said, voice steady.

Julian lifted the first board with a bone folder, slid a gloved finger under the flyleaf, and eased it open. Inside, a hand. Not the clumsy imitation that had come through the museum door yesterday in its moralizing disguise. This hand lived. The ink had browned to the warm of tea left too long under a winter window; the pressure of the nib was rain and argument both. The date at the top of the first page belonged to the year they had already learned too well: *September 4, 1846.* Beneath it:

I am asked for silence. I am married into it. Yet my mouth is a door and will not stay shut. If there is a God who likes truth better than peace bought with fear, let Him read this when I cannot speak it.

Miriam exhaled a breath that had waited under her ribs for a century and a half. The pendant at her throat warmed the way courage warms a room.

Elijah's hand went to his heart, and for a moment Miriam saw not an obstacle but a man who had spent himself keeping people from breaking when he had only hymns to bind them. "Leah," he whispered.

The next entry ran brokenly, as if written in a kitchen between interruptions:

The window: it is twelve to common sight. But I saw thirteen in the glazier's paper—drawn in faint pencil and rubbed at as if he had been told to stop. I touched the place with my finger and the journeyman looked at me and the world ran the way sugar runs when you add heat. He said, *You see.* I said, *I do.* And then I said nothing.

Further down the page, in a tighter, angrier line:

They say unity and mean obedience. They say charity and mean hush. They say *households*—always plural—so no one is guilty and everyone is. I am told to sign what I do not consent to: a recalculation of minutes, a settling of "Appendix C." I would not sign if not for the peace of my own—my mother who cannot bear a son's scorn, my sister who will lose her roof if we defy.

Julian's breath stuttered. He steadied it. The page turned with the care one offers a sleeping baby's head. More dates.

More sentences that made the present stand up in the room and listen.

September 20 — My wedding day. Pastor Nathaniel asked me whether I came freely. I said yes with my mouth and no with my bones. Matthias is not unkind. Unkindness is not the only way to be cruel. After the vows we stood below the glass and the men talked about money. Henri D. said we should say a prayer for the rose. I opened my mouth to say thirteen. The prayer did not give me room.

October 1 — Elise A. made a necklace of the glazier's hidden attempt. She said, *If we cannot keep the petal in the window, we will keep it on a throat.* She gave it to me first and then pressed it into cedar with me watching so I could swear what we did if I was asked later by the truth itself. We sealed the cedar with a scrap of hymn and I bent my head until I could hear the wood decide to hold.

The pendant, against Miriam's sternum, quickened. She felt rather than saw Julian glance at it and then back to the page as if to verify that the room had not rearranged itself into theater.

October 8 — The men have called what we did "peace." I call it grammar. The sentences we write now will be read by girls who do not choose the verbs. If a girl reads this, let her know: I saw it. I did not imagine it. If I sign, it is not consent. It is hunger. It is winter thinking through my skin. I am ashamed. I will keep a copy of the minutes that told the truth and fix them under the floor. If the floor is later broken and the paper lost, let this stand.

Julian sat back hard on his heels, as if his body had stepped off a stair it thought was there. He closed his eyes—one second, two—and opened them again to the discipline that had saved so many fragile things from becoming interesting dust. "We have to move," he said. "From wonder to protocol."

"Protocol is reverence," Miriam said, and reached to stabilize the board so he could slip Mylar under the first gathering.

They built a small clean world on the muslin: gloves, sleeves, weights, barriers. As they lifted one leaf at a time they discovered the narrow ledger of a woman's fight to stay decent while telling the truth. In November, Leah recorded the first whisper of a baby inside and the first ache of a conscience she could not paralyze. In December she wrote, *I am tired of the peace of households. I want the peace of being right.* In January she recorded a thaw and a quarrel. In February the handwriting faltered and returned, bolder, as if she had found someone to speak to and taken courage back from her own mouth.

At the back an inserted slip of thinner paper, different color, different decade. *1892.* The same hand, older, rimmed with tremor. *We are asked to recast. I will not. I have already recast God into a friend who prefers truth. I am tired of borrowing a piety that does not like daylight.* Underneath, a first name: *Leah,* and a very small rose drawn with thirteen short, stubborn lines.

The room was not only a room by then. It was a threshold. Everyone breathed as if their ribs had finally been given permission to widen.

THEY CARRIED the journal to the reading room on a cradle of muslin and care. The square had started to stir—the sound of a broom against brick, the bakery bell, Theo dragging his chalkboard outside with a groan that passed for morning greeting. Elijah locked the chapel himself, slowly, like a man closing a door he hoped would hold the warmth until he could build a better fire.

At the museum table they arranged the book under glass, not to imprison it but to slow hands that would love it too roughly. Julian made notes in his tidy block script—date, condition, dimensions, anomalies; Miriam wrote Leah's lines on index cards as if copying them into a pocket would make her voice easier to carry. Mrs. Mathers sat with her hands folded and her eyes unguarded, a posture that made her look like a girl and a judge at once.

"Read them," the older woman said to Miriam, when they had built enough safety into the room to bear the sound. "Read them as if she were still waiting to hear her voice in someone else's throat."

Miriam read.

My mouth is a door and will not stay shut.

The sentence moved through Miriam like an organ note, began in the floor, rose through the table, lived in her mouth for a beat, and then seated itself in her chest. She read another.

They say unity and mean obedience. They say charity and mean hush.

She didn't have to tell the room what it already knew—that those plural *households* had never been vocabulary but architecture; that piety and patriarchy had done what they tend to do when the room is well set and the stakes are disguised as linens. Leah's lament sounded like a woman trying to stay inside a marriage and outside a lie. It sounded like Miriam's last weeks and Ruth's last letter and Elise's sketched thirteenth petal and Mrs. Mathers' napkin folded around a cedar shaving.

Julian turned a page. His knuckles had gone pale under the glove. "Here," he said softly.

November 2 — Henri D. is kind in the way of women who manage men. Vivian will be like her if we live that long. Elise A. says there is a fifth sacrament and it is keeping. I asked Pastor whether the church would know itself better if it liked truth. He said truth divides. I think silence does.

Miriam looked up at Elijah. He didn't flinch. "I have said those words," he admitted. "I meant them as a balm. I see that they were also a brace."

"You braced when a bandage was needed," Mrs. Mathers said, not unkindly. "And you bandaged when what was needed was a surgery. We all did."

More lines. *A child is not a witness against her father. A wife is not a witness against her husband. But a woman may witness for truth against anything that lifts itself up against mercy.* Leah's theology read like someone finding God in an empty kitchen at midnight and liking Him better for not needing a choir.

"She writes past the men and to the girl who will read," Miriam said. "She is writing to us."

"To you," Julian corrected gently, and Miriam understood his distinction: she was the mouth that had found the door; he was the hand that set the hinge.

Miriam read the entry about the pendant and felt the silver pulse at her throat. She read the description of sealing the cedar with a scrap of hymn (*There is a balm in Gilead...*), and she heard her aunt's voice humming half a stanza in a room upstairs. She read the late entry written with shaking hand when Leah chose not to sign the 1892 recasting. The older woman's refusal reached through paper and into Miriam's ribcage, struck a tuning fork that had hummed since the day she turned the shop key.

"What does it do to you?" Julian asked, because his care always began with attention.

"It makes me less lonely," she said. "And more responsible."

He nodded, like a sailor watching wind shift to a more honest direction. "Then it's doing its work."

The next page had a stain, the shape like a leaf or a tear. Leah had written through it as if refusing to let a spill edit her. *I have been told that my words will be used against my husband, against the town. I say use them for the truth, and the truth may break what needs breaking and mend what can be mended. I cannot tell which is which. That is not my job. My job is to make the true thing visible to the living.*

Miriam laid her palm on the table and felt the grain under the finish. "She solves the equation I've been exhausting myself trying to solve," she said. "I kept wanting to keep the peace and tell the truth. She says the order is wrong. Tell the truth; then see what peace is possible."

Elijah drew his chair closer, leaned in as if to warm himself at a small fire. "If the town had been given these pages in 1846," he said, "we would have had a different church."

"Or no church," Everett said from the doorway, where he had appeared without announcing himself. "We would have had a crisis."

"We have a church and a crisis," Mrs. Mathers replied, unsentimental. "It takes less faith to say both than to pretend one erases the other."

Everett's gaze took in the cradle, the glass, the gloved hands; the bureaucrat in him was comforted by procedure. "Chain of custody," he said, trying the phrase out in a room that had never required him to say it. "Is it established?"

"We can document what we can't domesticate," Julian said. "You may write that sentence down; it will be useful at the council."

Everett pressed his lips, then nodded as if forced into admiration against his better habits. "What do you intend?" he asked Miriam, and for once the question lacked accusation.

"To read," she said. "To decide, with the living, what to do with the dead's courage."

Everett glanced at the window, at the hill he loved to approach with clipboards. "The families..." He did not finish the sentence. The plural had learned to finish itself.

THEY DID NOT GET to finish the book in reverent silence. It is the nature of turning points to call their own audience. News moved through Cedar Creek the way water finds culverts. By mid-morning Vivian stood in the doorway with Claire at her shoulder, Graham with his ring beside Mack with his patience. Nadia slipped in to stand behind Elena; Theo leaned on the jamb with a tray of lemon bars in case courage decided not to be aesthetic. Pastor Elijah had not left. Mrs. Levine arrived under pretense of delivering scones and stayed because her face had already undone what decorum asked.

Julian lifted his head. His voice found a register between host and herald. "We have made a discovery," he said. "Leah's journal. Evidence, not rumor. Humane, not theatrical. We will read from it, and then we will decide what to do next together."

"That assumes," Graham began, "that the museum—"

"—keeps faith with truth and the town in one act," Vivian finished, eyes on Leah's script as if reading over their shoulders. Her voice had lost its peach gloss; underneath was oak. "Read," she said.

Miriam read Leah's opening lines; she chose the entry

about the window and the petition; she read the sentences about *households* and the differences between unity and obedience; she read the paragraph where Leah wrote *I am ashamed* and then the one where she wrote *I will not be.* When she reached the description of sealing the cedar with the pendant and a hymn, she stopped and put her palm over the silver at her throat.

Claire's chin lifted at the word *pendant.* "You kept it," she said, and her voice carried both awe and accusation. "You—women—kept it."

"We did," Mrs. Mathers said with the calm of someone elected by no one and governed by everyone. "We do."

Graham's hand found his ring. "This will divide households," he said, voice low and full of a fear that had kept marvelous company with him for sixty years.

Mack shook his head, not in rebellion but in recognition. "It already has," he said. "We simply stopped naming the lines."

Vivian's eyes shone with the tears of people who learned early how to hide them. "Leah was a Dubois by marriage," she said. "Which makes this our ledger, too." She looked at Pastor Elijah. "I have dependent faith," she said. "I need you to say grace."

He did, surprising Miriam by choosing not the usual words but a sentence that began, "Blessed are those who mourn what they built badly," and continued with lines that did not spare any house. When he finished, the room had the quiet of a kitchen after an argument that ends with someone agreeing to start over.

Everett cleared his throat, bureaucratic instinct rousing for useful duty. "We require a process," he said. "This is a document. There are donors. There is the council. There will be petitions. We must—"

"—set a table large enough for the whole town," Mrs. Levine cut in, hands on hips, apron frequenting the room like a flag. "And feed people while they listen. No pitchforks on an empty stomach."

"Paper & Pie," Theo said from the doorway, already half-turning to go chalk. "But with Guards for Civility and a Bell for the Speaking Order."

"We might begin with the families," Elena suggested, practical mercy compressing itself into a plan. "A closed reading with representatives. Then the town. Diffuse the voltage where the load is heaviest."

"And we need allies at the council meeting," Nadia added. "People who can say words like *chain of custody* without losing the rest of the room."

"Write the phrases on cards," Walter offered. "Hand them to the men who love to make speeches. Let them feel useful while they carry the truth." He grinned at Everett, who tried not to grin back and failed humanely.

Julian had kept still through the clamor, the way a beam keeps still while people decide what walls they want to bear. He touched the glass lightly. "Before any of that," he said, "we stabilize and we scan. We make a copy robust enough to be read while the original rests. We establish the history of the object in a way no argument can undo. We preserve Leah's voice from our handling as much as from our enemies."

The word enemies settled uneasily, like a bird unsure whether the tree is welcome. Miriam looked at it square. "We will have some," she said. "Let's not pretend otherwise."

Graham raised a hand, an old habit. Everyone looked. "I have spent a lifetime keeping a certain shape," he said. "I do not know how to stand if you take it away." The admission stripped him. It was the most generous thing he could have said.

"Then keep the shape of being decent," Mrs. Mathers replied. "Let the shape of being right change around it."

Vivian inhaled, held it, released it. "I will sit with this in my house," she said. "Claire, you will sit with me. Mack, you will come and tell me what the Wagners hear when this is read aloud. Pastor, you will make your church ready to be less afraid."

Elijah nodded, as if he had been waiting to be told something that gave him back his job.

"Tonight," Theo announced, leaning back through the door with chalk already on his fingers, "Paper & Pie becomes *Paper & Proof*. No speeches longer than a pie slice. Anyone using the words *hysteria* or *witch hunt* pays a scone fine to the library."

"Tomorrow," Everett said, recovering his vocation, "the council will schedule a formal session. We will need copies. We will need summaries. We will need, God help us, bullet points."

"We will need Leah's sentences intact," Miriam said, speaking to the room she would eventually have to stand in alone. "We will not paraphrase her into comfort."

Julian placed his hand flat on the table next to hers, the way he always did when the room tilted. Not touching, not claiming—anchoring. "We will present the evidence," he said, eyes on her, giving her his steadiness to borrow. "We will ask the town to be as brave as a bride."

Pastor Elijah cleared his throat. "And if the town refuses?"

"Then we will have told the truth," Miriam said, the shrug in her voice not indifference but resolve. "And the truth will have begun to work without us. It always does."

The afternoon banked itself against the windows. They scanned the first pages, breath held while the machine's light moved. They logged, labeled, wrapped, agreed. When they finally returned the cedar bundle to its muslin cradle and set the stone carefully back into the wall—yes, back; the cavity would hold another night without panic—Elijah stood with his hand on the nave door as if to ask permission of the building before he locked it.

On the hill, the rose window took the late sun and laid it down the aisle in long unbroken bars. The crack translated brightness into something more articulate than glare. For a second—a trick of refraction, or hope—Miriam saw a thirteenth shimmer again, less shy than before. She touched the pendant and felt it answer.

In the square, Theo wrote **PAPER & PROOF • 7PM • NO PITCHFORKS.** Mrs. Levine stacked plates. Everett drafted an agenda. Vivian went home to set a table that had held too much silence and was now going to be asked to hold speech. Graham took off his ring, just to see how his hand felt without it. Mack walked to the hardware store with purpose shaped like relief.

Miriam and Julian stood a long minute on the chapel steps, not talking because talking would have turned the air back into a corridor they had already walked. When they did move, they moved together, down into the town that was about to learn the difference between peace and wholeness. The journal waited on the museum table, fragile and intact, the way courage waits in a room that doesn't think it will be used. The families would be confronted. The town would be asked to choose. The thirteenth petal, at last, had a mouth.

18

DOUBTS AND DEFENSES

By late afternoon the square had the brittle sheen of a storm that chooses whispers over thunder. The chalkboard outside the Riverlight café read **PAPER & PROOF • 7PM • NO PITCHFORKS**, but the town arrived with implements more efficient than forks: opinions sharpened against decades, alliances polished thin as cutlery. Someone had strung lanterns between the bakery and the post office, an optimistic garland that trembled each time the river wind pushed up the hill. Miriam stood in the museum doorway beside Julian and watched Cedar Creek take its seats the way a jury does when it already knows the verdict and wants the shape of the performance anyway.

The room filled by family order without anyone announcing it—Wagners on the left as if gravity pulled them, Dubois on the right like a counterweight; Adlers scattered through the middle to be accused by both sides; everyone else choosing benches as if neutrality were a plot of land to be purchased with politeness. Everett laid out agenda cards like sutures. Pastor Elijah stood near the back, as if distance might pass for restraint. Theo positioned his bell and a plate for scone fines with the theatrical solemnity of a bailiff.

Miriam's pendant lay warm and steady at her throat. The journal waited on its cradle, pages scanned twice and printed once, copies stacked like invitations to a wedding that might not end in a marriage. She could feel the town's attention on the silver more than on the paper, and she realized with a pang that people were braver about staring at her than at Leah's handwriting.

Everett cleared his throat into the microphone, the way officials bless rooms. "We'll begin with remarks from Ms. Adler," he said. "Then statements from representatives of the families. Questions will follow. Civility is not optional. Theo has a bell."

Theo rang it gently. The sound walked the air and sat down.

Miriam stepped forward. The podium had been borrowed from the high school; it smelled faintly of varnish and late adolescent speeches. She touched her notes and felt the familiar tug toward apology. She refused it. "Thank you for coming," she said. "What we unearthed is not a scandal. It's a record of honesty that was too brave for its time. Leah wrote what she could not say aloud. I'm going to read three passages and then ask this room to decide whether Cedar Creek prefers peace that costs the truth or truth that costs our old arrangement."

She read the entry where Leah wrote *my mouth is a door and will not stay shut*. She read the line about *households*—plural, the word that had grown loud as a bell. She read the paragraph where Leah described sealing the pendant and a hymn into cedar. She didn't dramatize; she didn't whisper. She let Leah's sentences sit on the room the way evening sits: evenly, without panic.

Then came the responses—the town's other instrument. Graham rose with the careful dignity of a man who has never liked microphones. "Unity has been our proudest habit," he said, and the word *habit* revealed more than he intended. "We owe it to our children not to make our grandparents' quarrels their weather." He glanced at Miriam only once, and in that glance was a plea disguised as a principle: do not make me learn a different way to live.

Vivian stood next, capable even in fatigue. "If a wrong was done," she said, "I know—because I have tried to keep a house—that women did the most work to patch it. I am not opposed to the truth. I am opposed to spectacle." She looked at the pendant as if it were both a claim and a kindness. "Some symbols belong in rooms, not on stages."

Others followed—Mrs. Levine in favor of the reading, Elena advocating for process and copies, Nadia reminding everyone that children hear what adults say and what they refuse to say, Walter offering the levity that keeps rooms from melting into dread. Then a voice Miriam didn't expect, brittle with fear: a woman from the back row—Mrs. Pritchard, who taught handwriting at the school—rose and said, "You are tearing everything," and sat down too hard as if she had been startled by her own sentence.

The fear spread through the benches like a shiver passed between bodies on a pew when winter refuses to leave. Two men near the aisle muttered about *outsiders*, the word tossed like a small stone in the direction of Miriam's ribcage. Another asked whether *these women* understood the meaning of *reverence*. A younger man with a Wagner profile and a Dubois mouth demanded, "What gives you the right?" and when she answered quietly, "Inheritance and obligation," he shook his head as if she'd spoken a foreign language.

The bell rang. Theo raised it once, twice, like a pastor's hands collecting the room for prayer. "No pitchforks," he reminded, voice light but eyes unamused. "And no tearing anything we can sew."

Miriam read one more line from the journal—*I am ashamed; I will not be*—and the sound that came back was not applause or boos or even a decision; it was the animal murmur of a town reaching the edge of its old map.

Elijah stepped forward then—smooth, almost a relief to those who wanted a familiar cadence. "We have loved our peace," he said, looking at the floor rather than at Miriam, "and perhaps—perhaps—we have mistaken quiet for wholeness. Ms. Adler has asked us to listen to the dead. That is not sacrilege. It is grief done properly. But I warn us all: we will hurt each other if we do not proceed with reverence. Please—" He turned to Miriam at last. "Please consider yielding some of your zeal for the sake of those who cannot breathe under the dust you stir."

The plea landed like a curtain. Portions of the room exhaled in relief—ah, the pastor has said it; the brave will be quiet now and spare us. Miriam felt alone in that particular way you feel when the person who means well asks you to be less yourself.

She reached for the pendant. Before she could speak, a new sound split the room's tired music: Julian's chair scraping wood as he stood.

JULIAN HAD PRACTICED discretion for months; he had worn his neutrality like a uniform that says *I am here to carry paper, not torches*. He removed it now as simply as one removes a coat. He didn't go to the podium—he stepped into the open space beside Miriam, a small tactical decision that read as something larger. He faced the room, glasses catching a stripe of lamp light, the lean, deliberate scholar who had convinced the town he would never choose the heat over the archive.

"I am going to say this plainly," he began, and the square tensed the way a violin does when the bow lands exactly where it must. "I am the one who chose to catalog the letter slid under our door yesterday as *In Dispute*. I am the one who dated the paper and the watermarks. I am the one who traced Leah's hand to the marriage record and found that the forgery mimicked it crudely. If you want a librarian to scold, scold me. But if you want to accuse a woman of spectacle, you will have to explain to me why our evidence in her hands scares you more than the quiet we kept in yours."

A ripple—shock, then a scatter of small laughs that sounded like oxygen returning to lungs. He went on, voice even. "Miriam has not asked you to believe in miracles. She has asked you to recognize a thirteenth line in a drawing and a paragraph in a journal that says a woman saw what we have preferred not to. We can disagree about what to do now; we cannot pretend nothing has been said. If you want to carry on in peace, say openly that you prefer peace to truth and let your children decide whether they want to inherit that choice. Do not hide behind the pastor and call it reverence."

Elijah flinched at the edge in the sentence; Julian turned to him in the same breath. "With respect. You have kept people from breaking. Tonight I'm asking you to help us break an arrangement that is killing us politely."

He modulated then—the scholar's instinct to steady a room he had just shaken. "There will be a process. There will be copies and councils and, God help us, bullet points. There should be. But there must also be a sentence we teach ourselves to say straight. So here is mine: I stand with Ms. Adler. I believe Leah. I believe the women who kept what the wall was asked to keep. If that costs me donors, so be it. If it costs me comfort, good. I'm tired of reading Cedar Creek as if it were fragile china. It is a working bowl. Let's use it."

The room tilted. You could see the change—tiny recalibrations across faces, as if someone had tilted a map and rivers remembered which way gravity goes. Vivian's mouth softened; Claire's chin rose. Mack allowed himself one smile with his eyes. Graham set his hand flat on his thigh, as if teaching it to stop reaching for the ring he had left on his dresser.

The resistance concentrated where it always does when a town is cornered by honesty: around the word *outsider*, around the specter of *hysteria*. A man in the back stood and said both. Theo rang the bell so hard it jumped. "No fines," he said. "Just shame."

Miriam felt a pulse rise against her wrist—her own heartbeat arguing for speech. But Julian was not finished. He lifted a folder from the table behind him and held up a single page. "You want neutrality? Here it is. Exhibit A." He read: *Appendix C—concerning window design, spousal counsel, and admonitions to discretion—sealed by key, copy noted to be placed with Pastor; also, note of a cedar reliquary placed within south wall, vestral side.* He lowered the page. "We did not conjure a reliquary to enjoy our own cleverness. We found it where your great-grandparents wrote they put it."

He set the paper down and took one small step closer to Miriam—subtle enough to escape most eyes, obvious to hers. "I will be here when you are angry," he told the room. "Save some for me. Miriam's hands are busy carrying Leah."

Silence met him like an intake of breath. Then, from the left bench, Mrs. Mathers: "Well," she said, "that's the first useful speech we've heard since the mill closed." The room laughed, grateful for the release valve, and in the laugh a decision began to form—not final, not unanimous, but real.

Everett found his voice and his gavel-less authority. "The council will convene tomorrow at ten for formal receipt of the journal," he said, words clipping back into order. "Tonight we will hear three questions—only three—and then we will conclude. Ms. Adler, Mr. Roth, you will be prepared with a summary and a plan."

Julian looked at Miriam; Miriam nodded. He answered the first question about provenance; she answered the second about motive without using the word *sin* or *patriarchy* and still managed to say both. The third question wasn't a question; it was Mrs. Pritchard's apology to the room for having used the word *tearing* when what she meant was *frightening*. "I was afraid I would lose my place," she said. "It appears I have been standing in the wrong room."

The bell rang once more, Theo pressed lemon bars into people's hands as if citrus could buffer candor, and the museum exhaled strangers back into neighbors. On the sidewalk, someone started humming *There Is a Balm in Gilead*, and the hum became a thread that looped the square and tied off somewhere near the fountain.

THEY DIDN'T LEAVE RIGHT AWAY. You don't step away from a room that has just rearranged itself and expect to walk straight. They returned the journal to its case, logged the small fingerprints of the evening in Julian's tight hand, and stood for a minute in the quiet that follows a departure as significant as an arrival.

"Thank you," Miriam said, the two words exhausted and precise.

"For what?" Julian asked, genuinely curious.

"For stepping out of your uniform," she said. "For choosing heat with me."

He looked at his hands, then at her. "I didn't choose heat," he said. "I chose light. You were already carrying fire." He hesitated, the way careful men do when they've practiced silence as virtue. Then he crossed it. "It is easier to be brave in a room with you in it."

The sentence landed between them and built the kind of pause that makes a third thing possible. She reached to close the journal's case and their hands collided in that old, accidental choreography that had started as clumsiness and matured into fluency. They didn't withdraw immediately this time. The contact held long enough to translate into the body's other language—*I see what you risked for me.*

He cleared his throat and ruined the solemnity in exactly the right way. "Theo assigned me cleanup," he said. "We are to fold chairs and store pitchforks we didn't use."

She laughed, and the laugh unknotted something in her chest. "Then we should begin."

They folded chairs; they stacked the lectern behind a curtain that would not quite hide it; they collected pencils that had rolled under benches when people's hands shook. He moved the way he read: steady, attentive, unwilling to assume a corner hadn't trapped something worth keeping. When they reached for the same stray pencil, their knees bumped and stayed. He looked up; she did too. The room was dim except for the desk lamp on the journal. The light caught the edge of his mouth, made a small grammar there —a contraction that said *don't run.*

"Can I ask you a selfish question?" he said.

"Please."

"If you decide to leave this town because it asks too much—if it becomes the wrong house for you—tell me before you go. Don't disappear and write me a tidy note. I would rather suffer your doubt in person."

The request startled her with its humility. "I'm not leaving," she said, surprised at how quickly the truth arrived to answer him. "Not because the town is gentle. Because it is mine."

He nodded, slow relief moving through his face as if it had been needed there for years. "Then I'll stay in it with you," he said. "Even when it pours sugar in my research budget."

She touched the pendant. He noticed and let the smallest smile rise. "That thing," he said, "has better instincts than I do."

"It is made of thirteen yeses," she said. "It took me awhile to hear them."

When they stepped into the square, night had settled into competence. Lanterns shook themselves into steadiness; the fountain performed its unremarkable miracle; the chapel rose like a shoulder exhaling a day's held tension. Townspeople lingered in knots that looked less like factions and more like families who had moved their furniture around and discovered the floor was sturdier than they feared.

Elijah approached them in the half-light and spoke before Miriam could brace. "You were right to resist me," he said, words thick but clear. "I mistook my weariness for wisdom. I will not again." He turned to Julian. "And you were right to refuse neutrality. I will use your words on Sunday and give you no credit."

"Good," Julian said. "They'll hate me less."

Elijah's laugh came out like a cough; then he sobered. "There will be people who try to make you regret tonight. I will not be one of them."

"Walk with us tomorrow," Miriam said. "When we take the journal to the council. Start as you mean to continue."

He nodded once, grateful for an assignment he could keep.

When he had gone, they crossed to the river's rail because water is the only thing that understands the labor of changing shape while keeping course. They stood without leaning and let the chill work its old cure on fevered nerves.

"Your defense surprised me," Miriam said, not teasing, naming. "Not because I doubted you. Because I know what it costs you to stand in public."

He turned, and the lamps brought out the gray at his temples in a way that made the moment honest. "I have been careful my whole life," he said. "Care is good. But tonight I realized my carefulness had started apologizing for itself. That's not scholarship. That's fear." He let his hand hover near hers, then let it rest, palm down, on the rail a finger-width from her own. "Your courage made my caution look like a lie I was telling myself. I don't like being lied to, even by me."

She slid her hand the distance between their fingers until the backs paired lightly. The contact was almost nothing. It registered like proof. "Thank you," she said again, hearing how insufficient the phrase is and deciding to keep saying it anyway.

He looked at the chapel and then at her. "Tomorrow is going to hurt," he said.

"It already does," she answered. "But tonight felt like the right shape of pain."

They walked back up the street with the slow, satisfied exhaustion of people who have lifted an awkward thing and discovered it was, in fact, built to be carried by two. In front of the shop, he stopped without prelude. "I know we're obligate to the town in the morning," he said, "but would you allow me one selfish request?"

"Try me."

"Let me be the first person you see when you open the door," he said. "So if you have to be brave immediately, you don't have to do the first minute alone."

She unlocked the door and stood in the frame, facing him, the pendant bright as a heartbeat in the lamplight. "Be here," she said. "And bring your stubbornness. We'll need both kinds."

He tilted his head, a small bow that managed to be formal and fond. "Goodnight, Ms. Adler."

"Goodnight, Mr. Roth."

When she closed the door, she leaned her forehead against the wood—not with despair, but with the simple bliss of rest earned. In the window, their reflections stood for a beat longer—the slow-burn outline of two people who had chosen loyalty in public before tenderness in private. Behind her, the shop breathed. Above her, the rose window kept its thin crack, not yet mended, already speaking. And somewhere in the square, Theo erased **NO PITCH-FORKS** and wrote **BRING FORKS FOR PIE** because rooms that tell the truth should also learn to laugh again.

19

PIECING THE PUZZLE

The museum's reading room still smelled faintly of cedar dust and lemon polish from the council meeting, as if wood and citrus had tried together to steady a body that had been rattled too long. Miriam sat with Leah's journal open before her, gloved hands hovering over its fragile pages, while Julian paced the length of the long oak table, muttering fragments under his breath like a scholar rehearsing a sermon.

On the table lay three objects, aligned not by chance but by the gravity they exerted on one another: the pendant, silver and stubborn, etched with thirteen petals; a tracing of the chapel's rose window with the faint crack sketched in red pencil; and Leah's words on the page, small but insistent: *If a girl reads this, let her know: I saw it. I did not imagine it.*

Miriam leaned back in her chair, rubbing her forehead where fatigue collected. "We've been looking at them as three separate witnesses," she said. "But maybe they're a single testimony."

Julian stopped pacing, pushed his glasses higher on his

nose, and bent over the pendant. He touched the etched lines with the soft end of a brush, not his finger, the way one checks a pulse without disturbing the body. "Thirteen," he murmured. "When every drawing, every carving, every commission ordered twelve. You can forgive a community for thinking it was superstition."

"Except Leah wasn't dreaming," Miriam countered. "She saw the thirteenth drawn. She named it. And when it was erased from the glass, she carried it here." She touched the pendant's chain lightly, then spread her hand over the journal's open page. "They took away wholeness and replaced it with symmetry."

Julian's gaze flicked to her. "Symmetry comforts," he said.

"And wholeness wounds," she answered. "Because it demands truth."

The words sat between them like an ember. Julian exhaled, slow. "So the crack in the window is not just physics. It's testimony."

"The glass couldn't hold their silence any more than Leah could." Miriam rose and moved to the tracing. She put the pendant in its center, letting the etched petals fall across the drawn circles. The thirteenth petal extended where the crack ran, completing the shape that the artisans had been told to erase. "The fracture is not a flaw," she whispered. "It's a finger pointing."

Julian lowered into the chair beside her. For once he didn't rush to annotate, to cross-reference, to catalog. He simply looked—at the overlay of silver on paper, at the small tremor in Miriam's hand, at the way the pendant and the journal seemed to breathe in the same rhythm.

"It's more than a symbol," he said at last. "It's a grammar. Twelve is order. Thirteen is a sentence unfinished. They chose silence instead of completion, and the silence itself cracked the glass."

Miriam nodded slowly, the truth clicking into her like a key finally cut to fit. "The pact wasn't only between families. It was between the town and itself. They decided to hide the part that made them whole. And they've been living as if wholeness were dangerous ever since."

Julian leaned forward, his elbows braced on the table, hands steepled. "So the thirteenth petal isn't superstition. It's a record of what was denied. And Leah—" He tapped the journal with reverence. "Leah was brave enough to say so."

Miriam felt a weight shift inside her chest, not leaving but resettling. "She passed it forward. And now it sits here. Not just as history. As an instruction."

The pendant caught a shaft of afternoon sun through the museum's high window, and for an instant, the silver shimmered like colored glass. Julian looked up and smiled —a small, astonished thing. "I think we've finally stopped chasing fragments," he said. "We've heard the sentence whole."

THEY MOVED the objects into a circle on the table—pendant, tracing, journal—like the spokes of a wheel. Miriam spoke first, her words slow, each one chosen as if she feared they might evaporate if spoken too quickly.

"The pendant is survival. A woman's refusal to let truth be erased. The journal is witness. A testimony hidden but not silenced. The window is the public face of the town— beautiful, symmetrical, cracked because it is incomplete." She glanced at Julian. "Together they don't just tell us about the past. They tell us what the town has to do now."

Julian nodded, pulling his notebook closer. He began

sketching, the way some men pray. Circles, petals, annotations. "In iconography, twelve is cosmic order—months, tribes, apostles, zodiac. Always twelve. But thirteen—" He tapped the page with his pencil. "Thirteen says: the circle can hold more than you're comfortable with. It is the reminder that symmetry is not the same as truth."

"And that women were the thirteenth," Miriam said, her voice firm. "Leah, Elise, Ruth. Each saw what was left out, carried it, waited until the day someone would open the cedar."

Julian paused, then drew a line across his sketch: the crack in the rose window. "What if the shimmer you saw," he said softly, "was the glass remembering the thirteenth?"

She felt heat at her throat where the pendant rested. "Not a ghost," she said. "A promise. A petal waiting to be acknowledged."

The room fell quiet. Even the museum's old clock seemed to tick with reverence. Miriam thought of the night whispers, the voices that had pressed *whole* and *below* into her bones. She remembered Leah's trembling script, the late entry from 1892 where she refused to sign the recasting. Every thread, every symbol, every moment of doubt was converging into a single demand: wholeness named aloud.

Julian closed his notebook and set it aside, his eyes steady on hers. "You realize what this means. We can't just preserve this in a case. It isn't artifact. It's imperative."

"I know." Miriam straightened. "The families must be brought together. Not just to argue, but to listen. To see the thirteenth petal revealed, not erased again."

The decision sat in the air, solid as cedar. Miriam felt fear brush her like cold air under a door, but the fear had a strange companion: clarity.

"I've spent months being tested," she said, half to herself.

"Welcomed and doubted, mocked and defended. But this —" She laid her palm over the pendant. "This isn't just about me. Leah's voice has chosen its echo. If I stay silent now, I betray her as surely as the pact betrayed the truth."

Julian's face softened, the scholar folding into the man. "And you won't be alone," he said. "Not again."

The window's tracing, the pendant, the journal—they looked like an altar. Miriam breathed in the scent of cedar rising faintly from the cloth. "Then we tell them," she said. "All of them. In the chapel. Where the silence began."

DUSK FELL with the hush of expectation. Miriam closed the shop early, turned the sign to *Resting*, and carried the pendant openly against her sweater for the first time, no longer tucking it under fabric as if ashamed of its light. Julian walked beside her, journal secured in its muslin, his satchel clinking with the careful weight of glass slides and preservation sheets.

The square greeted them with sidelong looks. Some faces wary, some curious, some already loyal. Miriam met their gazes without apology. The air carried the low murmur of disagreement, but it no longer cowed her. She realized, with something like wonder, that she no longer needed universal approval. She carried Leah's truth, and that was enough.

At the chapel steps, Pastor Elijah waited again. His posture carried the familiar tension of a man torn between protection and prophecy. "You mean to speak there?" he asked quietly.

"Yes," Miriam said. "The silence was made here. It will be broken here."

He searched her face, found no hesitation, and bowed

his head. "Then may God grant you gentleness even as you wound."

Inside, the rose window loomed, its crack a river across the glass. Miriam walked straight down the aisle, pendant shining in the dim light, journal held steady in Julian's careful hands. She stopped before the south wall, the place where cedar still whispered *below*.

People followed—Vivian with Claire at her side, Graham heavy with resistance, Mack steady as a post, Mrs. Mathers composed, Everett scribbling, Theo juggling his bell. The pews filled, the murmur rose, but Miriam turned and faced them as if she had been standing at that altar all her life.

She lifted the pendant, letting the lamplight catch its thirteen petals. She laid Leah's journal open on the lectern. She gestured toward the cracked window where the thirteenth shimmer waited to be acknowledged.

"Three witnesses," she said. "A pendant made to preserve what glass erased. A journal that spoke what households would not. A window that fractured because truth cannot be silenced forever. Together they testify to one thing: Cedar Creek chose symmetry over wholeness. It is time we choose differently."

The room hushed. Even the children, restless on their benches, stilled as if the air itself had commanded them. Miriam felt a strength move through her that wasn't hers alone—Leah's hand steadying hers, Elise's whisper, Ruth's watchful gaze.

"I cannot force you," she continued. "I can only guide you. But I tell you this: the thirteenth petal is not superstition. It is us—all of us—whole, not twelve households pretending, but thirteen voices, each heard. If we deny it again, the crack will widen. If we accept it, the glass may heal."

She laid her hand flat on the journal. "Leah asked for one girl, someday, to keep her mouth a door that would not stay shut. That girl has been found. And I will not be silent."

For a heartbeat, no one breathed. Then a ripple of voices rose—some in protest, some in assent, some trembling with the shock of recognition. But Miriam stood calm, pendant gleaming, crack shimmering faintly behind her. For the first time since she had arrived in Cedar Creek, she felt not like an outsider tested but like a guide chosen.

Julian's gaze found hers, steady, loyal, unguarded. And in his eyes she read not only defense but devotion.

The thirteenth petal had spoken. Now the town must decide if it would listen.

20

PIECING THE PUZZLE CONTINUED

The reading room of the Cedar Creek Museum had grown into their workshop of truth. Papers, sketches, fragments of Leah's journal, and the silver pendant lay spread across the long oak table. The pendant glowed faintly in the lamplight, the etching of thirteen petals catching shadows like hidden veins. Miriam stared at it as though it were breathing. Julian sat across from her, his posture half-collapsed with fatigue, yet his eyes alive with the same stubborn fire she felt pulsing through her own chest.

"We've been circling around it for weeks," Miriam said, her voice low, her fingertips brushing the journal's fragile pages. "The pendant, the window, Leah's words—they aren't three mysteries. They're one."

Julian leaned forward, elbows braced on the table. His pencil tapped against his notebook as though rhythm might shake meaning free. "Three artifacts, three witnesses, if you prefer the language of history. We've treated them separately because that's what curators do: classify, contain. But you're right. They belong to a single sentence. We've only been hearing fragments."

He adjusted the tracing of the rose window that they'd laid out on paper—concentric rings of glass, twelve symmetrical petals, the faint red pencil line showing the fracture across the north quadrant. Miriam took the pendant from where it rested and laid it directly on the center. The silver gleamed, the thirteenth petal extending beyond the line of symmetry, falling exactly where the crack had spread.

Julian's sharp intake of breath broke the silence. "Look at that," he murmured. "The crack doesn't destroy the design —it completes it. It's as if the window itself has been trying to reveal what was erased."

Miriam pressed the pendant flat against the tracing, her heart pounding. "Leah said she saw thirteen drawn on the glazier's paper. They made him erase it. But she carried it anyway—here, on this chain. The crack, the shimmer I saw, it's not accident. It's testimony."

Julian rubbed his brow, the scholar in him wrestling with awe. "In every sacred geometry, twelve is the number of order. Apostles, tribes, months. Twelve keeps the world symmetrical. But thirteen—" He stopped, considering. "Thirteen means surplus. Refusal. A wholeness that symmetry can't handle. No wonder they feared it."

Miriam's voice steadied as she spoke the truth that had been pressing against her for days. "It wasn't only superstition. It was a pact. They chose silence over honesty, symmetry over wholeness. That pact was broken the moment Leah refused to stay quiet. And the crack in the rose window is the town's scar for that choice."

Julian stood, restless with discovery, and began pacing, one hand running along the spines of the books that lined the shelves. "So the thirteenth petal isn't an embellishment. It's the missing truth. The symbol of what the town couldn't carry in daylight. Families signed unity, but what they agreed to was omission."

Miriam closed the journal gently, her palm resting on the leather as if blessing it. "And Leah bore the cost. She called herself ashamed, then she called herself free. That transformation is what we've been circling too. She passed it forward to us."

They looked at one another across the table, the silence no longer strained but charged. The objects formed a triangle between them—silver pendant, cracked rose, trembling words. Three voices speaking the same sentence, waiting to be spoken aloud.

Julian stopped pacing. His eyes found hers with rare certainty. "Then that's our resolution. The thirteenth petal is not invention. It's remembrance. It's the wholeness they tried to suppress. And if the town doesn't claim it now, it will keep fracturing until it does."

Miriam's pulse steadied, clarity flowing through her like a tide that no longer fought the shore. "We have to carry it into the chapel. Into the place where silence began. And we have to say it in front of them all: the pact of silence broke us. The thirteenth petal can heal us."

Her words did not tremble. And for the first time, Julian didn't hesitate either. He simply nodded.

THEY CLEARED THE TABLE, arranging the three artifacts deliberately as though preparing an altar: journal to the left, tracing of the rose window at the center, pendant resting in its heart. Candles flickered on the sill, the only light aside from the desk lamp.

Miriam drew a breath, her hand hovering over the pendant. "It's more than metal. It's inheritance."

Julian, seated again with his notes, spoke like a teacher, though his tone carried reverence instead of detachment. "In iconography, roses have always meant unity. Petals radiate from a single center. Twelve petals speak of perfect order—everything in balance. But the thirteenth..." He tapped the pendant lightly with the eraser of his pencil. "It defies completion. It says: wholeness isn't tidy. Truth doesn't divide evenly."

"And yet it's truer," Miriam said softly. "Symmetry is beautiful, but it isn't whole. Wholeness is messy. It includes the voice that says no when everyone else says yes."

She opened Leah's journal again and read aloud from the September entry: *They say unity and mean obedience. They say charity and mean hush.* The words fell into the room like stones into water, ripples touching everything they had gathered. "That's what the thirteenth petal stands for," Miriam continued. "Not a superstition, not rebellion for its own sake. Wholeness that costs comfort."

Julian's expression shifted—skepticism dissolving into something close to wonder. "You've been insisting from the start that symbols don't lie. I thought you meant intuition without evidence. But this—" He gestured at the journal and pendant. "This is evidence. Symbols are evidence carved by people who didn't have minutes or legal codes to protect them."

Miriam smiled faintly. "You defend history with parchment. I defend it with intuition. Turns out Leah gave us both."

They fell silent, the kind of silence that listens rather than hides. Outside, the river's low current whispered against the banks, a hymn Cedar Creek had been singing since before the town had a name. The cracked rose window, invisible from here yet present in their minds, seemed to hum with them.

Miriam set her hand flat on the tracing. "The shimmer I saw that night—it wasn't a vision meant only for me. It was a sign that the glass still remembers. The thirteenth petal is already there, waiting to be named. When we speak Leah's words aloud in the chapel, the truth will not just be history—it will be revelation."

Julian leaned closer, his voice quiet. "You believe the rose will glow again."

"I don't just believe it," Miriam said. "I know it."

The words startled her as much as him. But they held.

For the next hour they mapped connections like cartographers drawing a coastline. The pendant etched in silver, the crack aligning perfectly with the erased petal, Leah's refusal to sign the recasting, the pendant hidden in cedar for a century. Each thread converged, pointing toward the same truth: Cedar Creek's unity had been built on silence. The thirteenth petal was the key to breaking that silence without breaking the town itself.

When at last they sat back, their notes a constellation of arrows and circles, Julian removed his glasses and pinched the bridge of his nose. "Do you realize what this makes you?"

Miriam tilted her head.

"A guide," he said simply. "Not just an heir. Not just an interpreter. A guide for all of them. You're the only one who can carry this forward."

The word hit her chest like both a burden and a benediction. Guide. Not seer, not prophet, not meddler. Guide.

"I don't know if I'm ready," she whispered.

Julian's gaze was steady, unwavering. "Neither was Leah. She wrote anyway."

Miriam looked at the journal, then at the pendant. Fear still curled in her, but it no longer owned her. She was beginning to understand: readiness is not a prerequisite for calling.

The next evening, Miriam and Julian carried their work into the shop. The back room smelled of dried herbs and incense, her great-aunt's old bottles lined neatly along the shelves. She cleared the table, laying out the pendant, tracing, and journal once more.

She stood in the center of the room, Julian at her side, and spoke as if Leah herself were listening. "You asked for one girl to keep her mouth a door that will not stay shut. I am that girl. And I will not be silent."

The pendant warmed against her chest, as though acknowledging the vow.

Julian stepped forward, his voice low but certain. "Then you're ready. You've stepped into the role whether you meant to or not. The town is waiting, Miriam. They're afraid, divided, uncertain. But they're also listening. You're the one who can lead them to wholeness."

She turned toward him, her eyes luminous in the lamplight. "You'll stand with me?"

His answer was immediate, without hesitation: "Always."

The word steadied her more than she expected. She nodded once, then gathered the journal to her chest, the pendant gleaming faintly above it. The tracing of the rose window lay between them, the crack running across it like an invitation rather than a wound.

"Tomorrow," Miriam said, her voice calm, resolute, "we bring them into the chapel. All of them. We tell the truth Leah could not say aloud. We show them the thirteenth petal. And we let the window decide whether it will glow again."

Julian reached for her hand, not with urgency but with quiet solidarity. Their fingers intertwined, scholar and seer bound by a truth larger than either could have carried alone.

Miriam lifted her chin, her fear transmuted into something fiercer—conviction. For the first time since she had stepped into Cedar Creek, she felt not like an intruder or an heir, but like a guide.

The thirteenth petal was ready to be revealed. And she was ready to lead them into it.

21

THE GATHERING AT THE CHAPEL

The chapel had never looked so solemn. Evening light seeped through the fractured rose window, scattering slanted beams across the pews where generations of Cedar Creek's founding families now sat—faces taut with suspicion, apprehension, and the brittle sheen of pride. The crack in the glass caught the last of the sun, glowing faintly, as though waiting to see whether truth or silence would win tonight.

Miriam stood at the front, pendant gleaming at her throat, Leah's journal laid carefully on the lectern. Julian stood a few steps behind her, steady as an anchor, his satchel full of preservation supplies and notes—symbols of order in a night ruled by memory.

She scanned the room. Vivian sat near the aisle, her daughter Claire stiff at her side. Graham's large hands clenched and unclenched against his knees, his ring absent but his authority heavy in the air. Mack leaned forward slightly, eyes shadowed yet open. Mrs. Mathers perched upright, hands folded in her lap like both witness and judge. Pastor Elijah occupied a seat near the center, shoulders bowed under the weight of decades of compromise. Around them clustered cousins, spouses, grandchildren—faces that bore the echo of the pact though none had signed it.

Miriam cleared her throat. The sound felt too small for the burden of what she must carry, but she spoke anyway.

"Thank you for coming. This gathering isn't about choosing sides—it's about telling the truth. Leah's words, the pendant, and the rose window have waited over a century for this night. The silence that bound our families has cracked. We cannot pretend anymore."

A low murmur rippled through the pews. Graham rose first, as Miriam expected. "And what exactly do you intend to do, Ms. Adler?" His voice carried both contempt and fear. "Reopen wounds? Humiliate us in front of the town? Some of us worked our entire lives to keep Cedar Creek whole. Do not undo that in one evening."

Vivian followed quickly, her words laced with exhaustion rather than venom. "We are not children needing correction, Miriam. What's past is past. Leah's complaints may have been sincere, but they don't belong in the present. We've built something here—businesses, homes, traditions. Must we tear it all down because of one voice?"

Miriam rested her hand on the journal. "One voice that spoke for many who could not. Leah was silenced by her marriage, by her church, by her community. She wrote because her mouth could not stay shut. That voice is not past. It's present. You can feel it."

The pendant pulsed warm against her skin. She lifted it into the fading light, the thirteenth petal glimmering faintly as though responding. Gasps fluttered through the pews— fear, wonder, disbelief.

Julian stepped forward then, his voice calm but cutting. "This isn't spectacle. It's evidence. The pendant, the journal, the crack—they corroborate one another. We have the tracing, the hidden entries, the watermarks. We know Leah wasn't imagining the thirteenth petal. It was erased, deliberately, by men who preferred symmetry to wholeness. And that pact—the one you're so eager to call peace—was silence disguised as unity."

Mack shifted, the first to break the posture of defense. "So we've been living under a false peace," he said slowly, his voice carrying to every corner. "That's the truth, isn't it?"

"Yes," Miriam said. "And truth is the only foundation strong enough to rebuild on. If you keep pretending, the crack will widen until the whole window falls."

The chapel seemed to breathe in unison, air charged with centuries of unsaid words.

Claire's voice broke it. "And if we acknowledge it? What then? Do we just live with shame?"

"No," Miriam answered, her eyes meeting the girl's. "You live with honesty. Shame festers in silence. But when truth is spoken, healing can begin. Leah wasn't asking us to live forever in her pain—she was asking us not to bury it."

Her words hung in the nave like a bell still ringing.

THE RESISTANCE CAME sharp and fast. Graham rose again, his voice like gravel. "You don't understand, Miriam. You came here with nothing to lose. The rest of us carry legacies, inheritances, names. If we let Leah's words redefine history, everything we built collapses. Businesses tied to these families, reputations beyond this town—gone."

Miriam met his fury without flinching. "Then maybe what was built needs reshaping. Leah didn't destroy Cedar Creek—she told the truth about it. You're afraid of collapse because you know the foundation was flawed."

Vivian stood, her hands trembling though her voice remained composed. "And what of loyalty? We protected each other, sometimes through silence. That was how we survived. Women learned to hold households together by not speaking what would tear them apart." Her eyes glistened. "You think that was cowardice. I call it endurance."

Miriam softened her tone. "I honor your endurance, Vivian. But endurance is not the same as healing. You kept the roof from falling. Leah wanted more—she wanted the house rebuilt so it wouldn't keep cracking."

Pastor Elijah shifted uneasily, then rose, his tall frame casting a long shadow. "I told Miriam once that some truths should stay buried. I see now I was wrong. But I also see the danger here. If we force every wound open at once, we may not survive the bleeding."

Julian spoke before Miriam could. "And if we cover the wound again, it will rot. Survival isn't the same as living, Pastor. You know this."

The pews erupted—voices overlapping, accusations flying. Some shouted about protecting children from scandal, others muttered about outsiders stirring unrest. A few—Mrs. Mathers, Nadia, even Theo from the back—raised words of support, insisting the truth was long overdue.

Miriam let the noise crest, her hand steady on the journal. Then she opened to the page she had chosen and began to read aloud, her voice clear, cutting through the cacophony.

They say unity and mean obedience. They say charity and mean hush. A girl may not be witness against her father, nor a wife against her husband. But I will be witness for truth against anything that rises against mercy.

The voices faltered, stilled. The words of a long-dead bride rang louder than any present protest.

Miriam closed the journal gently. "Leah risked everything to put those words on paper. She was not tearing families apart—she was trying to save them from silence. If we refuse to hear her now, we betray her twice."

Silence, thick and trembling. Vivian pressed a hand to her mouth, eyes wet. Graham sat heavily, the fight draining from him like water leaving a cracked basin. Claire leaned closer to her mother, whispering something Miriam couldn't hear. Mack nodded once, his gaze meeting Miriam's in quiet agreement.

Elijah lowered himself back into his seat, his face weary but softened. "Perhaps the time for reverence is to let her words speak fully."

Mrs. Mathers spoke next, voice strong despite her age. "We have feared this night for too long. Let it be done. Let it be spoken."

The tide had shifted. Resistance remained, but it no longer controlled the current. Leah's words pressed forward, undeniable. The families could either yield or drown in their own silence.

MIRIAM STEPPED DOWN from the lectern, carrying the journal in her hands. She walked slowly to the center aisle, turning so that she faced both sides of the chapel—Wagners on her left, Dubois on her right, Adlers scattered in between. The pendant shimmered faintly, catching the dim light like a small flame.

"I know you are afraid," she said, her voice gentle now. "Afraid that telling the truth will unravel everything you've worked to hold together. But listen: it is already unraveling. The crack in the rose window shows it. The distrust between you shows it. Leah's words show it. You have been carrying silence like a heavy trunk, and it has bent your backs. You don't have to carry it anymore."

She moved closer to Vivian, meeting her eyes. "Vivian, you spoke of endurance. You held your family together. Now you can rest. The truth can do the holding for you."

Vivian's lips trembled, then pressed tight. She nodded once, eyes glistening.

Miriam turned to Graham. His fists clenched, his face taut with old pride. "Graham, you fear collapse. But collapse is not the only ending. Sometimes it's the beginning of rebuilding. You don't have to lose your name to gain wholeness. You only have to stop guarding silence as if it were treasure."

His jaw worked, but he did not speak. Still, his shoulders eased, just slightly.

Miriam looked to the younger faces—Claire, Nadia, others her own age and younger. "And you—you've inherited these divides without choosing them. Leah wrote for you. She asked for one girl to keep her mouth a door that would not stay shut. I am that girl, yes—but so are you. Every one of you has the right to speak truth without fear. You are not bound to the pact anymore."

The pendant pulsed with warmth, and for a moment, Miriam thought she saw the faint shimmer of a thirteenth petal ripple across the cracked rose window above them. Gasps confirmed she wasn't the only one.

Julian stepped forward, his voice measured but strong. "This isn't about blame. It's about inheritance. You can choose what you pass on—silence or truth. Tonight is your chance."

Miriam raised Leah's journal high enough for all to see. "These words are no longer hidden. The cedar has released them. The thirteenth petal has spoken. Now it is up to us to listen."

Silence held the room, but it was a silence transformed —not oppressive, but reverent. Slowly, Vivian stood, her hand clasping Claire's. "I will listen," she said simply. Claire echoed her, voice unsteady but sincere.

Across the aisle, Mack rose as well. "I will listen too."

Even Graham, after a long pause, gave a grudging nod. "I can't promise comfort," he muttered. "But I will hear her out."

The chapel exhaled, tension softening into something more human. The first cracks of compassion spread across hardened surfaces.

Miriam returned the journal to the lectern, laying it open as if inviting everyone to approach. She stepped back, pendant still glowing faintly at her chest.

"This is only the beginning," she said. "Tomorrow, we continue. But tonight—we have broken the silence. Together."

The rose window shimmered faintly once more, light bending across the fractured glass until it seemed, just for a breath, that thirteen petals bloomed whole above them.

And for the first time in generations, Cedar Creek sat in the chapel not divided by silence, but bound by truth.

22

THE TRUTH REVEALED

Miriam stepped forward and placed the journal on the lectern and faced them all—women who had learned endurance as a first language, men who had mistaken vigilance for virtue, children with faces uncreased by the town's practiced hush.

"This isn't a trial," she said, voice steady. "There is no culprit to punish. There is only a practice to end."

A murmur moved like wind over dry grass. Graham Wagner's jaw worked; Vivian Dubois hands tightened in her lap; Mack's attention leaned forward as if it could help carry weight. Miriam opened the book. The leather made a sound like a sigh.

She read without theater—no pauses for effect, no angling for pity—only the cadence a truth finds when it is finally allowed its full measure:

They say unity and mean obedience. They say charity and mean hush. A girl may not be witness against her father, nor a wife against her husband. But I will be witness for truth against anything that rises against mercy.

A creak, a cough, then stillness. She turned the page.

The glazier drew thirteen. He rubbed it out at a man's word. Elise made a necklace of what was erased, and we pressed it into cedar with hymn and tears. They sealed the minutes with a key and put our silence in the church like a saint. I am ashamed; I will not be.

The words struck the room with that paradoxical gentleness hard truths sometimes wear. No one looked away. The children did not stir.

Miriam kept reading. *Appendix C. For the peace of households. Recasting. Signatures taken from women who could not afford dissent.* The journal did not name a single villain. It named a habit grown into architecture. It described a vow not to a God of light but to a fear of fracture. The culprit, Miriam realized as she read, had never been a person; it had been a consensus.

She closed the book and let silence follow its echo. "You see it," she said softly. "Not a crime to prosecute. A practice to release. Generational silence—our town's favorite idol."

Elijah's eyes shone. "I helped keep it polished," he said into the hush, confession like warm bread. "We called it pastoral care. Often it was simply quiet."

Vivian rose half an inch and then the rest. "We called it endurance," she said. "We carried it because the men would not, and because we were told the roof would fall if we set it down." She swallowed. "It has fallen anyway, a little every year, where we could not admit it."

Graham looked at his empty ring finger as if it were a map he hadn't learned to read. His voice arrived rough. "We thought we were sparing our children." He took a breath that sounded expensive. "We asked them to spare us instead."

Miriam nodded—not absolving, not accusing. "We can

stop," she said. "Not by choosing new villains. By choosing a new vow."

A child in the back whispered, too loud and perfectly timed, "What vow?" The smile that ran through the room was the first breath of spring through a house shut too long.

Miriam set her palm on the journal. "To tell the truth and keep each other. In that order."

The crack in the rose window seemed, impossibly, to gather what remained of daylight and lay it down the aisle in a thin, steady bar.

RECONCILIATION DID NOT ARRIVE as a chorus. It came in single, careful voices, as if the town were learning a new hymn from the alto line up.

Mrs. Mathers stood. "I loved my mother and I loved my father," she said, simple as bread. "I learned to be loyal by not naming what hurt us. I am still loyal. I will also be truthful." She turned to Vivian. "Our grandmothers kept a roof. Now we will build beams."

Vivian rose fully this time. She took Claire's hand and faced the Wagners, the Pikes, the Adlers, the handful of families whose names stitched the town's civic minutes. "I cannot keep you from shame," she said, meeting Graham's gaze without flinching. "I can offer you mine, so we don't carry it alone." She looked to Miriam. "And I can stop asking the bravest woman in the room to be quieter so I do not have to be braver."

Mack cleared his throat. It sounded like anger and relief shaking hands. "We'll open the boxes," he said, meaning the attics, the file drawers, the trunks at the back of closets that held unsigned copies and addenda no one had wanted to catalogue. He put his hand flat on the pew rail, a carpenter's vow. "No more secret minutes. If a paper shaped us, it will be read in daylight."

Everett, who had arrived ready to defend an agenda against feeling, stood as if surprised by his own legs. "The council will accept the journal formally," he said. "We will commission a public record of what was done and what will be undone. We will fund the window's restoration with the thirteenth petal included. If you wish to petition, bring pie and bullet points in equal measure." A ripple of laughter—grateful, threaded with tears—gave him courage. "And we will hold a town meeting where every household—" he stopped, corrected himself—"every person—may speak."

Elijah stepped beside Miriam. "I will preach repentance," he said. "Not for history. For habits. We have spent years choosing quiet over neighbor-love. We will choose again."

Graham rose slowly, a man walking onto a floor he had not laid. He faced Miriam, then Julian, then the room. "I was trained to keep a shape and call it integrity," he said. "Perhaps integrity is keeping the person beside you." He looked down at his hands and then up at the rose window, eyes wet in a way no one present had seen. "I have been wrong for a long time. I am tired of being wrong alone. If we are to be wrong as we learn, let us be wrong together."

A murmur of assent. Nadia, a twin on each hip, called out, "We will bring casseroles. No one fights hungry." Theo rang the bell—one bright, ridiculous note that made the pews smile. Mrs. Levine lifted a wrapped loaf from her bag, set it on the rail, and said, "Bread for the truth," as though such phrases were common in Cedar Creek.

Not all consent arrived sweetly. A man near the back stood to invoke *outsiders* and *hysteria* in the same skittering sentence. The room did not jeer; it did not applaud. It waited. The man faltered under the weight of their waiting, sat down, and whispered into his hands. A woman beside him—his wife, or his sister—put a palm between his shoulder blades and held it there while his breathing evened.

Miriam did not press. Reconciliation is not spectacle; it is stamina. She simply lifted Leah's journal again. "We will not all change at once," she said. "But we will all be changed by the truth once it is spoken. That is how truth works."

She looked at Julian; he nodded, then reached into his satchel, drew out the tracing of the rose window, and held it up where everyone could see the red pencil line and the ghost-circle where the thirteenth would live.

"We propose," he said, "that the restored window carry thirteen. Not as provocation. As wholeness. The town that chose silence will choose completion instead." His voice warmed. "And we propose that the pendant be worn not by one owner but by a procession—passed from house to house each year at the festival, a sign that no family will be asked to carry what belongs to all."

Vivian's shoulders loosened; Claire's mouth turned upward the smallest degree; Mack nodded, relief visible as daylight. Even Graham's stern face softened into something like wonder.

"Agreed," said Mrs. Mathers, and in Cedar Creek, when she says *agreed*, a quorum appears.

Everett, half laughing, half crying, scribbled *ROTATING PENDANT RITUAL* on an index card as if ritual could be minuted and minutes redeemed. Theo wrote **THIRTEEN = WHOLE** on his palm in ink and held it up for the back pews.

Miriam waited for the inevitable last test. It came from a woman near the center—Mrs. Pritchard, who had once accused them of tearing. She stood again, voice trembling, and said, "I was wrong the other night. I didn't mean tearing. I meant frightening. I am still frightened." She swallowed. "But I can be frightened and consent."

"That is the bravest sentence we have spoken this week," Elijah said, and the room believed him.

THE AIR CHANGED. Not warmer, not brighter—just truer, as if the room had been tuned. Miriam could feel it on her skin, in the way the pendant steadied its heat, in the breath that moved through the pews like a shared tide. She laid Leah's journal open again, turned to the page that had waited for this precise hour, and read the lines that made bridges across time:

If I sign, it is not consent. It is hunger. It is winter thinking through my skin. I am ashamed; I will not be. I will keep a copy of the minutes that told the truth and fix them under the floor. If the floor is later broken and the paper lost, let this stand. If a girl reads this, let her mouth be a door that will not stay shut. Let her speak, and may the house not fall but right itself.

She closed the book and looked up. "Leah," she said to the quiet, "it is spoken."

As if the chapel itself had been waiting to hear its name, the crack in the rose window caught a last invisible seam of light and let it spill—first a thin thread, then a gentle pane, then a soft undulation that moved across the colors like breath across a sleeping child. It wasn't spectacle. It wasn't a miracle you could sell tickets to. It was a building remembering its design.

A shimmer gathered along the fracture, the sort of glow stained glass makes when sunset and confession meet. For a heartbeat—and then for several—an extra curve of light bloomed where the erased petal would have arced. Not a trick of eyes, not wishful seeing: a patient geometry, briefly visible, consenting to be seen.

People wept without embarrassment. Vivian's hand found Claire's. Graham's found Mack's shoulder. Nadia's twins reached for the air and laughed, grabbing at color. Theo leaned his head against the rail and made the small exhale men make when they have been holding themselves upright too long. Everett forgot his index cards and simply stood with his mouth open, which, for Everett, was also worship.

Elijah whispered a word that might have been *amen* or *again*. Mrs. Mathers sang one line of a hymn Leah had quoted—just one line, enough: "There is a balm in Gilead." Others joined, not with volume but with that soft, sturdy tone kitchens use when they sing over work.

Miriam felt tears and did not wipe them. She let the salt mark her face the way the river marks stone: not damage; shaping. She lifted the pendant in her palm so the light could touch it. The thirteenth petal in silver answered the thirteenth shimmer in glass like two notes resolving into chord.

Julian stepped to her side, not to explain, not to protect —only to be. His hand hovered, then rested at the small of her back, a steady warmth that said *present*. She looked at him, and in the look they exchanged the long, careful arc of the last weeks folded into something simple: we carried this; we will keep carrying; together.

"Say it," he murmured.

She turned to the room and, with Leah's journal open, the pendant bright, the window shimmering its quiet assent, spoke the new vow she had promised:

"We will tell the truth and keep each other. We will put

wholeness before symmetry. We will let our children inherit completion, not quiet."

Voices answered—first a few, then many, then most: "We will." Not in unison but together—thirteen, not twelve.

The shimmer thinned, as all visitations do, and settled back into glass. The crack remained, but it looked different now—not a wound, a seam. The chapel exhaled, and the town exhaled with it.

Elijah raised his hands, not in benediction exactly but in gratitude. "Go in truth," he said. "And take one another with you."

People drifted into aisles that did not separate so much as braid. Apologies braided with plans: Vivian and Graham speaking low and earnest about ledgers and letters; Everett promising copies and public minutes; Mack already drafting a work order in his head for scaffolding and gentle hands; Mrs. Levine pressing loaves into arms that had just put burdens down; Theo scribbling **THIRTEEN = WHOLE** on the chapel chalkboard as if to teach the building its new arithmetic.

Miriam closed the journal and held it for a moment against her heart. She whispered, "Thank you," not to the town, not to Julian, but to the woman whose sentences had made this night possible. She slid the book into its muslin, set it in Julian's waiting hands, and let herself be emptied of fear.

On the steps, the evening had softened into that particular Cedar Creek blue that makes even brick look forgiving. The river spoke its old grammar. Lanterns came alive one by one along the square. Behind them, the rose window held its quiet, dignified glow—twelve petals and the memory of a thirteenth, soon to be glass, already a promise.

Julian touched her elbow. "You did it," he said.

"We did it," she corrected.

He inclined his head, accepting the plural the way a town accepts rain after a long hush. "Tomorrow we start the work," he said.

"Tonight we start belonging," she answered, and for the first time since the key had turned in her great-aunt's shop door, the word fit in her mouth without wobbling.

They descended the steps into a town that had chosen, at last, to be whole.

23

THE FIRST KISS

They left the chapel together without agreeing to; their feet simply found the same stairs, the same cool air. Behind them, voices braided into softer shapes—apologies, plans, someone humming *Gilead* in a kitchen-honest key. Ahead, the river kept its grammar, clauses of current punctuating the evening with small, right sounds.

The square's lanterns had come alive. Theo had chalked **THIRTEEN = WHOLE** on a board outside the Riverlight and drawn a lopsided rose that would have made a glazier wince and Leah laugh. Mrs. Levine, refusing to let anyone go home empty-handed, pressed a warm heel of bread into Miriam's palms as they passed. "For after," she said, as if *after* were a country you needed provisions for.

They said little on the hill. Words that had been brave in a room felt suddenly too loud under stars. The pendant lay quiet against Miriam's skin, as if it, too, had done its part and now consented to rest. She tucked the bread into her bag and let her hands be empty.

At the river rail they stopped. The water wore a thin

seam of moon. Downstream, a heron lifted—too slow for surprise, exactly the pace of relief. The air held that cleaned-out feeling chapels sometimes leave behind when a confession has done its work.

Julian set his satchel on the bench and exhaled like a man discovering he'd been standing without knees. "You spoke a sentence," he said, not looking at her yet. "And the building changed shape to fit it."

Miriam kept her eyes on the water. "We all did. You stood beside me when it cost you."

"I said words," he answered. "You said them like a beam."

They stood with the kind of silence that is not empty but full—the space after a bow releases a string and before the note decides whether to linger. The river kept time. Somewhere behind them a child laughed the way children do when the adults have decided to live rightly again.

He turned then, gentle as if approaching an animal he hoped to be allowed to touch. "Tell me where you are," he said. It was the question he had asked her on the night of the forged letter, when doubt had taken up residence in her ribs. Tonight it meant more. Or perhaps it meant the same thing, and more was simply what honesty always turns out to be.

"I am..." She searched for a word that wasn't performance. "Emptied but not hollow. Strong the way cedar is—flexible, not brittle. Scared that tomorrow will start asking for proof again." She smiled a little. "Hungry. Grateful."

"Hungry," he repeated, tasting the word because words had fed him longer than food had. He opened the paper around the bread Mrs. Levine had handed over, broke it with his hands, gave her the larger piece without comment.

He took his smaller half and did not pretend not to be content with less.

They ate leaning on the rail, not speaking. The bread was still warm enough to feel human. When they finished, she brushed crumbs from her fingers and did not tuck her hand back into her pocket. It stayed near his on the rail, not touching, in the way of things that have already made up their minds.

"You carried Ruth's house into a shape it can live in," he said after a while, voice low. "I watched you become the exact person Leah wrote toward."

"You carried the town to the edge of fear and asked it to look," she said. "And you let it see you choosing me."

"That surprised you." He didn't make it a question.

"It relieved me," she said, and felt the honesty land with a small click in both their bodies. "And it frightened me, because relief is so close to need."

He turned, leaned his hip against the rail, and faced her squarely. The lamplight had a way of finding the gray at his temples and making it look like decision rather than age. "I have tried, for years, to need no one," he said. "It made me efficient and untrue." He let a beat pass. "Tonight I would like to need you, if you will allow me the risk."

Her laugh surprised itself out of her, not for humor but for release. "You are very bad at romance," she said, "and perfect at it."

"Field-trained," he admitted. "Not school-taught."

She set her palm, finally, over his on the rail. The contact traveled up her arm like a remembered song—nothing dramatic, everything precise. He did not move to seize it; he received it as if she had placed a fragile thing there and he meant to keep its shape.

The kiss arrived the way certain weather arrives over

water—signaled long before it happens. He shifted half a step closer; she tilted her face not in invitation, exactly, but in consent; the world narrowed to the width of a bench and widened to include everything that had brought them here: the pendant's weight, Leah's lines, scaffolding yet to be built, bread still warm on their tongues.

He touched her cheek first with his knuckles, a scholar's carefulness even now. "I am going to be clumsy," he warned softly.

"I'm not," she said, and the thread of play saved them from reverence so intense it would have paralyzed. She set her free hand lightly against his chest—bones, breath, heartbeat—and lifted her mouth to his.

It was not fireworks. It was not the river leaping its banks. It was a hinge sigh, a seam closing correctly for the first time in years. He kissed her with the restraint of a man who understands preservation and the warmth of one who understands finally what objects are for. She answered with steadiness rather than hunger; she had waited long enough to know that the first meal after famine should be simple.

When they stepped back it wasn't to flee; it was to see. They looked at each other like people reading a page they thought they already knew and finding a new sentence written in the margin. He cupped the side of her neck with one hand, thumb resting at the chain's clasp, and smiled a little, almost startled. "So this is what belonging feels like," he said.

"Like bread and breath," she said. "And a river not in a hurry."

He laughed under his breath, looked down as if to steady himself, then up again. "I'm going to ask again," he said. "Where are you?"

"Here," she answered, and for the first time since she

had carried a ring she no longer wore, *here* meant one person as well as one town.

THEY WALKED the path that flanked the river, where cedar gave way to alder and back again, where the boardwalk remembered every festival and every quiet grief. He kept his pace half a measure behind hers, then beside it, then in front for a few steps when the boards wobbled, learning the choreography of care without making a show of it.

"I was nineteen when I learned endurance," Miriam said, the words opening like a window you have to push past old paint to lift. "It is a skill and a curse. When David died, endurance saved me from drowning. It also built a room I forgot to leave." She glanced sideways, checking whether the name would bruise him. It didn't; it warmed him by the way a candle on a windowsill warms a passerby who never knocks.

"My marriage taught me a different curse," Julian said. "Control dressed as kindness. I tried to make the house safe with rules—calendars, budgets, a color-coding of affections. It turns out love prefers grammar to formatting." He smiled, rueful but not bitter. "When she left, I thought the worst thing was the empty. Now I can see the worst thing was what I had been calling full."

"Do you want it all back?" Miriam asked, not to test him but to measure his own seam for strength.

"No," he said gently. "I want the parts that were true, and I have them already." He nodded toward the pendant. "Words that fit their objects. Hands that ask permission. Bread that is better when shared. And—" He hesitated, as if approaching a line he might trip over. "A woman whose courage recalibrates a room."

She let that sit where he had put it. He did not reach to adjust it. They crossed the little footbridge where children had thrown a thousand wishes into the slow eddy and adults had pretended the wishes were physics.

"I am afraid of being the town's instrument," she said after a time. "Of becoming a mouth no longer connected to a body. Leah asked for a girl whose mouth would not stay shut. She did not ask for a tool."

"You are not an instrument," he said. "You are a musician. You decide where the bow goes." He stopped them with a hand at her elbow, not possessing, only pausing. "If anyone begins to play you, including me, take the violin away and walk out. I will follow you into the alley and apologize properly."

"That's a very particular plan," she said.

"I've had practice," he said. "With apologies."

"And alleys?"

"Those too." He looked out over the water, the way men do when the right sentence arrives and needs space to land. "Miriam, when I defended you tonight, it wasn't a grand gesture. It was a correction. Of my habits. Of the town's. You have made me better at the moral version of fieldwork."

She breathed in. The air smelled of damp wood and a distant cinnamon from a bakery that never actually sleeps. "You have made me steadier," she said. "When the letter arrived, when the wall breathed, when Elijah asked me to be small—your presence made the difference between performance and courage."

They reached the low bend where the boardwalk came closest to the water, where children liked to squat and point at minnows that always darted out of reach. She stopped and touched the rail with her fingertips, feeling the little scars left by a hundred summer bracelets and pocketknives.

"If I am honest," she said, "I wondered if kissing you would change the work."

"It changes everything," he said promptly, and then, seeing her face, laughed softly. "For the better, Ms. Adler. The work is the work. We just won't do it from opposite ends of the same table pretending the stretch is noble."

"Shared side," she said, as if ordering from a menu.

"Shared side," he confirmed. "I'll even let you mark my papers with your red pen."

"I don't use red," she said. "It looks like punishment. I use a soft pencil and write *again* in the margin."

He made a pleased sound she had not heard from him before, something that belonged to a younger decade and had survived in him anyway. "Then teach me to try again when you ask."

They kissed once more, not because drama required it but because tenderness did. It was different now—less careful. His hand found the back of her neck with the knowledge of a man who has learned that steadiness is an intimacy. She answered with a thumb along his jaw, a small mapping of a coastline she planned to know by heart. The night accepted them without changing its weather.

When they parted, she leaned her forehead against his and spoke into the quiet between their mouths. "I like that you're not afraid of my dead."

"I am afraid of many things," he said, the truth so clean it felt like a dare. "But not of the way love dignifies what came before it."

"Field-trained," she said again.

"Field-trained," he agreed, smiling against her smile.

· · ·

THEY TURNED BACK toward the square, not because the night had spent itself, but because morning had already sent a note ahead: scaffolding schedules, council logistics, a town learning to speak with adults' voices instead of inherited whispers. The first work of belonging is always tomorrow.

At the foot of the hill, the chapel kept its posture—twelve petals and a seam that now read like intention. Everett crossed with a folder clutched like a sacrament and nearly collided with them, then bobbed, abashed. "Minutes," he said, tapping the folder. "Readable ones." He looked from one to the other and, for once, chose not to make it official. "Goodnight." He hustled off, the way men do when they sense a private weather and are kind enough not to stand in it.

Theo had left the café door propped with a milk crate and a note—**KEY UNDER THE SUNFLOWER**—that was either an invitation or a dare. He had also drawn an arrow pointing to a pie safe labeled **STAFF ONLY** and underlined *Only* twice, which told Miriam there was at least one slice inside he hoped would fail to be protected.

"Tomorrow," Julian said, nodding at the chapel. "We meet the stained-glass guild. I've already emailed descriptions and scans. They'll balk at an addition. They always do. Then they'll remember what art is for."

"We'll need volunteers to strip the beadboard carefully," she added. "And a watch schedule. Whoever came to the wall last night has a conscience but not enough sleep. Let's not tempt him with early morning loneliness."

He grinned sideways. "I'll make a sign-up—*Guardians of Civility, Night Watch edition.* Theo will insist on capes."

"Absolutely not capes," she said, horrified and delighted, and he laughed, the easy kind, relieved of the labor of proving anything.

They reached her shop. The front window made a quiet mirror in the lamplight, throwing back two figures who had learned the difference between being alone and being solitary. She unlocked the door and paused on the sill, turning to him not as a threshold you cross or do not, but as the person you consult before you decide where to sleep.

"Come in," she began, then stopped. The town was small. Its appetite for commentary was large. She lifted a hand, palm up, to revise. "Tea tomorrow morning. Before the guild. Before Everett's bullet points. We'll plan. And you can be the first person I see."

His face, listening, did that quiet settling she had already come to trust. "Yes," he said. "And I'll bring stubbornness, per your standing order."

"And lemon bars," she bargained.

"Those, too," he said. "Payment for services already rendered."

He stepped closer then, one hand braced lightly on the doorjamb, an old-world gesture that made the present sweeter. "Before I go," he said, "I want to say something unbeautiful."

"Please do," she said. "The beautiful has had a long night."

He took a breath. "I admire you. Not as a preface to desire. As its companion." He shook his head once, as if to clear any dust of rhetoric. "I like the way your mind refuses spectacle and chooses precision. I like the way your courage rubs my fear until it warms. I like that you laugh at me when I deserve it. I like that your first language is care."

She swallowed, because praise offered this cleanly can be harder to bear than insult. "I receive that," she said. "And I return it. I like that you put your body between me and a room you loved enough to argue with. I like that your hands ask before they do. I like that you keep choosing we when I am tempted to go back to I."

They did not kiss again. Some nights ask to be sealed; this one had already been signed and witnessed.

"Tomorrow," he repeated.

"Tomorrow," she said.

He turned down the street, and she watched him go not with the panic of someone left, but with the calm of someone accompanied even in absence. When he reached the corner, he lifted a hand without looking back—the gesture of a man who trusts the person behind him to still be there when he returns.

Inside, she set the bread on a plate, poured water into the kettle, and leaned for a moment against the counter with her eyes closed, letting the day inventory itself. The pendant cooled slowly, then found her temperature again, a small silver consent. She wrote a card and slid it under the glass by the register beside the others:

- **Tell the truth and keep each other.**
- **Thirteen is whole.**
- **Shared side.**

The kettle sang. She made tea and took it to the window, sat on the stool Ruth had always insisted was bad for posture and perfect for people-watching. The square exhaled; the river continued; the chapel kept its seam. Somewhere in the dark, a man who had stood at the back of the room and said *outsider* shifted in bed and thought of his mother; somewhere else, a girl who had never seen her name in a ledger drew thirteen petals in the margin of her homework and felt a little less alone.

Miriam sipped and smiled, not at the town, not at the

window, but at the idea that love could be work's ally and not its competitor. She was not naïve; tomorrow would ask for proof again. But she would answer from a different grammar now. Not I. We.

When she set down the cup, the glass in the front window caught a passing breeze and made a tiny, familiar sound. The hinge-sigh again. The night answering. The future opening no wider than a mouth and exactly wide enough.

24

REBUILDING THE ROSE

By breakfast the scaffolding already laced the chapel's south wall like a careful exoskeleton. Mack's crew moved with the economy of men who had learned patience from lumber; their hammers spoke in measured iambs. A white van from the stained-glass guild idled by the curb, its doors swung wide to reveal crates of lead came, trays of mouth-blown glass, and a wooden box stenciled **FRAGILE / LIGHT** that made everyone smile.

"Roll call," Everett announced, clipboard in hand, earnest as a metronome. "Glass team, carpentry, safety, food." He glanced up and, catching his own self-importance, added, "And... joy. Volunteers for joy."

"I run joy," Theo said, hoisting a string of pennant flags in unapologetically mismatched colors. "Also hydration. Also capes for the Night Watch." He winked at Miriam, who leveled a look that said *absolutely not capes* and then ruined it by smiling.

Vivian arrived in work boots and a linen shirt with sleeves already rolled. "We'll cover the guild's rental and insurance," she told Everett before he could ask. "And the festival committee voted last night: all booth fees go to the window fund." Claire, at her side, lifted a fabric-wrapped bundle. "Donation jar covers," she said. "Thirteen-petal motif. I figured we could be literal just this once."

Graham came later, walking like a man trying not to startle a skittish horse. He carried a thermos of coffee and two boxes of doughnuts, which he deposited by the sawhorses without speech. When Mack nodded a thanks, Graham nodded back, the smallest treaty written in grease and sugar.

Pastor Elijah stood near the vestry door, blessing without speech whoever passed. Mrs. Mathers pinned a list to the chapel notice board: **TOOLS THAT DO NOT WOUND** followed by a neat inventory—bone folder, nylon spudger, soft-bristle brush. Beneath it she taped a hand-drawn rose with thirteen petals; a child had added a face in the center, which made the old woman laugh in a way that made everyone else less cautious.

Miriam arrived with the pendant visible against her sweater and a paper bag from the Riverlight. She set lemon bars on the folding table and then pulled the muslin-wrapped journal from her satchel and placed it inside the roped-off nave with a handwritten sign: **ON LOAN TO THE PRESENT. HANDLE WITH CARE.** Her hands didn't shake. The pendant pulsed warm once, like a small assent.

Julian followed with his canvas kit: cotton gloves, Mylar, a string line, a pencil so soft it barely marked; the scholar's offering to a worksite. He touched the scaffolding, then the wall, as if greeting old friends he hadn't known he was missing. "We'll start with the damaged tracery," he told the guild's lead, a woman named Anita with sun-browned forearms and a wave tattoo that wrapped around and down her arm. "The crack traveled along a stress line, but the stone held."

"Stone keeps secrets better than glass," Anita said, squinting at the rose. "Glass is honest. It breaks where the lie is."

"Add that to the plaque," Theo called.

The guild laid out samples—reds like pomegranate skin, blues like deep river, a green with the modesty of cedar shade. Anita lifted a small, roundel-shaped sheet whose color was not color exactly but a clear with a whisper of gold at its heart. "For the thirteenth," she said, matter-of-fact. "Not bright. Not ashamed. Let the petal be visible when the light is honest."

Miriam looked up. The crack cut across the rose like a thin river map, already less accusation than instruction. She closed her eyes for a breath, listened for that now-familiar pressure that sometimes rose from wood or stone when a thing wanted to be found. Nothing dramatic came—only the practical silence of a town beginning again. It steadied her more than any shimmer could have.

Work took a shape. Mack's team eased out beadboard softened by humidity and years of paint, numbered planks in pencil, stacked them in sequence under a tarp, as reverent as archivists. Nadia organized the youth crew—teenagers in safety vests—into runners, pairing each with an adult so tasks were always shared: older hands guiding, younger hands carrying, both sets learning. Everett made a fresh sign-up sheet every hour because he liked evidence of willingness. Mrs. Levine circulated with sandwiches and the scolding affection that keeps people from skipping meals when they're being noble.

In the nave, Pastor Elijah pulled the pew cushions and set them aside, then knelt with a bucket and cloth and quietly cleaned the dust from the baseboards. The sight of it moved Miriam more than speeches had—contrition performed as mending.

Just before noon, Anita climbed to the center of the rose with a harness, a pencil, and a little paper template cut to the curve the thirteenth would one day occupy. "I'm not placing it today," she called down. "I'm teaching the window where it goes." She pressed the paper into the negative space, traced lightly, then lifted it away. From below, the gesture looked like liturgy: a promise made in outline so the day would keep lean toward it.

Theo's flags found the line of the scaffolding and the rail of the chapel steps. Children painted tissue-paper petals at the craft table and then ran in a solemn line up the aisle to tape their creations to a cardboard circle someone had labeled **PRACTICE ROSE**. One kid added a fourteenth petal; his mother moved to peel it off; Miriam shook her head. "Let it stay," she said. "We're training ourselves to be surprised."

When the bells in the square marked noon, people set down tools as if the town had one body. Elijah stood and lifted a hand. "We'll pray," he said, and then amended, "We'll pause." The distinction mattered; the room exhaled.

"In this work," he said into the hush, "teach our hands to be gentle, our words to be careful, our hearts to prefer completion to comfort." He looked at Miriam. "Teach us to tell the truth and keep each other."

"Amen," said Mrs. Mathers. "And pass the lemonade."

By afternoon, the nave had grown beautiful in a way that had nothing to do with stained glass. It was beautiful because people occupied it with useful bodies—hauling, measuring, steadying ladders, reading, laughing when ladders squeaked, apologizing when tempers began to fray.

Graham fetched a box of antique glass he'd salvaged years ago and never admitted he kept; Anita selected two pieces with a nod that looked as much like absolution as approval. Vivian stood beside Claire and accepted donations not as penance but as participation, saying thank you like a woman paying an old debt with joy.

Miriam kept moving—between wall and table, scaffold and pew. People asked things—where does this go; can I help; is it all right to feel too much—and she answered without haste. In her moving body the town found the new grammar it had promised: tell the truth and keep each other. Seeing it made the vow easier to say.

At dusk, they strung lanterns across the square for the resuming festival. Booths that had closed during the hardest week reopened with a lightness that surprised even their owners. Theo chalked **NO PITCHFORKS, ONLY PIE** and then, under it, **THIRTEEN = WHOLE** again, as if repetition were the muscle by which towns change shape.

From the hill, the unfinished rose watched like a patient elder. The crack no longer dominated. It simply showed where to mend.

Morning arrived bright as a brass bell. The guild returned with a second van and a young apprentice named Penny who had the best eyes anyone had seen since Leah's sketch. Penny held up a sample against the sun and said, matter-of-fact, "Not blue, not white—water-light," and Anita, who was learning not to be threatened by younger certainty, nodded without caveat.

Everett pinned the day's agenda to the chapel door and added a line at the top: **MIRIAM TO OPEN.** He handed her the marker. She stood on the steps, not behind a podium, not above anyone—simply visible—and welcomed people as if they were entering a house she was learning to love out loud.

"Thank you for coming back," she said. "Thank you for keeping each other yesterday. Today will be more of the same. We will add something small and precise and true to the window; we will add something large and quiet and true to the town. If you don't know where you belong in the work, ask someone carrying less than you are."

Laughter, easy and unafraid. Pastor Elijah, at the rail, smiled with the mien of a man happy to be seconded.

Claire stepped forward holding a small velvet pouch. "On behalf of the festival committee," she said, cheeks pink with purpose, "we vote to formalize the pendant rotation. First year: Miriam Adler, as keeper and guide. Next year: the youngest girl born after tonight whose family promises to let her speak. After that: pass it along where courage is needed."

Vivian tied the pouch to the pendant chain with fingers that did not quite shake. "If we ask you to wear it," she said to Miriam, "we also promise to see the woman bearing it, not just the symbol."

Miriam swallowed, then nodded. "I will wear it," she said. "Not as ownership—as stewardship. And when it is time, I will let it go."

Everett cleared his throat with the ceremony he loved. "The council met this morning," he announced, "and voted unanimously to accept Leah's journal into the museum's collection—permanently on display, with digital images for public study." He looked up, less official than moved. "We also voted to append the phrase **Tell the truth and keep each other** to the town's mission statement. It will look terrible on letterhead and very fine on us."

Applause broke like warm rain. Elijah rang the chapel handbell, the note bright enough to make children laugh and adults remember how.

Work resumed, and Miriam moved again through the cycles of asking and answering. In the lull between tasks, a woman she didn't know well—Mrs. Pritchard, who had feared tearing—approached with a wrapped box. Inside lay a calligraphed copy of Leah's vow, mounted under glass. *My mouth is a door and will not stay shut.* The letters were not ornate; they were sturdy.

"I made this last night," Mrs. Pritchard said quietly. "Hands know apologies faster than mouths." She glanced toward the nave. "May I hang it in the vestibule?"

"Please," Miriam said. "Where children can touch it with their eyes every time they come in."

At midday, Anita called for silence. She stood with Penny on the scaffold, each holding an edge of a small, curved panel assembled overnight: lead lines delicate as nerve, water-light glass at the center like a kept promise. "We'll dry-fit," Anita said. "Then rest. We place in ceremony after sundown."

The panel slid into its negative space with the relational satisfaction of a well-made sentence. A small sound rippled through the nave—someone's gasp, someone's laugh, the soft *oh* of a person recognizing a shape they didn't know they'd been missing. Penny grinned without permission; Anita let herself grin too.

"Good," Anita said. "The window accepts."

Miriam stood under the rose and felt, in her skin, a change that was not mystical so much as familiar—the alignment that comes when you move a piece into the place it was cut for. She lifted a hand without thinking and the pendant warmed once, then settled, as if to say *we are on time.*

In the afternoon, the square filled—not frenetic, not forced—just a town resuming its festival with the understanding that celebration can be sober without being sad. Pie contests recommenced with a gentleness that allowed two first prizes. The parade captain admitted he had planned a float lampooning the council and then thrown it out, confession earning him as many cheers as satire would have.

People stopped Miriam as she crossed—some to thank, some to ask, some simply to touch her sleeve the way people touch relics when they need an excuse to touch a person. She did not flinch. She let herself be held, which was the newer courage. A boy offered her a paper petal with **AGAIN** penciled in the center; she put it in her pocket like a vow.

Late afternoon shaded toward gold. Volunteers swept sawdust, coiled extension cords like sleeping snakes, laid blankets on the hill. Elijah carried a small lectern to the landing and set it aside, then turned to her. "Would you say the words tonight?" he asked. "After the guild places the petal."

"Yes," she said, and felt the nervousness arrive without the shame that used to accompany it. Nervousness meant she cared. It also meant she knew the sentences by heart.

Near sunset, Vivian approached with Graham in tow. He looked less armored than he had in a decade; his hands were empty. "I brought nothing," he said, a little wry. "Is that all right?"

"It's perfect," Miriam said, and he believed her.

"Thank you," he added after a moment, the phrase

landing clumsy and precious. "For not humiliating us while telling the truth."

"I told it because humiliation is a poor teacher," she said. "Grief and courage do better."

Graham nodded, glanced up at the window. "It's... beautiful," he said, wonder outpacing reluctance.

"It was always trying to be," she answered.

Under the lanterns, with work stopped and faces turned up, the town waited. Anita and Penny climbed once more, carried the finished petal between them like a child, and seated it. Lead pressed, solder pooled, a whisper of flux, a rag polished the seam. The panel held.

For a heartbeat the rose was simply a window again, awaiting light. For another heartbeat it was more.

THE FIRST EVENING with the thirteenth in place did not roar; it hummed. The river sent up a breeze that found the glass, and the glass, instead of guarding its color, gave it away. The new petal did not shout; it breathed—water-light at first, then a quiet gold as lanterns found it from below.

Anita signaled to Everett. He dimmed the square lights one by one—not to stage a miracle, only to teach eyes how to see. When the last lamp softened, Elijah lifted the small handbell. The note threaded the hill.

Miriam stepped forward to the landing with the pendant visible in the soft dark and Julian at her side—near enough to share breath, far enough to honor the room. She did not look at him before she spoke; she felt him the way you feel a sturdy rail in a stairwell you've only just begun to trust.

"We promised," she said, voice clear without strain, "to tell the truth and keep each other." She lifted a hand toward the rose. "This is our keeping—choosing completion over symmetry, wholeness over hush. The thirteenth petal stands for what we refused to lose again: the voice that says *I am here too*."

She let the quiet receive the words, then added, because it was honest to do so, "We will forget. We are human. So we will practice remembering." She held up Theo's chalkboard, where he'd copied the town's new arithmetic. **THIRTEEN = WHOLE.** Laughter moved like warm wind.

"Now," Elijah said, eyes bright, "let us look."

They did. The evening light, last of the day, caught the new curve and rode it like a promise to the far edge of the glass. People reached for one another's hands without shame. Children lay on the grass and pointed. Penny cried openly; Anita put an arm around her and did not pretend it was just solder stinging her eyes.

Julian leaned to Miriam's ear. "You did that," he murmured.

"We did," she answered automatically, then allowed herself the concession of his claim. "All right. I did a little."

He laughed quietly. On the hill, Theo's flags riffled. Mrs. Levine began distributing slices of a cake she had labeled *Rose Window* and decorated with thirteen petals of candied citrus. Vivian made a point of taking the smallest piece and giving the largest to Claire. Graham—softened, awkward, present—cut pie and asked children their names as if he were introducing himself to his own town.

The festival resumed around the worksite, less pageant than picnic. Fiddles lifted a tune that people knew how to dance to without practice. Couples turned—some careful, some exuberant, all relieved. Miriam felt a pull toward the square's center and stayed where she was; the hill was her place tonight. Julian stayed with her without asking if he should.

"You're staying late," she said when the first wave of cleanup started—Everett and Walter stacking chairs in companionable silence, Nadia carrying twins sagging with sleep, Elijah returning the handbell to its hook. "There are minutes you could be writing."

"I like undocumented time," he said. "I plan to make more of it." He tipped his head toward the shop. "And besides, I still owe you lemon bars."

"You owe me nothing," she said. "But I'll take lemon bars."

They walked down together, the pendant cool now against her skin, not extinguished—rested. The shop's front was dark, but inside the back room a lamp burned; she had left it on because she knew how the end of public work can feel like a cliff. He followed her through the aisles of crystals and cards and herbs Ruth had labeled in a hand Miriam was learning to imitate without betraying.

"I've been thinking," Julian said, setting his satchel by the door more comfortably than he had the first time, when everything he did felt provisional. "If you want, we can make a small table upstairs—half library, half workbench. For scanning notes, mounting the pendant schedule, writing together. Shared side."

She liked the phrase enough to set it on the table like a vase. "A workbench in Ruth's attic," she said. "She would have called that sacrilege and then stocked it with pencils."

"I was hoping she would approve," he said, and for a second the room held her aunt's laugh.

They climbed the narrow stairs and stood in the low-ceilinged space that looked down over the square. She switched on the lamp. The circle of light made a room inside a room—enough. She pulled a small table from the wall and, with the competence of a person who has moved furniture alone, angled it under the window. He held the other end and didn't overhelp.

He set out the first objects of their shared life—not a toothbrush, not a drawer's worth of socks, but the tools by which they made meaning: a notebook, a soft pencil, an envelope of photo corners, a square of Mylar. He placed them without ceremony, the way you place things you plan to use again tomorrow.

"You'll need a key," she said, surprised by the calm in her voice. "For mornings when you arrive before me."

He looked up, careful even when receiving. "Yes," he said simply, not pasting gratitude over the obvious welcome. She found the spare under the little ceramic bird Ruth had always kept on the sill. He took it and didn't make it a vow. That would come later; this was enough.

From the square floated the tail of a tune and the steady soprano of Mrs. Mathers counting teens into a tidy line for slices. The town had its own pulse again, irregular and healthy. Miriam stood at the window and watched the chapel light trim into its ordinary glow, the thirteenth petal now indistinguishable from the design except when the angle of light admitted you knew where to look.

Julian came to stand beside her. Not in front. Not behind. Beside.

"What did today teach you?" he asked.

"That belonging isn't granted," she said. "It's practiced. The town let me practice in public, and did not punish me for learning where everyone could see." She turned to him. "What did it teach you?"

"That scholarship is better when it's married to courage," he said. "And that I'm allowed to be happy out loud."

She smiled. "Permission granted."

They stood until the music thinned and the lanterns began to wink out. He touched the frame of the window with two fingers, a practiced benediction for wood that had done its duty and would do it again. Then he looked at her, and in his face she saw all the ways the day had folded them together—work, witness, a plan for a shared table, a key.

"Tomorrow?" he asked.

"Tomorrow," she said. "There's a town to keep."

He kissed her once—shorter than last night, more ordinary, which made it lovelier—and then left by the front, whistling a small fragment of the hymn the town had learned to sing in its new key. She watched him cross the square without hurry. At the corner he lifted a hand, not as farewell but as punctuation: more to come.

Upstairs, she set a new card under the glass by the register before she turned out the lights:

- **Completion beats symmetry.**
- **Practice belonging.**
- **Shared table, shared side.**

The hinge-sigh came again when she locked the door. It sounded, tonight, less like a threshold and more like a house settling around the people who would keep it. Outside, the rose held. Inside, the workbench waited. Somewhere between them, Miriam felt it quite clearly—the click of a life aligning—and knew, not as prophecy but as craft: the window would last; the festival would grow lighter; the town would forget and remember and forget and remember again; and when it did, she and Julian would be there, steady as stone, honest as glass.

25

———

QUIET EVENING AT THE SHOP

The square had emptied hours ago, but the echo of laughter still clung to the cobblestones. Miriam turned the key in the shop's lock, then left it dangling while she stacked the last of the crystal trays in the display case. The glass clinked softly, a lullaby of mineral and light. She wiped the counter with deliberate slowness, the kind of small ritual that told her body the day was done, even if her mind still hummed with unfinished lists.

The pendant rested cool against her chest. She'd stopped tucking it away; the town had seen it, named it, agreed to rotate it. Tonight it was hers to carry, and instead of feeling like a chain it felt like a hand resting at her sternum—steady, not heavy.

She dimmed the lamps one by one until only the back reading lamp glowed, its circle of light softening the room into intimacy. The shop, in this light, looked less like commerce and more like memory—a place where Ruth's handwriting still labeled jars, where cedar beams held whispers from three generations of Adlers, where even dust seemed reverent.

A knock, soft but sure, came at the door. She turned. Julian stood outside holding two paper cups with steam curling from their lids. He didn't raise them like a peace offering; he simply waited, shoulders hunched against the night breeze, as if the decision to admit him should remain hers.

She opened the door without words. The bell chimed, lighter than usual, as though even it had learned the town's new grammar.

"Tea," he said. "Strong enough to carry scaffolding, weak enough to drink before sleep."

She took one cup, the cardboard warm in her hands, and inhaled the faint notes of chamomile threaded with something sharper—ginger, maybe. "Theo experimenting again?" she asked.

Julian smiled. "No. Me. I can brew water without injury."

"That remains to be seen." She sipped. The ginger caught the back of her throat, surprising and welcome. "Acceptable."

His mouth twitched into what might have been pride. He set his satchel on the counter without asking, a sign of how much he had come to treat this space as shared ground. "I thought you might want company," he said.

She gestured at the lamp-lit circle. "Company is the right size tonight."

They sat opposite each other at the small wooden table Ruth had always said was too wobbly for paying customers but perfect for family. Their knees almost brushed under the table, the proximity both ordinary and charged.

Julian peeled the sleeve off his cup, fidgeting with it. "I keep replaying the look on Graham's face when Anita seated the new petal," he said. "Like a man realizing his sternness had been architecture, not essence. I almost pitied him."

"Almost," Miriam said.

"Almost," he agreed, then laughed. The sound startled them both—it was freer than anything they had heard from him in months.

Her own laugh followed, quiet but full. For the first time since she had arrived in Cedar Creek, laughter didn't feel like intrusion or defense. It felt like belonging.

They drank in companionable silence. The square outside dimmed to shadows, lanterns extinguished one by one. From somewhere down the street a fiddle hummed its last phrase, then stopped.

Julian leaned back, the chair creaking. "Do you ever wonder what Ruth would say if she walked in right now?"

Miriam glanced around the shop—the mismatched shelves, the faint aroma of dried sage, the journal locked in the display case for safekeeping. "She'd say I finally stopped dusting her bottles and started using them." She smiled faintly. "And she'd scold me for trusting you so fast."

He accepted the tease without defense. "And you?"

"I'd tell her I'm not trusting you fast. I'm trusting myself to know when someone deserves it."

The words surprised her as much as him. He looked at her then, truly looked, and the warmth in his eyes was steadier than the tea between them.

They sat until the cups cooled, the room holding them like cedar holds scent.

When Miriam rose to clear the cups, Julian reached instinctively to help. She stopped him with a hand on his wrist. "Sit," she said, not sharply but firmly, the way you speak to someone you've decided to share authority with.

He obeyed, smiling faintly, and she rinsed the cups in the sink with unhurried care.

As she wiped her hands, her gaze caught on the mirror Ruth had hung above the counter. For a moment she saw herself not as widow or outsider but as shopkeeper, guide, bearer of a town's reluctant hope. Her reflection wasn't softened by candlelight or blurred by tears. It was sharp, sure, entirely hers.

She returned to the table and sat again, folding her hands. "When I first unlocked this shop, I felt like an intruder in my own bloodline," she admitted. "Every jar looked like an accusation. Every whisper from the street sounded like a test. Tonight..." She gestured toward the shelves, the counter, the pendant. "Tonight it feels like mine. Not because I inherited it, but because I chose it."

Julian nodded slowly. "You've shifted from caretaker to keeper. There's a difference."

She considered that. "Keeper implies responsibility. But also choice. I am not here because Ruth expected it. I'm here because I expect it of myself."

"Which means the town can trust you," he said. "Because you're not obeying ghosts—you're listening to them."

Her throat tightened. "I never thought I'd get to say that. For years, I thought my story ended with endurance. Surviving loss, keeping going, nothing more. But Leah's words, the window, this pendant—they've shown me endurance is only the preface. The story is what you choose after you've endured."

Julian reached across the table, not dramatically, just steady. She let his hand cover hers. His skin was warm, rough at the edges from work, honest.

"You are different from the woman who arrived," he said.

"Not because Cedar Creek changed you, but because you changed Cedar Creek."

She met his eyes. "Do you believe that?"

"I saw it," he answered. "I watched silence shift when you named it. That's not observation—that's witness."

The word—witness—landed with the weight of Leah's journal. Miriam inhaled slowly, then released it, a sigh that wasn't fatigue but recognition. She realized she was no longer afraid of being seen.

They let the quiet linger. Outside, the square settled into its deepest stillness, the hour when even gossip slept. Inside, the shop breathed with them, cedar beams expanding and contracting in rhythm with night air.

Miriam stood and moved to the shelf where Ruth had kept her most esoteric volumes. She pulled down one—*The Geometry of Mercy*—and laid it on the table. Its pages smelled of dust and rosemary. She flipped it open to a diagram of a circle with twelve petals, an ancient pattern of sacred proportion. In the margin Ruth had scribbled, in her brisk hand: *What happens if you draw thirteen?*

Miriam traced the sketch with her finger. "Ruth knew. She always knew. She just didn't live to see it."

Julian studied the note. "And you did. That's legacy. Not inheritance—continuation."

Miriam smiled. "Continuation that I finally consent to."

Her own words startled her again. Consent. Continuation. Choice. She realized she was building a lexicon of self she hadn't owned before Cedar Creek.

She closed the book gently. "I feel like myself again," she said. "Not the widow, not the outsider—the woman who belongs to her own name."

Julian leaned back, admiration plain. "And that," he said,

"is the only foundation strong enough to share with someone else."

THEY LINGERED in that circle of lamplight until the clock above the door ticked toward midnight. Miriam stretched, the pendant glinting. "I should close," she said. "Tomorrow will be long."

Julian stood, collected his satchel, then hesitated. "Before I go..." He opened the bag and pulled out a small cloth bundle. "I found this in the archive today, slipped behind a drawer."

He unwrapped it carefully. Inside lay a fragment of parchment, brittle but legible. A diagram, crude but familiar: a basin carved into stone, marked with a symbol Miriam didn't recognize. Below it, words in faint ink: *When the water runs dry, the silence ends again.*

Her skin prickled. "The basin," she whispered. She remembered the ceremonial basin by the river, usually filled for festival rites. She had never seen it empty.

Julian watched her face. "It may be nothing. Or it may be the next sentence in Leah's unfinished story."

Miriam set the parchment beside Ruth's book, their edges nearly touching. "The rose was about silence. Maybe the basin is about voice. Or renewal. Or..." She trailed off, unwilling to name the unease crawling up her spine.

Julian touched her arm lightly. "You don't have to solve it tonight."

"No," she agreed. But the parchment's presence felt like a seed already rooting.

He shouldered his satchel. "I'll walk you upstairs. Make sure you don't dream of puzzles without sleep."

She laughed softly, grateful for his steadiness. Together

they climbed to the small apartment above the shop. At the landing he paused, not crossing the threshold. "Tea again tomorrow?"

"Tea again tomorrow," she echoed.

He bowed slightly—a habit from classrooms he had never broken—and descended, whistling faintly. She listened until his steps faded.

Alone, she set the parchment on the desk beside the pendant. The lamplight caught both, casting twin shadows on the wall. She thought of Leah whispering *my mouth is a door* and wondered what new door was opening now.

She drew a fresh card, wrote in her hand:

- **Endurance is preface.**
- **Belonging is choice.**
- **When the water runs dry...**

She slid it under the glass counter with the others. Then she turned off the lamp, climbed into bed, and let herself rest.

But in her last waking thought, she saw the basin by the riverbed empty, moonlight catching a carved symbol in stone, and she knew the story of Cedar Creek was far from over.

26

———————

MIRIAM'S BLESSING

By late afternoon the bakery's windows fanned heat into the square like warm breath. Inside, the smells built a layered chord: yeast lifting its long vowel, honey's low hum, sesame's brief bright consonant, and the clean mineral of river water boiled for tea. Cooling racks lined the wall like pews. On each, round loaves glowed the color of late wheat.

Miriam Adler paused at the threshold, fingers grazing the bell on the bakery door as if it were a small instrument she'd finally learned to play. The pendant lay steady at her throat—not a badge, not a dare, simply an ordinary brightness among ordinary things. She stepped in and found the town already gathered as if they had been waiting for a cue that was not a summons but an invitation.

Everett stood at the counter arguing cheerfully with Walter about the democratic distribution of poppy seeds. Mrs. Mathers had claimed a stool by the window and arranged napkins with the grave pleasure of a woman who has waited her whole life to assign dignity to the small. Pastor Elijah stood near the back, sleeves rolled, laughing at something Claire had said; Vivian, beside her daughter, wore an apron she clearly kept for rare occasions and looked faintly pleased with its utility. Mack leaned against the doorjamb to the kitchen, clean towel thrown over his shoulder, the stance of a man who knows his hands will be asked for and is glad.

And behind the counter, sleeves dusted to the elbow, stood Mrs. Miriam Levine—the baker—her silver braid looped like a second apron string. The two Miriams had become accustomed to a shorthand that spared the town confusion: Levine for the oven, Adler for the shop. The baker cleared her throat; the room tilted toward quiet. "You're late," she told Adler with the kind of affection that sits right beside scolding. "Good. Blessings work better when the person being blessed has kept people waiting."

Miriam Adler laughed. "I stopped to look at the window."

"Everyone stops to look at the window," Mrs. Levine said. "That's what windows are for."

She reached beneath the counter and lifted a wooden board. On it lay lengths of dough like ropes of pale silk—strands numbered and resting. "We have braided six and eight and twelve all our lives," she said to the room. "Today we braid thirteen. Not for luck. For honesty."

"Is that... aerodynamic?" Everett asked, openly dubious.

Mrs. Levine shot him a look that could curdle milk into cheese. "Bread is for eating, not throwing," she said. "If it requires a new technique, we will learn a new technique. That's what weeks like this are for."

She beckoned Miriam behind the counter. "You will start it. Hands remember what mouths forget." She placed Miriam Adler's fingers on the strands, then hers atop, and together they began—the braid learning itself under pressure and patience. The room leaned in without crowding. Adler felt the tightness she hadn't noticed at the hinge of her jaw relax as dough warmed to her touch, as Mrs. Levine murmured a counting that was not arithmetic so much as choreography: over-two, under-one, carry, rest. When the seventh and the ninth strand tried to claim the same space, Mrs. Levine's thumb corrected them with a small, decisive kindness. "We make room," she said.

At the end, Mrs. Levine tucked the tails under and circled the long braid into a round, a galaxy with its own gravity. Then she lifted a thirteenth, smaller strand, rolled quick and sure, and set it in a gentle spiral on top—a visible thirteenth that did not dominate, only completed. "We won't hide it," she said, and brushed the surface with egg wash that gave the future crust a promise of gloss.

"Sesame or poppy?" Claire asked, holding two bowls with the seriousness of choice.

"Both," Mrs. Levine said. "And a little salt. The tongue must learn to tell all its stories."

She slid the tray into the mouth of the oven the way one returns a child to a bed well-made. The door closed with a snug, right sound. Heat exhaled in a wave across the room. The baker set the timer but everyone knew they were really watching the old clock over the register and their own hearts.

When the timer chimed, the sound lifted an old chord—anticipation, relief, hunger. Mrs. Levine opened the oven and the room filled with a scent older than speech. She rapped the bottom of the loaf and it answered with that hollow thump that bakers trust more than any clock. "It's ready," she said, and laid it on the board.

She covered the loaf with a white towel and set it in the

center of the shop on a table someone had dragged from the back. A simple cloth, a round of bread, a town.

"Shall we?" she asked the room. And the room, with a small, unanimous sound, said yes.

MRS. LEVINE SLID the towel off with a flourish that was not theatrical so much as delighted. The bread shone. The braid had baked into a landscape of curves and valleys, the sesame and poppy seeds finding their places like constellations. The thin spiral of the thirteenth sat patient on top, obvious and unashamed.

"Before we tear," Mrs. Levine said, "we bless." She lifted her hands over the loaf, and the room lifted its attention with them. "There are as many ways to bless bread as there are households," she went on, eyes sweeping the faces— faithful, doubtful, hungry. "I grew up saying a Hebrew sentence that thanked the One who brings bread from the earth. I still say it in my kitchen. Today we will speak Cedar Creek's sentence, because it is also true."

She nodded at Miriam Adler.

Miriam swallowed, felt the pendant warm once, then steadied. "Tell the truth," she said, "and keep each other."

"Tell the truth and keep each other," the room repeated, the cadence of a vow learning its own mouth.

Mrs. Levine tore the first piece from the edge and placed it in Miriam's waiting hand. "For the woman who came as a stranger and spoke as a friend," she said. "For the hands that opened a wall and closed no doors." She turned and put the next piece into Julian's palm. "For the man who argued tenderly." She tore again and gave to Elijah. "For the one who mistook quiet for reverence and then chose courage." To Vivian. "For endurance, now permitted to rest." To

Graham. "For sternness learning softness." To Claire. "For young mouths given permission to speak." To Penny from the guild, who had slipped in shyly at the door. "For eyes that see where the light wants to go." To Everett. "For minutes that finally mean what they say." To Theo. "For joy, unruly and necessary." To Mrs. Mathers. "For keeping what needed keeping and letting go of the rest."

Around the room the loaf became pieces which became hands, which became the small social physics of feeding: someone passing forward before eating for themselves, someone steadying a child's wrist while they wrestled a bite, someone saving the last seed-heavy corner for the person who said they weren't hungry and obviously was.

Pastor Elijah cleared his throat. "I would like—if the room permits—to say the blessing I should have said when you arrived, Ms. Adler." He met her eyes and the room's. "May the work you do in this town be met with steadiness, the courage you carry be matched by our own, and the truth you speak be softened by our love. May bread and words and windows do what they were made to do: make us whole."

"Amen," said Theo promptly, and the room, delighted by his eagerness, said amen again.

They ate. It was not ceremony; it was eating. Butter appeared the way grace does—unaccountable, exactly on time. Honey was passed with the carefulness that prevents stickiness turning into regret. Vivian laughed so suddenly at something Walter said about poppy seeds that she looked around as if to apologize for the volume and found no one asking her to hush. Graham took a second piece and did not pretend he hadn't wanted one. Nadia's twins sat on the floor cross-legged and demanded an inventory of sesame on their tongues like astronomers counting stars.

Mrs. Levine, satisfied that hunger had been addressed, reached under the counter and brought up a small, round, flour-dusted loaf scored with a simple rose—twelve petals cut shallow and a thirteenth marked as a tiny cross at the rim. "For your counter," she told Miriam. "A daily reminder that completion beats symmetry because it feeds more people."

Adler held the loaf in both hands like a gift that changes the person who holds it. "Thank you," she said, and the words did not wobble. She looked around the room—the faces she now recognized first by voice and then by history—and felt something shift, not in the town exactly but in herself, to make space.

Julian's shoulder touched hers—an accidental anchor. He was talking to Penny about lead came and to Elijah about annotated minutes and to Theo about the ethics of capes, absorbing and reflected in equal measure. He fit here, not as an accessory to her acceptance but as a participant in it. The sight loosened an old knot under her ribs that she'd been too busy to notice had remained.

Mrs. Levine brushed seeds from her palms and lifted the knife. "One last slice," she said, and cut the heel—the piece some families saved, some fought over, some offered to the newest guest. She put it in Adler's hand and, for the first time that evening, placed her other palm briefly against Adler's cheek, flour cool as a blessing. "From my house to yours," she said. "No one leaves hungry, and no one eats alone."

"From my house to mine," Miriam answered, surprising herself with the pronoun's certainty.

The baker smiled, something like mischief and pride sharing space, and the shop exhaled in the way rooms do when they've held the right people and the right work without theatrical strain.

 AFTER THE CROWD THINNED, after the last paper napkin had been tucked into the bin and the broom had found the flour that insists on being found, the bakery's hum settled into its after-music. Lights dimmed to a version of themselves that always reminds a town what stillness sounds like. Adler lingered at the counter with Levine, helping wrap the loaves that would be left on the free shelf near the door.

"I thought belonging would feel like being applauded," Miriam said, working brown paper around the round with an efficiency inherited and learned. "It feels like being expected."

Mrs. Levine tied twine with a butcher's knot, deft. "Applause is for people who plan to leave. Expectation is for family."

Miriam considered that, considered the last weeks— how the town's gaze had changed from testing to trust, how hands reached for her now not to weigh her but to give her something to carry. "Family means obligation," she said, less complaint than inventory.

"It also means you can ask someone else to sweep when your back hurts," Mrs. Levine said. "Which it does. So ask."

Miriam laughed and called Theo, who appeared from the alley as if the town had a bell for mischief. He swept with absurd vigor while singing two lines of an unplaceable song until Mrs. Mathers shushed him for the satisfaction of it. Elijah stacked chairs. Everett took home the clipboard to write minutes of a blessing because he said if it wasn't written down it would turn into rumor and he was tired of rumor.

Julian washed the large mixing bowl at the sink and dried it with care, then set it where Levine pointed without pretense of knowing better. He had learned when to lead and when to follow and when to make tea. He made tea.

Mrs. Levine poured two cups and handed one to Miriam. "Drink," she commanded. "I'm old enough to take a tone."

They stood side by side at the window, looking out at the square. Lanterns winked. Somewhere, faintly, someone practiced a fiddle line that would be ready by festival's end. On the hill, the rose window caught a sliver of moonlight, the new petal answering the angle with a patient, water-light curve. No shimmer tonight, nothing theatrical—just the ordinary miracle of a thing finally permitted to be what it is.

"I was afraid," Miriam said, because the hour asked for honesty, "that if the town embraced me I would disappear into its embrace—become a mascot, a mouth, a useful myth. Tonight it felt... human. Specific. I didn't vanish. I showed up."

"The trick," Mrs. Levine said, "is to keep showing up. And to let them show up for you."

They drank and said nothing for a while, knowing silence no longer required defense. It was not the old hush. It was rest.

Then Mrs. Levine's tone shifted—still warm, a thread of something older woven in. "My mother's mother braided blessings into bread," she said. "Not fancy words, just wishes kneaded quiet—health for a neighbor, a baby sleep-ing, a quarrel cooling, the price of flour not rising. When she tore the loaf, the wishes went to work. I don't argue the theology. I argue the results." She nodded at the round with the small thirteenth spiral for Adler's counter. "There's a blessing in that, braided and ready. You'll know where to tear it."

Miriam thought of the girls who would cross her threshold with their hands stuffed in their jacket pockets and their mouths set against crying; of the boys who would pretend not to read the sign about truth and keeping each other and memorize it anyway; of Vivian, who would stop by in the morning with a question she thought was about invoices and was really about grief; of Graham, who would learn how to ask for help without making it look like a favor to the helper; of her own heart, which, though steadier, would still wobble on some days and need a piece of sweet, ordinary bread to remind it that being human is not a mistake.

"I'll tear it," she said. "I'll know."

Mrs. Levine nodded once as if they had made a business arrangement and then, satisfied, turned to scold Theo for attempting to balance an empty mixing bowl on his head. "You cannot bless and juggle at the same time," she informed him. "It sends the wrong message to the yeast."

When the shop finally emptied, Adler stood for a moment in the doorway with the loaf for her counter in both hands. Julian came to stand beside her—near, not leaning; beside, not behind. He didn't reach for the bread. He reached for her empty hand, and when she gave it, he held it like a promise that had already been kept.

"You were claimed tonight," he said, voice low.

"And I did some claiming," she answered. "It goes both ways."

They walked across the square to her shop at a pace that made no apologies to the hour. Inside, she set the round on a plate with a small card that read, in her newly tidy hand: **If you need a piece, take a piece. If you have a piece, share it.**

She tucked the thirteenth spiral into the honey jar and left the lid loose.

Julian hung his jacket on the peg as if it had always been meant to live there half the week. "You're smiling," he observed, pleased and certain.

"I am," she said, and felt the truth of it pull at her cheeks and not let go. She reached for the light switch, then paused. On the counter lay the fragment he had brought last night —the parchment with the carved basin and its cryptic line: *When the water runs dry, the silence ends again.* She set her palm over it, felt the whisper of future work like the first cool breeze after a hot day. "Tomorrow," she told the parchment. "Tonight we eat."

They split the heel, dipped it in honey, and stood at the counter chewing like people who had rebuilt something with their hands and were content to be simple about it. Outside, the square settled. Inside, the shop held.

Miriam turned the sign to **RESTING** and locked the door. The hinge sighed, not with fatigue this time but with that small domestic bliss houses make after good conversation and the right dishes drying by the sink. Upstairs, a shared table waited. On the hill, the rose kept its new curve. And in her chest, finally, something that had been waiting longer than she could measure said yes and meant it.

27

NIGHT BY THE CHAPEL

Miriam climbed the hill alone, the square behind her settling into the kind of quiet that belongs to towns after a feast. Lantern ropes clicked softly in the breeze; the last vendor rinsed his ladle under a spigot and left the bucket upturned to dry. Above, the chapel kept its simple posture, stone dark as bread crust against the thin ribbon of moon. She had told Julian she wanted to walk up by herself—no reason offered, none required. He had nodded, as he always did when her reasons were the sort that lived wordless.

The new rose waited, the thirteenth petal finally seated where the crack had insisted it belonged. During the day the glass held color like a reservoir; at night it returned light to whatever gave it—moon, lamp, or the ordinary glow of the town's windows. When Miriam reached the landing she paused not out of hesitation but to let her body catch up to the quiet already gathered there. Cedar leaned in from the edges of the lawn; the stone steps kept their own cool wisdom. She laid her palm against the door. It had the patient give of a thing that has been asked to be both boundary and welcome for a long time.

Inside, someone—Elijah, she guessed, or Mack heading home late—had left one low lamp burning in the nave. The pews inhaled it and made of it a kindness. The rose was not loud; it would never be. But the thirteenth curve caught the lamp's breath and folded it back into the window with a calm that made her hands unclench.

She stood under the window the way one stands under a sky, head tipped, allowing awe to operate on the places ordinary thought cannot. Up close, the solder lines looked like ink that had dried exactly where it should—no flourish, no apology. Penny's hand was in that steadiness, and Anita's. The guild had given the thirteenth a glass that was less color than permission: water-light by day, a soft honey when evening found it from below. It looked like something made to be seen and something made to last.

"Leah," she said, not loudly and not as an invocation. As acknowledgment. The name had become less a secret and more a member of the room. "Thank you for speaking across time. I heard you. We heard you."

The pendant warmed once against her throat. She let it be. An earlier version of herself would have sought signs the way a child tests magic by doing it twice. Tonight she did not test. She received. In that receiving she recognized the difference between hunger and gratitude.

A draft lifted from the floorboards, usual in a building this old, and yet it carried the faint sweetness of cedar sap and old paper. Miriam closed her eyes. Behind her eyelids the window lived again, petals aligning around a center that did not claim them so much as welcome them into the circle. She thought of the bread Miriam Levine had broken that afternoon, the thirteenth spiral set aside with honey for whoever came hungry and uninvited. In her mind, bread and glass kept each other.

"Your mouth became a door," she whispered, repeating Leah's sentence, "and it taught mine how to open." The words left her without effort. There was no tremble in them now, only the clean edge of a thing that has found its fit.

She sat in the second pew as Ruth had once done when the bakery was closed and the square too loud. Her hands lay open on her knees as if to show the room she had brought nothing to barter, nothing to wave as proof. The truth had done its work; the proof would be tomorrow's errands—minutes, scaffolding receipts, a sign-up for Night Watch with no capes allowed. Tonight belonged to gratitude not for results but for presence. She had asked to be guided and had been. She had asked to be held and had been—by a town, by a man, by a sentence older than both.

The rose held steady, not demanding attention, trusting the eye to come when it was ready. The thirteenth curved quietly into the pattern—the kind of bold that looked, from a distance, like belonging. Miriam smiled, small and true. She had come to thank a bride. She found herself thanking a building, a team, a town, a history, and a God she was not in the habit of naming but had begun to notice in the seam where courage met mercy.

"Thank you," she said again, and meant every direction she meant.

SHE DID NOT LEAVE. The room kept being a room, so she kept being a person in it. The first nights after the wall had breathed, her body had wanted to name everything—every creak a message, every shadow a visitor. Grief teaches you the habit of searching. Tonight she did not search. She let the mystery be the size of the work and the work be the size of a person. It was enough.

Her calling had once frightened her because it felt like disappearance—seer, guide, vessel: words that implied emptying, as if her own life were a cost paid to rent an hour of clarity for others. Even Elijah's early caution had fed that fear: be careful, be reverent, be small. The week had loosened those knots. Leah had not dissolved to speak. She had concentrated. The pendant did not erase Miriam's heart; it steadied it. The work of a guide was not to vanish but to remain, to keep a body in the room so the room could find its courage.

She stood and walked the aisle, fingers brushing the pews not as a superstitious touch but as a checking-in, a gratitude to wood that had held so many tired backs. At the vestibule she paused before Mrs. Pritchard's calligraphy: *My mouth is a door and will not stay shut.* It looked less defiant now, more like craftsmanship. A door is not only for leaving; it is for entering.

The chapel's little side door tugged at her curiosity the way a thread snags a ring. She opened it and found herself in the narrow passage by the vestry where the stone kept cool even in July. Somewhere below and beyond, the river worked through its sentence without needing applause. Miriam stood a while with the ordinary brooms and the extraordinary quiet and tried on the knowledge that she was a woman who heard things. That hearing would not ruin her life. It would arrange it.

"What do you want from me," she asked, and did not mind that the question had more than one listener—God, Leah, her own brave self. "Every day, I mean. Not just at peak moments when the town arranges itself in pews and I am asked to speak."

Return, she heard without thunder. Return to the simple. Clean baseboards when nobody is looking. Feed people who forgot they are hungry. Read what was hidden. Rest. Tell the truth and keep each other.

She breathed. The pendant had cooled. It lay against her skin with the ordinary comfort of a necklace. She wore it as stewardship now, not as spectacle. There would be a day—coming sooner than she thought, perhaps—when she would settle it around a young girl's neck and bless courage in a face that had not yet had to use it. She would know when. The pendant would, too.

At the back of the nave she stopped at the glass case where Leah's journal would soon live with its images available to any curious twelve-year-old with a school project and a parent patient enough to explain. She rested her fingertips on the case, then pulled back; oils and paper do not keep each other. "We won't lock you away," she promised the book and the woman. "We'll read you and clean the fingerprints with care and then read you again." It felt right that all of it belonged to the museum and the chapel and the town, not to her alone. Possession had never been the point; continuity had.

Returning to the center aisle, she let her attention widen. The window hummed its yes. The pews offered their long, bare patience. The boards remembered footsteps—brides and pallbearers, toddlers and men who limped from ladders, women who sang when their husbands would not. She could feel the room's history the way fingers feel grain: in one direction smooth, in another resistant and telling its truth.

"I accept," she said aloud, and surprised herself by laughing softly at the formality. "I accept without becoming a mouth that forgets it is a body. I accept with a bedtime and a breakfast and friends who correct me. I accept with lemon bars." The last made her grin, and the grin made her human, and being human made her brave again.

On the landing outside, the night had cooled further. She sat on the top step and watched the town's windows go out—Mrs. Levine's first (bakers sleep like farmers), then the Riverlight (Theo never closes so much as he stages intermissions), then Everett's back office light at the museum (it lingers because minutes cannot tuck themselves in). She texted a single word to Julian—**here**—and put the phone back into her pocket before it could reply. It buzzed once: **me too.** Enough.

From her purse she pulled the slip of parchment he had found—a crude diagram of the ceremonial basin and the line *When the water runs dry, the silence ends again.* The square had kept her day too full to brood. Night gave her permission to look without surrendering to worry. She studied the symbol cut into the drawn stone, a kind of spiral that did not quite return to itself. A mystery, yes; a demand, not yet. She folded it carefully and returned it to her bag. The next book would write itself when it was time. This chapter wanted its proper end.

She went back inside and stood once more beneath the rose. "I will listen," she said to all the voices that had claimed her, "but I will not let listening unmake me." The room knew the difference. So did she.

SHE LINGERED until the chapel taught her how to leave. Some rooms make an exit feel like betrayal. This one made it feel like release. The thirteenth petal wore the lamplight like a shawl; the lead seams tucked it into the circle; the old stone accepted the new decision with the unceremonious grace of matter that has outlived a hundred arguments.

Before she turned to go, she did something Ruth would have teased and approved. She lifted her hand and touched—just once, just lightly—the stone sill beneath the window. "For you," she said to the bride who had kept her courage in cedar. "For all of you whose names I don't know. We will keep what you kept. We will let go what you could not."

On the hill, the grass had cooled enough to hold the day's leftover warmth without burning it off. She crossed to the low wall and sat with her feet on the stone, a posture half child, half queen. The river spoke from below, phrases catching on rocks the way grief catches on years and keeps going. A fox or a cat—night's little uncertainty—moved at the edge of the trees and left her unbothered. Farther down the street, a porch swing creaked in a rhythm that suggested a promise in progress rather than a marriage in peril. She let herself think of Julian only as much as the night seemed to enjoy. There was a sweetness in leaving that chapter to write itself in daylight.

The town had always sounded like itself. Tonight it sounded like itself after becoming more itself. She pictured the shop's counter with the honey jar and the thirteenth spiral tucked under lid, a small edible liturgy for frightened days. She pictured Vivian asleep with her phone charging and her shoes finally off. She pictured Graham lying awake and unafraid of not knowing, the rarest courage. She pictured Penny's hands restless with a new design and Anita letting them be. She pictured Elijah's sermon notes with more crossed-out hushes than underlined warnings. She pictured Theo drafting a chalkboard pronouncement about pie that was really about mercy. She pictured a girl she did not yet know tracing petals in the margins of her math homework and learning the geometry of wholeness before someone taught her symmetry instead.

Miriam stood. Reverence that sits too long turns to theatre. She walked to the door and, because it felt right, locked it behind her with Elijah's spare key, then slid it back under the mat and smiled at the trust in that domestic gesture. At the bottom of the steps she turned once more. The rose received the night. The night received her thanks.

On her way down the hill she passed the ceremonial basin at the path's bend, the stone lip dark and wet with the day's poured water. She did not stop, but she did notice the way moonlight found a shallow carving in the inner ring—a spiral that did not quite return to itself. She carried the noticing the way you carry a smooth stone—no heavier for the keeping, made ready by the holding.

The square looked different from above and below; that was its small magic. From above, it was a bowl. From below, a stage. From the chapel steps, it was a table. Miriam crossed it without being observed because the hour had taught the town to let its good woman walk home in peace. She unlocked the shop and listened to the hinge breathe. Inside, the little round Levine had given her sat under a cloth by the honey jar with a handwritten card that said **If you need a piece, take a piece. If you have a piece, share it.** The card looked like a vow and a joke—a perfect dialect for Cedar Creek.

She lit a single lamp in the window so the square could borrow a little light and the light could borrow a little square. She poured water, not tea. She set the parchment fragment beside the cup and did not read it again. She stood at the workbench upstairs for a minute just to feel the pleasant ache of a table made for two.

At the glass she wrote three lines on the small card under the counter:

- **Gratitude is also work.**
- **A door opens both ways.**
- **Whole, not hush.**

She slid the card into place as if she were installing a tiny pane in a quiet window. Then she turned out the lamp, and the room remembered where all its edges were. In the dark, the pendant lay against her skin and adopted her temperature like a tame and faithful thing. She pressed her fingers to it, not as a superstition, as an amen.

Before sleep took her, a message arrived from Julian, brief, exactly as much as night could hold: **The rose was beautiful from the street. You were seen. Rest.** She did not reply; there would be time for words in the morning. The last thing she saw before she closed her eyes was not a shimmer or a broken wall or a crowd waiting to be guided. It was the calm weight of a town at rest under a window that finally knew its own design.

Miriam lay still long enough to hear the room settle, then let sleep carry her with the same steady cadence as the river. If there were voices, they sang like wood cooling. If there were signs, they kept the kindness of staying small. Night folded itself around her. Somewhere, a clock took its own deep breath before beginning another day. The chapel waited with its new curve. The basin cupped the moon and kept its secret an hour longer. And Miriam—guide, shopkeeper, keeper of a pendant and a promise—slept in the simple knowledge that gratitude and courage can share a bed and call it peace.

28

JULIAN'S CONFESSION

Morning arrived clean, the kind of light that wipes slate and counter both. The square breathed out steam from bakery vats and first-kettle tea; a broom stitched neat lines on the café's stoop; somewhere a ladder locked into place against the museum's cornice. Miriam flipped the shop's sign to **OPEN** and stood a second with her palm on the glass, as if agreeing to her own invitation.

Julian appeared in her reflection before he reached the door—shoulders, then the careful line of his jaw, then the small lift at the corner of his mouth that meant he'd rehearsed something and decided not to say it exactly as written. He held two paper cups. He didn't raise them like peace offerings. He simply waited.

She let him in. The bell chimed, precise as a small promise.

"Tea," he said, setting one cup by the register. "Not heroic. Competent." He hesitated, then found the sentence he wanted. "May I ask for ten minutes I can't get back?"

"You may," she said, leaning a hip against the counter,

pendant cool against her collarbone. "But you can keep the cups."

He smiled, grateful for the ledge of play. Then he put his hands flat on the counter—not to take possession of the space, but to anchor his own. "I have realized something," he said. "And realizing it has made the rest of my sentences untrustworthy until I say it aloud."

She waited, the way she'd learned to wait when the river was the one speaking: still, but not passive.

"I thought I was drawn to you because of history," Julian said. "Because you carried the archive into air. Because your presence turned evidence into proof. Those are true and too small. The truth is I am drawn to your courage. Not the public kind—the efficient speeches and the tidy minutes." He shook his head once. "The domestic courage. The kind that chooses people over symmetry. The kind that will tear bread before there's a consensus and trust the room to catch up."

He let breath in, then out. "It has been a long time since I admired someone in a way that asked anything of me besides praise. You ask for change. I want to change toward you."

Miriam didn't speak at once. She let the words move through the rooms they needed to move through: grief, skepticism, relief. She remembered all the brittle compliments she'd endured in other lives—*you're so strong* meant *please keep absorbing my work*. This was cleaner. It named the thing and promised to carry weight.

"Thank you," she said. It wasn't modest, and it wasn't the gratefully-embarrassed little laugh women get trained to perform. It was acceptance. "I thought you were drawn to how I help your work make sense."

"I am," he said. "But I want you when there's no work, too. I want your courage near me when we are ordinary."

She absorbed that tenderness like a second cup of heat. "You've already shown yours," she said. "In the chapel. In the way you stopped explaining and stood next to me."

He nodded once. "That was the first time I've chosen a person over a room I loved. It felt like relief." He stepped around the counter then and stopped an arm's length away, enough to be seen, not enough to require a decision. "I would like to touch your hand," he said, almost wry. "Field-trained consent."

She offered it, palm up. His fingers closed—not possessive, not theatrical. They carried the texture of work and ink and the river's humidity, and she felt the yes arrive from the practical parts of her: shoulders, breath, the small place behind the knees where fear had lived.

They left the cups to steam and stepped into the square because confessions require a sky. The town accepted them without commentary, which is a form of blessing rare enough to count as miracle. They walked in the direction their bodies already knew—past Theo's chalkboard (**THIRTEEN = WHOLE** framed by a cartoon heron), past the free-shelf loaves on Levine's stoop with the small note **If you need a piece, take a piece**, past Everett carrying an armload of folders like a man escorting a flock of geese.

Hands still linked, they crossed toward the river. Julian's voice found its quieter register. "I have admired many people for their minds," he said. "It made me comfortable. Admiring your courage makes me better."

"You're good with my dead," she said. "That made you necessary. This makes you mine."

It was braver than any of the speeches she'd given with a

lamp behind her. He took it without negotiation. "Then I am yours," he said simply. "Not as possession. As direction."

The river wore its cool sentence. The pendant rested warm. They did not need to kiss to seal anything; they had already become an "and" walking.

THEY CIRCLED BACK through the square with the unhurried pace of people testing how an ordinary day fits two sets of feet. A child with a paper crown tried to sell them a map to the best puddles; Miriam bought one and asked for a revision; Julian took notes as if puddles were a subfield of cartography and the child the leading scholar. The errands of a life accrued: return Bishop's borrowed step stool; speak to Penny about the next round of restoration; a box of tea for Elijah; cinnamon for Vivian; lemon for Theo's experiments; a new pencil cup for the shared table.

At the shop, they climbed to the attic workbench and set objects in their places. The table looked more itself with two mugs rings and a scatter of photo corners and a short list stuck under the lamp with a magnet:

- **Night Watch sign-up: no capes.**
- **Pendant rotation ledger.**
- **Basin research: who carved? when? why spiral not-closed?**

"The basin," Julian said, tapping the note. "I've flagged three references. One is a half-sentence in a flood report from 1911. One is a diary that mentions 'the old cup' by the bend. The third is a drawing—poorly scaled—but it includes the spiral you showed me."

"And my piece is the whisper that won't leave," Miriam

said. "*When the water runs dry...*" She didn't finish the line. She didn't need to. The air finished it with her.

"We don't have to start tonight," he added. "But I'd like to propose a rule. When the work turns large, we reduce it to something domestic and repeatable."

"Such as?" she asked, interested in how his logistics braided with her longing.

"Tea at eight. Two hours of reading. One walk. A rule for argument: first person to raise their voice must name a fear. Second person must name a hope. Then lemon bars."

She laughed, delighted by the structure that protected the softness. "Add: when I say I need quiet, you don't make quiet into a test I have to pass. And when you say you need evidence, I don't take it as a challenge to my worth."

He held out the pencil like a little scepter. She wrote the additions under his suggestions. The list looked absurd and holy. "What about Sundays?" she asked.

"Unhurried," he said. "Half the shops closed, the other half pretending. Church or no church; window-gazing mandatory; bread required; no minutes."

"Night Watch?" she said.

"Shared," he answered. "If you go, I go. If I go, you go. If neither of us should go, we say so aloud and find a third."

"You're imagining a life," she said. It wasn't accusation.

"I am," he admitted. "But I will not outpace you. We can live in outline and fill it one careful wash at a time."

She considered the shape of it: two kettles, a spare key, a drawer that contained both his soft pencils and her folded index cards; the boring joy of lists they both revised with the same pen; the possibility that one day, without ceremony, a pair of gloves that fit his long fingers would live in a bowl by her door; the choice, again and again, to say **we** as a discipline and not lose **I** as a name.

"Long-term," she said, tasting the word. "You, too?"

"Yes," he said. "Not as demand. As desire." He looked down, smiled a little, then looked up again. "I want to be the person who locks up the shop when you forget. I want to be the call you make when the plumbing sulks. I want to be the reason Theo rolls his eyes and pretends we're unbearable. I want to read you the boring parts of ledgers until the boredom makes us giddy. I want to learn your bad moods by their footsteps and do the dishes they keep making."

"Permission granted," she said, and the smile that followed had nothing to prove. "In return, I want to learn the names of your nervous habits and teach them how to sit. I want to put my thumb on your jawline when you are about to over-explain and have you forgive the interruption. I want to keep the town from using you as a podium when what you need is a porch."

"Porch," he echoed with evident fondness, as if the word itself had a rocking motion. "Then it's settled. We're an—"

"—us," she finished.

He held out his hand again—ceremony and practice at once—and she took it. They went back down to the street to see what the day would give **us** to do.

By AFTERNOON the square had warmed into work. Mack's crew finished re-seating beadboard; Penny and Anita cataloged scrap glass with a solemnity that made even shards feel useful; Everett pinned **PUBLIC MINUTES: ROSE WINDOW** on the museum corkboard and added, under it, **COMMENT HERE** with a pencil on a string. The town had discovered civilized argument and was nearly intoxicated by it.

Miriam and Julian walked hand in hand through this

ordinary carnival. The handholding lacked spectacle; it had the dignity of a tool that fits the work. People greeted them with the new dialect—trust, a little teasing. Vivian passed a paper sack over the bakery counter. "Lemon bars," she said. "For research." Elijah tipped the brim of a hat he did not usually wear and did not explain. Theo drawled, "Disgusting. Adorable. Carry on," and chalked **SHARED SIDE** under the day's pastry list as if it were a menu item.

They turned toward the chapel at the hour when the new petal stops pretending it is shy. Light eased along the curve and made a clean hinge where fracture had once been. Julian, with the reflex of a man who takes notes as apology and celebration both, pulled a thin notebook and sketched the arc; Miriam, with the reflex of a woman who listens for pressure in wood and air alike, closed her eyes and let the quiet speak.

"What do you hear?" he asked, not to test, to include.

"Not names," she said. "Textures. Relief. Stone letting go of bracing it didn't need. Glass practicing breathing." She paused, tilted her head. "And us. The room has moved its chairs to make room for us."

He grinned, pleased with the accuracy of her extravagance. "The room is a genius."

"So are you," she said. "In a very particular way. Maps and scales and an index of the unglamorous true."

"The way you say that feels like poetry and not mockery," he said.

"It is," she answered. "And also a contract. When the basin starts telling stories, you'll keep me from drowning in metaphor. When the records refuse to yield, I'll keep you from mistaking quiet for absence."

They walked on, rhythm easy. At the bend where the

path meets the river, they paused by the ceremonial basin. Children had left petals in it; a dragonfly rehearsed its own geometry. The spiral carved in the inner ring held a smudge of silt; the water moved like breath over it.

Julian crouched, practical. He took a rubbing with the soft pencil he now carried as habit, the lead catching on the spiral's shallow, stubborn groove. "It doesn't close," he said, "by design."

"Which means it's not a trap," she answered, "but an invitation."

He folded the paper and slid it into his notebook. "We'll test its history without testing its patience."

"Good," she said. "I like our version of science: kindness first, then curiosity."

He stood and dusted his hands; she brushed the graphite from his fingers with her thumb, an intimacy small enough to pass unnoticed by anyone who wasn't looking and large enough to lay claim.

They returned to the square with the afternoon's long shadow walking ahead of them. The town made a sound Miriam hadn't known towns could make: collective contentment. Not triumph. Not defended cheer. Contentment, the quiet kind, shaped like chores crossed off and apologies kept.

Julian stopped them in front of the shop and turned her gently so she faced him and the square and the chapel all at once, the way a compass faces more than one cardinal truth. "I have another sentence," he said.

"Proceed," she said, smiling already.

"I used to think reason was the instrument and awe the orchestra," he said. "Now I think they trade chairs. You taught me that."

"You taught me awe doesn't have to be lonely," she said. "And that reason is allowed to be tender."

He nodded, as if accepting the grade from a teacher he admired. His hand tightened around hers, a small affirmative. "Shall we walk this town as if it is ours to keep and not ours to control?"

"We shall," she said. Then, because clarity had become their habit, she added, "Hand in hand until one of us needs both hands, and then we braid."

They set off again—not for drama, for groceries. Mrs. Mathers needed envelopes; the guild needed beeswax; Nadia needed five minutes with her hands free; Everett needed to be told to go home before the light went out in the museum basement. The work of harmony is not performed; it's done.

At dusk, they crossed the square one last time, and the rose window took their shadows and returned them as pattern. Julian kissed her temple—short, competent, the way you cap a pen you intend to use again soon. She turned her face and met his mouth, not to prove anything to the square, but because the square had become part of the sentence they were writing.

He pulled back first, as if to model restraint; she tugged him a fraction closer, as if to model joy. They laughed into the kiss. Harmony doesn't erase edges; it lets them fit.

When they separated, the pendant lay warm, the notebook had a new rubbing, and the day had room left in it for dinner. "Tomorrow we start the basin in earnest," Julian said.

"Tomorrow," she agreed. "Tonight we practice belonging."

They walked hand in hand through the town that had

decided to keep them, a rational man and a mystical woman moving in the same key. The chapel hummed its yes; the river kept its grammar; the square, for once, asked nothing more of them than to pass through it slowly and together.

29

FESTIVAL FINALE

By nightfall, Cedar Creek's square was transformed. Lanterns swayed from lines strung between storefronts, each painted glass globe glowing like a captured sunset. Some bore roses—twelve petals, thirteen petals, and even a few drawn by children that defied counting altogether. Others showed rivers, loaves, foxes, and stars. The square had become a gallery where every hand had added a mark, every house a story.

Music spilled from the bandstand: fiddles bright, guitars steady, a drum that thumped like a heart running uphill but never winded. The air tasted of cinnamon and yeast, of wood smoke curling from small braziers placed at the square's corners. People crowded benches, leaned from windows, perched on the bakery steps. The town had gathered not out of duty, but desire.

Miriam stood at the edge of the circle, hands folded loosely, watching the first dance unspool. Couples stepped, spun, and laughed when their feet tangled. Children wove between adults like darting minnows, holding paper lanterns that bobbed in time with their energy. Someone pulled Miriam into the circle—Theo, with his dramatic bow. "A guest of honor doesn't get to brood on the sidelines," he declared. "Dance is not optional. It is minutes of joy, and I am recording them."

She laughed—an unguarded sound—and let herself be pulled. Her shoes caught the rhythm more easily than she expected, as though the stones had been waiting for her feet. Theo twirled her with theatrical flourish, then passed her to Nadia, who spun her once before being claimed by her husband. A child caught Miriam's hand next, and she stooped to match the quick, gleeful steps, lanterns bobbing like fireflies around them.

Julian leaned against the bandstand rail, arms folded, watching. Admiration softened the lines of his face, but he didn't intrude. He knew this was not his moment to guard her, or even to guide her. This was hers alone: the step from participant to belonging.

Vivian joined the circle, skirts swinging, her daughter laughing as she tried to keep pace. Graham—grudging at first—allowed himself to be coaxed by Mrs. Mathers, who clapped in rhythm until he gave in and matched her steps. Elijah tapped his foot in time at the edge, then surprised himself by stepping forward, coat discarded, moving with a grace that reminded the town he had once been a young man with music in his blood.

Miriam moved through partners, her laughter growing less cautious, until she realized she was no longer counting steps. She was simply dancing. The lanterns turned above her, constellations in motion, and for the first time since she had set foot in Cedar Creek, her body forgot to wonder if she was welcome. It simply was.

The fiddles rose in unison, then cut off sharp. Applause burst like a wave against the stones. Miriam found herself beside Nadia, both breathless, both glowing. They grinned at each other, conspirators in joy.

Julian stepped forward then, offering a cup of cider. She took it, her hand brushing his. "You've been smiling," he said softly, "and not the careful kind."

"It feels new," she admitted, her chest still rising with laughter. "And it feels like it has been waiting a long time."

He didn't answer with words. His eyes were enough.

The music started again, this time slower, a reel with the rhythm of river water. Couples paired. Theo found another willing partner, Graham danced stiff but willing with his niece, and Vivian clasped Elijah's hand, surprising both of them. Julian extended his arm, not theatrical but steady. Miriam took it. Together they stepped into the current of the dance, and the town moved with them, lanterns flickering above like the blessing of a hundred small suns.

THE SQUARE'S stones carried the rhythm the way riverbeds carry current—by shaping it, by holding it, by never trying to own it. As Miriam moved, she noticed not just her own joy, but the town's: Graham's sternness easing into a grin when his niece spun too fast; Vivian throwing back her head in laughter that startled her as much as anyone else; Elijah letting himself forget sermons long enough to clap in time with the beat.

Children wove between dancers with ribbons tied to sticks, painting the night air with bright arcs. The bakery had set out trays of challah, sliced thick and drizzled with honey; the café countered with lemon bars stacked like bricks in a sweet wall no one wanted to breach alone. Mrs. Mathers distributed napkins as if orchestrating an opera of crumb control.

The rose window, lit from within by lanterns arranged along the pews, glowed above the square like a participant rather than a monument. Its thirteenth petal caught the lantern light and bent it outward, scattering honey-gold across the dancers. More than one person looked up, caught the shimmer, and returned to their steps with renewed laughter.

Julian and Miriam moved easily through the dance, their steps aligning not because they had practiced but because they listened. He leaned close once, murmuring, "Do you realize this is what wholeness looks like?" She tilted her head toward the crowd: neighbors holding hands, rivals trading smiles, children teaching their elders new moves with fearless glee.

"Yes," she said. "It looks like this."

At the song's end, the square erupted into applause again. This time, no one hurried away. The fiddlers struck up a softer tune, almost a lullaby, and people swayed where they stood, some singing under their breath. Miriam closed her eyes a moment, letting the melody press into the cracks silence had once filled.

Everett approached with a clipboard raised like a torch. "I have recorded that Graham smiled," he declared, "and I intend to file it under Historic Events." Graham rolled his eyes but didn't deny it. Vivian teased that she would testify under oath. Laughter swelled—not forced, not nervous, but real, rolling through the crowd like a tide.

The night grew deeper, but no one spoke of leaving. Lanterns burned low, replaced by fresh ones from baskets carried by children who loved the excuse to run errands at midnight. The square's center became less a dance floor and more a hearth: people gathered, broke bread, traded stories. Someone passed a guitar; someone else joined on flute.

Voices wove a net of sound that caught every ear and held it tenderly.

Miriam sat for a while on the bakery steps, Julian beside her, their hands still linked. She watched the people she had once feared would never welcome her now carrying her laughter in their own mouths. The town was not perfect, nor suddenly free of its grudges. But tonight, its bonds showed mending in motion.

A girl of twelve approached shyly with a plate of honey-drizzled bread. "Mrs. Levine said you should have this," she said, offering it like an offering.

Miriam accepted, tore the piece in half, and gave one back. "Eat with me," she said. The girl grinned and sat beside her, swinging her feet. They ate in silence that was comfortable, then returned to the music when the fiddles called again.

By the time midnight bells chimed, the square felt less like a festival and more like a living room that had simply spilled outdoors. The lanterns bobbed overhead, the rose window gleamed, and Miriam knew she was watching not just a celebration, but a restoration—the bonds of Cedar Creek knotted tighter, stronger, because they had been tested and chosen anew.

THE LAST SONG of the night began slow, a circle dance that asked for every hand. One by one, people stepped in— Vivian, Graham, Elijah, Theo, Everett with his clipboard tucked under one arm, Nadia with her twins, even Mrs. Mathers reluctantly giving up her post by the napkins. The circle grew until it filled the square.

Miriam hesitated for a moment at the edge, memory tugging at the old fear: the outsider's ache that one step too bold would unravel acceptance. Then she felt Julian's hand at her back, not pushing, simply present. She stepped forward. Hands clasped hers on both sides—one child's, one elder's—and the circle closed, whole.

The music rose, feet moved in unison, lanterns swayed as though nodding approval. Miriam felt the weight of the pendant, light and steady, against her chest. She had carried it as a burden, then as a duty. Tonight it felt like what it had always wanted to be: a gift meant to be shared.

Her voice joined the others, not leading, not lagging, simply part of the whole. She realized with a start that she was laughing—not the cautious laugh of politeness, not the brittle laugh of defense, but laughter free and unmeasured. It rose out of her like a spring that had been sealed too long.

Julian, across the circle, caught her eye. Admiration softened his face, but more than that—relief. As if he'd been waiting for this sound, this lightness, all along. He mouthed the word *finally*, and she grinned, answering with *yes*.

The song ended not with a flourish but with a collective exhale, the circle loosening into embraces and promises of bread tomorrow, tea next week, scaffolding help when needed. People clapped Miriam on the shoulder, thanked her without ceremony, included her in plans without pause. She was not guest, nor interloper, nor experiment. She was theirs.

As the crowd dispersed, she remained a while in the square, lantern light soft on her face. Julian came to her side, his hand finding hers again. "You're inside now," he said, voice low.

"I am," she admitted, marveling at the ease of the words. "And it doesn't feel like I lost myself to get here. It feels like I found her."

They walked slowly across the square, past Levine's

Hearth, past Theo chalking one last absurd proclamation, past the fountain where children floated lanterns shaped like petals. Above, the rose window glowed, thirteenth petal steady in its circle.

Miriam paused, looking up. "I used to think wholeness was something you inherited, something fixed. Tonight I see it's something you choose, over and over."

Julian squeezed her hand. "And you chose. They chose you back."

They walked on, their steps unhurried, the night wrapping around them like a quilt sewn from laughter, bread, and lantern light. The festival's music faded behind them, but its echo remained in their breath, their hands, their quiet.

For the first time since she had set foot in Cedar Creek, Miriam did not wonder if she belonged. She knew. And knowing, she laughed again—freely, fully, as one of them.

30

THE BASIN RUNS DRY

The square still hummed with echoes of fiddles and laughter when Miriam slipped away. Lanterns bobbed above the cobblestones like sleepy fireflies, their flames shrinking as midnight stretched thin. Families trailed home in clusters, children carrying the last scraps of bread or ribbons rescued from the dance. Miriam's hair clung damply to her neck, her cheeks warm from dancing, but her chest felt astonishingly light. For once, she had not carried the night—she had lived it.

Yet her feet carried her not toward the shop, but down the slope to the river. The current whispered with the steady patience of water that had seen centuries of vows and silences, and the moon hung swollen above the bend, spilling silver across the basin that marked Cedar Creek's oldest ritual.

The ceremonial basin sat carved into the bedrock at the river's lip, a wide bowl chiseled by hands nearly two centuries gone. Miriam had seen it filled countless times since her arrival: with spring water during the festival, with rose petals on weddings, with candles on nights when grief needed light. The basin was always full, whether by ritual, rain, or the generosity of the river itself.

Tonight, though, as she reached the riverbank, she halted. The basin was empty.

Her breath caught. The air cooled sharply, as if the night itself drew closer to listen. Moonlight revealed smooth stone, bare and dry, its inner spiral traced with silt and moss. The absence of water looked wrong—like a lung forgetting its breath, like a mouth frozen mid-prayer.

Miriam descended the slope carefully, heart thudding. Kneeling, she touched the basin's floor. Cool, not cold. Damp in places, but not pooled. As though the water had not evaporated, but fled.

And there, in the deepest curve of the spiral, the stone gleamed.

A symbol glimmered faintly under the moon, carved deeper than weather would allow. Not the rose, not any petal. This mark was angular, almost jagged, a shape both alien and familiar. She traced it with trembling fingers and felt the same pulse she had felt before the rose window cracked—an ancient resonance, a truth waiting.

Her mind leapt unbidden to Ruth's notes, to Leah's journal, to the whispers she had recorded on index cards. *Endurance is preface. Belonging is choice.* And now, here was another fragment: *When the water runs dry, the silence ends again.*

Her shiver wasn't fear alone. It was recognition. The rose had spoken its truth; now the river claimed its turn.

She heard steps behind her and half turned, but no one appeared. Only the sound of water lapping at the bank, strangely distant from the dry basin at her feet. She closed her eyes and whispered, "Not tonight. Please, not yet." But the air answered with stillness, as if insisting mysteries obey no calendar.

She stood slowly, brushing damp stone from her hand, and gazed back toward the square. The lanterns had dimmed further; voices had dwindled. Only one figure remained visible—Julian, standing at the edge of the square, searching for her. He raised a hand as if to call, but seemed to sense she needed this moment alone. He let his hand fall and waited, patient, watching.

Miriam looked once more into the empty basin. The carved symbol shimmered again, then dulled as a cloud crossed the moon. She drew a slow breath. The night had given her joy and belonging, but it would not let her leave without a reminder: Cedar Creek was not done with her, nor she with it.

She turned back toward Julian, her steps unhurried but certain. Behind her, the basin lay bare, waiting for the town to see what she had seen.

The next story had begun.

By the time she reached Julian, the square had nearly emptied. He stood with his satchel slung across his shoulder, arms folded, lantern glow catching in his eyes. "You wandered," he said gently, no reproach in it.

"I needed to see something," Miriam replied. She glanced over her shoulder, but the basin was hidden by shadows and slope.

Julian studied her face. "Something unsettled you."

She almost told him. Almost pointed to the river and the spiral and the carved mark that seemed to breathe under her touch. But memory of the rose reminded her: some truths had to unfold at their own pace, not under the press of midnight exhaustion.

Instead, she said, "The river has more stories than we've heard."

His mouth quirked. "And you intend to listen."

She nodded once. "Yes. Even if it means the festival isn't the only thing stirring this year."

They walked together toward the shop, steps slow, silence between them not empty but thoughtful. The night air smelled of spent firecrackers and baking bread, the scents of celebration lingering like blessings. But Miriam's thoughts circled back to the basin.

The rose revealed silence. The basin reveals thirst. What is left unspoken when the water vanishes?

At the shop, Julian paused before the door. "Whatever it is," he said quietly, "don't carry it alone."

She met his gaze, warmed by the weight of loyalty in his words. She had learned enough to know he would stand beside her when the time came. And she had learned enough to know that moment would come soon.

Upstairs, sleep took her in fragments. She dreamed of chains clinking beneath clear water, of hands raising bowls that crumbled like ash, of a river splitting to reveal stone marked with names she could not read. She woke before dawn, heart hammering.

Crossing to the desk, she pulled out her stack of index cards and wrote by lamplight:

- **When the water runs dry, silence ends again.**
- **Chains beneath current.**
- **Mark = not rose. Something older.**

She pinned the card under glass beside the others, a

map of mysteries that stretched now beyond the rose window. It had begun with belonging, but it would lead into something else—something older, deeper. Redemption, perhaps.

Julian's satchel rested against the chair where he had left it earlier. She traced its worn strap and smiled faintly. He had already become part of the pattern—reason and warmth, anchor and witness. Together, they had faced silence. Together, they would face water.

Outside, dawn painted the river pale gold. Miriam stood at the window and whispered, "I hear you." The basin lay hidden beyond view, but she knew it waited, as patient as stone, for the town to notice its thirst.

THE FESTIVAL GROUNDS by morning were scattered with ribbons and crumbs, lantern shards and chalk faded by dew. Children's laughter carried faintly as they chased each other along the river path. Life resumed, practical and cheerful.

But word spread quickly: the basin was empty.

By midday, half the town had drifted to the river to see for themselves. Some muttered of drought, though the river ran strong. Others whispered of sabotage, of rival families, of omens. Everett scribbled notes furiously, labeling the absence *a phenomenon of communal concern*. Theo chalked on the square's board: **RIVER KEEPS SECRETS. SO DO WE.**

Miriam stood apart, arms folded, pendant warm against her chest. She watched faces shift from amusement to unease as people leaned over the basin's lip, seeing only dry stone. None remarked on the faint carving—perhaps it was visible only to her. Perhaps that was the gift, or the burden.

Julian found her in the crowd. "You knew," he said quietly, not accusation but certainty.

"I felt it," she admitted. "Last night. Before anyone else came."

He exhaled, steady. "Then we begin again."

The words settled in her like both promise and warning.

The sun climbed, warming the square, drawing people back to booths and chores. By evening, the basin remained empty, the carving glimmering faintly when the moon rose again. Miriam lingered, brushing her hand along the stone rim.

"You've given me belonging," she whispered. "Now you ask more."

A wind stirred from the river, cool against her cheek, carrying with it the faintest echo of chains breaking, water rushing, silence cracking open.

She shivered, but did not step back.

Cedar Creek had called her once through the rose. Now it called her again, through water. The mysteries had only deepened, and with them, her place among them.

Miriam turned, lantern light flickering at her back, and walked toward the shop where Julian waited. Her heart beat not with dread, but anticipation.

Because she knew: a new story had begun.

And she would be ready to meet it.

AFTERWORD

It began with *The Thirteenth Petal*. She saw herself then, cautious and uncertain, holding her aunt's manuscript like a shield. Cedar Creek had seemed foreign, half-ghosted by old stories and whispered suspicions. The thirteenth petal was still hidden then, its mystery unsolved, its promise untasted. She had been an outsider, searching the past for answers to questions she had barely begun to ask herself. Yet even then, the land had whispered to her, the river had tugged, and the petals of prophecy had begun to stir.

Waters of Redemption rose in her memory next—the basin running dry, the first covenant tested. She recalled how frightened she had been by the silence of water, by the possibility that her search was folly. But she also remembered the strength she found in listening, in daring to stay rather than flee. That was when Cedar Creek first began to claim her, when she learned that redemption was not about possession but about presence.

Then came *The Silent Bell*. Miriam saw herself again standing beneath the old tower, hearing absence louder than sound, sensing that silence was itself a summons. It had been a season of division, fear, and mistrust. Yet within it, she had heard something more: a call to endure, to wait, to stand even when answers were withheld. Julian had drawn closer then, his loyalty steadying her steps even when her own faltered.

The memories folded into *The Fifth Cup*, when the goblet gleamed and the town's faith was tested by falsehoods and shadows. She remembered how she had nearly lost her trust in herself, in the manuscript, even in the possibility of belonging. But the fifth cup had reminded her: covenant was not about certainty, but about choosing to lift the cup even when hands shook. That act had prepared her heart for deeper mysteries still to come.

The arc curved forward into *The Bride's Lantern*, when love and sorrow mingled on the riverbank, and the grief of generations still pressed upon the town. Miriam remembered how she had felt that sorrow in her bones, how it had nearly undone her. But the lantern's glow had also shown her a way through—how grief could become light, how remembrance could become release. And in that glow, her heart had turned more fully toward Julian, not as ally only but as beloved.

And in *The Rose Reborn*. She saw it all as if laid upon the window: the manuscript sealed and then opened, the prophecy spoken aloud, the carving uncovered, the pendant glowing with memory, the council divided and then healed, the people fractured and then mended. She saw her own fear of leadership, her hesitation to love, her doubt that she could belong—and she saw how each had been answered, not by spectacle, but by covenant kept through trial.

WATERS OF REDEMPTION

Cedar Creek Legends, Book Two: *Waters of Redemption*

The town of Cedar Creek has always lived by its rituals. For generations, the river has carried its lanterns, the basin has blessed its people, and the bell at the fort has tolled dawn into every new day. But when those rituals begin to falter, long-buried secrets stir, threatening to break the fragile harmony of a community bound by memory, loyalty, and unspoken betrayals.

In *Waters of Redemption*, Miriam Adler—widowed newcomer and reluctant keeper of mystical gifts—finds herself at the heart of Cedar Creek's most unsettling mystery yet. At the opening ritual of the Rivers Festival, the ceremonial basin runs inexplicably dry before the entire town. Panic ripples through the crowd as an ancient symbol carves itself into the riverbed, shimmering with meaning too old for the present and too urgent to ignore.

Miriam's tentative bond with Julian Roth, Cedar Creek's earnest young historian, is tested as they search for answers. He clings to records, ledgers, and reason; she is haunted by visions and dreams that speak in chains, water, and silence.

Together they wade into the contested territory of the town's rival families—each quick to blame the others for sabotage, each carrying wounds from forgotten promises. As suspicion deepens, even the sheriff and pastor cannot keep hostilities contained.

Dreams lead Miriam to see the river not as a victim of sabotage but as a witness to betrayal. Whispers of an old oath broken during Cedar Creek's founding echo through her nights. Oral histories, ancestral confessions, and long-hidden ledgers reveal that the fracture at the heart of the town is not new—it has been waiting, century after century, for truth to be spoken aloud.

The deeper Miriam and Julian dig, the more their partnership sharpens into something more intimate. Vulnerability, conflict, and quiet confessions kindle a slow-burn romance at the very moment the town demands they carry the weight of its divided past. Each step forward means choosing between secrecy and exposure, safety and courage, silence and witness. And with every answer uncovered, the water seems to answer back.

When the truth of the old betrayal is finally spoken before the gathered families, Cedar Creek itself responds. The basin refills, lanterns flow downstream like absolution, and for one luminous night the town tastes reconciliation. But even as love and belonging take root for Miriam, a final twist refuses to let peace settle.

At dawn, the fort bell—faithful voice of Cedar Creek—refuses to ring. Its silence chills the town and casts a shadow across the green. For Miriam, the dream of the silent bride becomes prophecy. For Julian, the historian's doubt bends into something more personal and urgent. And for Cedar Creek, the hush marks not an ending but a summons.

Waters of Redemption is a sweeping blend of mystery,

romance, and myth woven into the fabric of small-town life. It is about what happens when a community dares to confront the truth it has hidden for generations, and what it costs to listen when silence speaks. With lyrical prose and unforgettable characters, the second volume in the **Cedar Creek Legends** series draws readers into a world where rituals are alive, history is personal, and the river itself carries the memory of every promise kept—and broken.

At once intimate and epic, *Waters of Redemption* is both a love story and a reckoning. And as the final pages close on the silent bell, readers will know with certainty: Cedar Creek's greatest mystery has only just begun.

ABOUT THE AUTHOR

Jordan Jace is a Pacific Northwest author whose mysteries and heartwarming tales are set against stunning landscapes. With a deep connection to the PNW region's natural beauty, Jace infuses each story with the magic of misty mountains, lush forests, and tranquil coastlines. Jace believes that joy can be found in the smallest moments and the most unexpected places. When not writing, Jace is exploring the world, seeking inspiration in every corner for the next unforgettable story. Discover more at jordanjace.com

www.ingramcontent.com/pod-product-compliance
Lightning Source LLC
Chambersburg PA
CBHW021220310726
48971CB00006B/1627